The
Runaway
Wife

The Runaway Wife

Dee MacDonald

Bookouture

Published by Bookouture in 2018

An imprint of StoryFire Ltd.

Carmelite House
50 Victoria Embankment
London EC4Y 0DZ

www.bookouture.com

ISBN: 978-1-78681-355-8
eBook ISBN: 978-1-78681-354-1

To every woman who's ever dreamed of running away.

CHAPTER ONE

RESOLUTION

One evening in early August, while she was mashing the potatoes for dinner, Connie McColl decided to leave home. Looking out of her window at the newly planted, pocket handkerchief-sized garden, she *knew* she had to go. Connie hesitated, considering the implications of this momentous idea, and then wondered whether or not she should add a dollop of cream to the potatoes, remembering her husband Roger's diet. But – sod that – she added it anyway. And, all the time, while she was mashing and smashing, exciting thoughts kept whirling around in her head. Of course, she'd considered this before during her long, long marriage – well, what woman *hadn't?* And, like most other women, she'd never acted on impulse, until now.

Because yesterday had been the final straw. It was twenty-three years ago, to the day, and no one had remembered Ben. No one. Except Wendy, her dear friend who used to live next door and who sent the card: 'Thinking of you'. But not a word from Roger; no bunch of flowers, nothing. Nothing at all. Not even from the children. That was the catalyst. The trigger. The reason for her resolve. Well, that and Roger's remark that morning.

'I don't know what you find to do all day,' he'd said. 'This place is brand new – must look after itself.'

Since they'd moved into this wretched modern bungalow she'd papered it, painted it, curtained it and planted the virgin flowerbeds, not to mention taking care of the daily cooking, cleaning, shopping and the rest. Oh, and babysitting the grandchildren for at least three whole days a week and, not least, ferrying Roger home at all hours of the day and night from the bar at the golf club, because it wouldn't do at all if he should lose his licence. Well, very shortly he was going to find out for himself exactly what she *did* do all day.

'You're knocking seven bells out of that saucepan!' Roger snapped, as he meandered into the kitchen, refolding his *Daily Telegraph*. 'I hope you haven't put *cream* in that. And have you seen my reading glasses anywhere?'

He was always losing something; if it wasn't his glasses it was his car keys or his wallet, and it was probably only a matter of time before he lost his marbles. Or she lost hers.

Connie continued spooning the creamy mash into the old blue Denby dish. It had been a wedding present; forty-one years she'd been spooning stuff into that dish. There was a small crack on the underside where it wasn't particularly noticeable. Rather like my marriage, really, she thought.

'No, I haven't seen your glasses,' she said. 'Perhaps you should be wearing them on a chain round your neck.' That was guaranteed to irritate him, but she said it anyway.

'That's what *women* do,' he said, right on cue. Forget that, then.

Roger wasn't a bad man, just a bit boring, predictable, dull; most likely she was too, so it was probably high time they both had some space.

He sniffed. When *had* he started that irritating habit, sniffing for no good reason? Had he always sniffed? She remembered the early days of their marriage and how proud she'd been of her handsome husband. It was a long time ago, of course, but she had no recollection of him sniffing then. Connie would love not to be constantly irked. Perhaps it really was she who was losing her marbles? She couldn't work out what, if anything, was wrong with their marriage – only that she now needed that space, away from the routine domestic chores, perhaps in order to re-evaluate her life and appreciate her husband again. And, at sixty-six years of age, how many more chances would she ever have to do anything so radical?

Not that there was anything dramatically wrong with her life; unlike her best friend Sue. Every time she lunched with Sue, Connie listened to her continuous bleating about her errant husband. Connie never bleated about Roger, but then again she didn't really have an errant husband. Instead, Connie McColl – dutiful wife, mother, grandmother, babysitter, chauffeur and great listener – had become more or less invisible. At times she was surprised to find herself still there in the mirror; a bored, jaded-looking woman staring sadly back at herself, having lost sight of who she was. Where had the once vivacious Connie gone? *When* had she gone? Was it too late to find her again? It was time to find out. A 'voyage of self-discovery', wasn't that what they called it? If she didn't set sail now, she never would.

'Diana rang while you were out,' Roger mumbled at dinner later, through a mouthful of boeuf bourguignon (à la Delia). 'She's got an assignment in Malawi – I think she said Malawi – for the *Sunday Times* travel section, so she won't be down to see us for a couple of weeks.'

Well, there's a surprise, thought Connie. Diana, their eldest, was always so busy jetting around, sorting out holidays for the uninitiated. Lovely life she's got, with not a care in the world. And any minute now Roger will say it's high time she settled down.

Roger sniffed. 'When is that girl *ever* going to meet someone and settle down?'

That *girl* is forty years old, Connie thought. 'Di doesn't need anybody.' She topped up her wine glass, the contents of which seemed to have disappeared somewhat rapidly. 'She values her independence.' And so she should – if she'd got a grain of common sense.

Roger glanced at her over the top of his glasses. 'You're knocking it back a bit tonight.'

Connie realised it was necessary to make plans quickly, and carry them out before she changed her mind. Her old green car would need to be checked over and filled up with petrol because she certainly wouldn't want to stop until she was a very long way from her life in Sussex. And a long way from Roger. She thought her daughter Di might understand. Lou certainly wouldn't and her son Nick would just worry about her safety. And what about Roger? She supposed Roger might still love her but, during the last twenty years or so, she couldn't recall him mentioning the fact; not in the way that he openly admitted to loving his golf, his gin and his Audi. Connie couldn't remember either when she'd last told him that she loved him. Did she still love him? She wasn't sure any more, her senses having become dulled and numbed over the years. Perhaps she'd become dull too? If so, it was high time to set off on an adventure, to go on a journey to who-knows-where, and to recharge her batteries.

The next day, with Roger safely at the golf club, Connie looked through her wardrobe and considered what to pack. She'd need T-shirts and jumpers and jeans. Perhaps a dress or a skirt or something. It all had to fit into her pull-along holiday suitcase, the one that Ryanair had charged an arm and a leg for putting in the hold last summer. And she'd need an overnight bag with toiletries, make-up and changes of underwear. Perhaps she'd take the folding garden chair too – why not? It was lying there, unused, unloved and faded, on the drive, waiting to be taken to the tip. She consulted the list she'd made earlier. Connie found lists to be a great comfort, even if half the time she lost them or forgot to take them with her. Then she picked up her phone and tapped Nick's number.

'Hi, darling. Dad's at golf, as usual, and I need my tyre pressures checked. Can I pop round?'

But, really, what she needed was an excuse to see him before she left.

Later, when he'd finished, Nick said, 'Your tyres are OK at the moment, Mum, but watch that front offside one because the tread's getting a bit thin. You should really replace it before you go too far. Mind you, you should be thinking about replacing the car as well, never mind the tyre. Why don't you just sell it, Mum? It must be worth quite a bit to someone prepared to do it up; old Escorts like this have become classics. It's got to be worth five hundred or even as much as a thousand to someone looking for a project. Anyway, why the sudden concern? Are you planning a shopping trip up to town or something?'

'I might just check out the sales,' Connie said, which was a possibility of course, so she didn't feel too guilty about lying.

'Good, good. Well, have you time for a cup of coffee? I think Tess wanted to ask you a favour.'

I'll bet, thought Connie, making her way into their large state-of-the-art kitchen.

As Tess created blasts of steam, along with much hissing and gurgling from the Italian coffee machine, she asked, 'Any chance you could have the boys next Friday, Connie?'

No chance whatsoever, Connie thought, and then, for the first time, she felt a little sad. She loved her grandsons Thomas and Josh, and she'd miss them. However, she'd made her plans and she intended to stick to them. And it wasn't as if she was going away forever.

'I'll have to come back to you on that,' she said, knowing that refusing now would only cause suspicion and, besides, she hadn't got a plausible excuse ready.

Tess looked quite thunderstruck, very nearly scalding herself. 'Why, what would you be doing?'

What could I possibly be doing? Having a life of my own? Doing all the things I've forgotten how to do.

'I have some plans,' Connie replied.

Shocked silence. She saw Nick and Tess exchange looks.

'OK, Mum,' said Nick, ever the peacemaker, 'just let us know when you can.'

She glanced back as she drove away. Nick was probably her favourite of her children. She knew she wasn't *supposed* to have a favourite, but there it was. And she so loved those two little boys. Why are we women always so plagued with guilt for one reason or another? She decided there and then that guilt was not to be part of her adventure. An adventure! That's exactly what it was going to be.

'Just to remind you,' Roger said later with a sniff, 'the golf tournament's tomorrow, so I'll be gone most of the day and I expect we'll end up in the bar – either celebrating or commiserating. So I won't take the car. You can drop me off in the Audi and then I'll give you a ring when I want picking up.' Standard practice this, usually around midnight, year after year, golf tournament after golf tournament, nights on her own in front of the telly. She saw more of Stephen Fry than her own husband. Maybe if he just said, 'Would you *mind* coming to pick me up later, darling?' then I wouldn't mind so much, she thought. But he didn't and I *do* mind. *You'll just have to get a taxi or walk, or stagger, more like, knowing the amounts of alcohol likely to be consumed.* She suppressed a giggle.

'What's so funny? Damn, that's the phone! Who's ringing up this late in the evening? I've got to sort out my clubs, so can you answer that?'

Connie sighed as she picked up the phone. 'Hello?'

'Hi, Mum, it's Lou. You weren't in bed, were you?'

'Not quite. What's the problem, Lou?' She refrained from add-ing 'this time'.

The problem was, as usual, that Lou, her youngest, wasn't get-ting any sleep because little Charlotte was bawling all night and every night, and Andy, her husband, had moved into the spare room along with his ear-plugs.

'It'll pass,' Connie said wearily.

She didn't sleep well either. Now they had single beds it didn't matter to Roger that she'd tossed and turned most of the night. Was she *mad*? And where the hell was she *going*? Would her old car break down? Would *she* break down, turn around and head straight back home again?

Still sleepless at 6 a.m., Connie surveyed a bedroom she didn't much like, a plastic window she didn't like at all, and a husband she didn't care for that much either. But was any of that a good enough reason to take off? As the sun rose in the sky, she felt that sense of resolution again and was determined to give up dithering as well as feeling guilty.

She got out of bed, tiptoed across the room and looked in the mirror. She didn't look too bad a specimen for her age – tall, rea-sonably slim (thanks to several seasons at Weight Watchers), not too wrinkly and nicely highlighted and lowlighted hair (thanks to Stacey at Fringe Benefits). She could surely pass for a little younger than her sixty-six years, but sixty-six she *was*, so it was imperative to get moving before she became too old and lethargic to contem-plate any adventure of this magnitude.

'I told you, didn't I, that it's liable to be quite a late session to-night?' Roger reminded her, smacking his lips as he scraped the muesli bowl at breakfast that morning. *Organic* muesli of course, because Roger had become very fussy about what he ate recently, all of which seemed to cost twice as much as the normal stuff. He was about to find out for himself the cost of these indulgences.

'Yes, dear.' Connie spread Marmite on her toast.

'So don't worry about saving me any supper.'

'I won't.'

Later they arrived at the golf club in Roger's Audi.

'Have a nice day, dear.' He sniffed, leaned over towards the driving seat and pecked her dutifully on the cheek. 'See you later.'

Unlikely, she thought. And there was that question again: did she love him at all any more? She wasn't sure. Often it was difficult to tell. But she didn't feel the slightest sadness as she studied his rear view heading towards the club house. And she certainly *did* plan to have a nice day.

She'd already filled up with petrol. 'Special promotion on Mars bars,' the cashier had announced cheerfully. 'Two for the price of one!' And Connie had driven off the garage forecourt with a full tank and a glove compartment stuffed with chocolate, which might be invaluable on the journey. Then she wondered if she should perhaps think of buying a tent, because just how often would she be able to pay for accommodation? She had some money in her own bank account, and her pension was paid in monthly, but she wasn't at all sure it would be enough. But she'd cross that bridge when she came to it.

After she'd written a note to Roger (and positioned it beside the kettle) and sent the same email to everyone else, she loaded up her old green Ford Escort, whose name was Kermit. He was a trusty friend. OK, so he was old. So was she, but so what? She had every intention of adding several hundred – or even thousand – more miles to his clock, despite what Nick had said. Connie even slipped her passport and Kermit's papers into the glove compartment, just in case. But could she face weeks, or even months, of driving on the *right*? There was a time, of course, when – carefree and confident – she'd taken her turn at the wheel as they headed off through France and Spain and Italy, when the children were small and life was fun; when even *Roger* was fun! Well, sort of. Then there was that time at Disney World when she'd driven miles and miles through Florida trying to find a restaurant that served alligator. 'We've got to find somewhere that's got 'gator!' the kids had yelled. And they had, eventually. As the cliché warned, it tasted just like chicken.

Connie wasn't ruling anything out because, if the weather at home was forecast to be lousy, she would definitely be heading towards *le continent*. She'd withdrawn eight hundred pounds from the hole in the wall at the supermarket, but how long would that last? She might even have to find a job eventually. A *job*! Was *any-one* employing sixty-six-year-olds these days?

It was a beautiful morning and Sussex sparkled in the early sun, so it wasn't quite as imperative to seek the Mediterranean as she'd first anticipated, and the forecast seemed good. After she'd dropped Roger at the golf club, she'd come home to finish loading Kermit and tidy up the house. Duty-bound to the end, she'd even unloaded the dishwasher.

She hadn't time to find a new home for all the junk that resided in her boot, so she just dumped in her case, bags and loose clothes, and stuck the garden chair on top. Nobody, as far as she could make out, had seen her preparing to leave. For a few minutes she stopped and thought about the enormity of what she was about to do. Should she go through with it? She consoled herself by deciding that she didn't have to be away for long and, if she got homesick, she could turn round and come right back. But once she got into the car and left the cul-de-sac behind, she began to experience a long-lost sense of freedom – and the thrill of being naughty. Yes, *naughtiness*.

It was easier than she expected to leave. At least poor Paddy wasn't around any more. There was no way she could have left her beloved old Labrador and she certainly couldn't have contemplated taking him and his leaky bladder along with her, so that final trip to the vet a few months ago was probably a blessing in many ways. And it wasn't even as if she loved the bungalow either, because she didn't, not like she'd loved their old house. She'd wept when they (Roger) decided to downsize. She didn't like retirement bungalows at all, although she knew it was the sensible option now that it was just Roger and her, heading for an arthritis-filled, telly-watching dotage – and it was a very nice, spacious bungalow, as Roger (and everyone) endlessly pointed out. But she still didn't like it. She didn't much like sleeping on the ground floor either. However, there was no disputing that it was *sensible*, and everything now had to be so bloody sensible: sensible bungalow, sensible manageable garden, nice, sensible, elderly neighbours in their little cul-de-sac. (What would they think of her now?!) Bugger that – she'd give up being sensible straight away. That, too! She was shedding 'sensible' along with the guilt and the dithering.

Nevertheless, she did feel a little guilty at not having contacted Sue, with whom she had so often discussed the minutiae of daily family life. Sue, who'd been threatening to take herself off and 'leave them all to it' for years, but was still there with her womanising husband. And now here was Connie actually *doing* it!

Connie felt a surge of excitement when she arrived at the T-junction. Now, *left* to the Channel port and *le continent*? Or *right* to middle England and all points north? She stopped and looked both ways, and then decided there was definitely less traffic heading north. A Royal Mail van had appeared behind her, a youngster at the wheel tooting impatiently. Even from this distance she could see 'typical-bloody-woman-doesn't-know-where-she's-going' written all over his spotty face. She turned right, after first giving him a two-finger salute. She hadn't done anything quite so rude since she was in school and she was relieved to see that he'd turned in the opposite direction. What *had* she been thinking?

The road ahead stretched long and straight, and dappled with sunshine. Connie was on her way.

CHAPTER TWO

DREAMING SPIRES AND ALL THAT

As she meandered along minor roads, the countryside had never looked lovelier; there it was in full-blown summer perfection to be enjoyed and not bypassed at silly speeds sandwiched between huge trucks on one side and reps in company cars, for the most part, on the other. Roger spent most of his life in the middle lane (well, of course; he *had* been an accountant) whereas Connie preferred the fast lane, but allowing for the fact that both she and Kermit were getting on a bit and she was in no particular hurry, there seemed little point in motorway driving. Anyway, she'd already got three points on her licence (that day shopping with Sue in Brighton) so she needed to take care.

As she drove, her feelings ranged from exhilaration that she'd actually *done* it, that she'd finally had the courage to up and leave, to fear of the unknown. Where was she going, for God's sake? It struck her that she hadn't had to make such a big decision in a very long time. Roger invariably planned their holidays, every route, every night-stop; it was easier to go along with it. He was, after all, very efficient.

Perhaps she and Sue should just have gone off somewhere for a week? Moaned about their marriages, eaten too much, drunk too much, then headed home again. Isn't that what bored women did? (To be greeted with a disinterested 'Nice time, dear?')

No, this had to be a solitary journey. Because there was only one person – Connie McColl – who could decide on exactly what she was feeling and exactly what she was going to do about it. She wasn't sixteen, though, she was sixty-six and, judging by the way her stomach was churning, she'd probably felt more confident at sixteen.

Then she saw the sign: Oxford! Oxford, where she'd first lost her heart and her virginity many, many years previously. The city occupied a special place in her heart, although she'd mostly viewed its dreaming spires from Dominic's musty attic bedroom, where she'd viewed them, and him, from some interesting angles. Really, sex had never been quite so good since and she'd done a fair bit of research – *before* she'd married Roger, of course.

Smiling to herself, she took the Oxford exit seconds before Ken Bruce informed his Radio 2 listeners of the road works, heavy traffic and long delays likely for all vehicles heading into the city from the south and the west. Too late she was aware of the panorama of red brake lights in the sea of traffic ahead. Half an hour later, having inched forward for less than a quarter of a mile, she began to wonder at the wisdom of her decision to visit this city. There she was, hemmed in on all sides, with no means of escape. She'd even become matey, in a shoulder-shrugging, eye-rolling sort of way, with a young woman in a silver Renault crawling alongside, and felt quite bereft when the Renault's lane moved forward and hers didn't. Silly things got to you when you were bored rigid. In need of soothing, she switched to Classic FM where they were in the middle of the 'Radetzky March', complete with hand-clapping. Not today, thanks, she thought, and switched back to Ken, who was about to go home. Only hope you don't live in Oxford, Ken, she thought.

By the time she got to the city centre it was mid-afternoon, and she was hot and exhausted and beginning to panic about finding accommodation. And then she saw it – the Randolph! She'd gone there, once only, with Dominic for afternoon tea. 'Do you suppose we'll ever be able to stay in places like this one day?' she'd murmured through her scone. 'I fully intend to,' he'd replied, and doubtless he had. She recollected he'd been studying law – or was it medicine? Well, it might have taken her nearly fifty years but she too was going to stay here tonight. And why not? she thought.

Having finally parked and given her payment details at the reception desk, she realised precisely why not. She'd be lucky if her money lasted a few days at this rate. This had to be a one-off.

Strolling in the afternoon sunshine, Connie found Oxford had changed a little; the atmosphere seemed more relaxed and less formal. She remembered locally owned, individual and interesting shops, but now here they all were – the usual selection of chain stores found in every city centre in the land. Pity. Having spent half the day cooped up in her car, Connie was glad to be able to stretch her legs and she walked until they began to ache. She remembered a tiny boutique where she'd bought a mini-skirt she couldn't afford, while Dominic had preened himself in the shop's mirror. He had been rather vain, with his carefully coiffed shoulder-length hair and ruffled shirts. She wondered what he looked like now. Elderly, like herself, and probably with a paunch.

She wandered off the main street and down some little lanes where there were still some boutiques and specialist shops. And independent bookshops. Yes, the old Oxford was still there, just hidden away.

Then it was time to head back to her beautiful expensive room and luxuriate in a soothing, scented bath. And *then* what?

As she cocooned herself in the enormous, fluffy bath sheet, Connie wondered how to spend her first evening as a woman alone. She decided she would have one drink, and one drink only, in the lounge downstairs and then head out to find somewhere cheap and cheerful to eat. And, after that, an early night. Jeans wouldn't do at all but, thankfully, she'd remembered to pack the white trousers. And, when covered by her long black silk shirt, her bum and tum didn't look big at all.

Soft music, comfy settees and attentive waiters! She ordered a gin and tonic and, feeling a little wobbly and self-conscious about being by herself, found a secluded corner from which she could observe the dark-suited businessmen, the laughing young couples and the barman wielding his cocktail shaker with not a little theatricality. She saw a short, plump lady in a similar black top and white trousers heading out of the bar with a face like thunder. Probably just had a row with her other half or something, Connie thought.

She'd almost finished her drink when she noted the arrival of a rather dapper and attractive man, probably in his late fifties or early sixties. He was looking wildly around, as if late for something. And then he spotted her and, much to Connie's astonishment, headed straight in her direction and said, 'Dorothy? So sorry I'm late! You can't *imagine* the traffic...'

'I'm not—' she began, but he'd already dumped his briefcase on the chair opposite and was heading off in the direction of the bar, calling over his shoulder, 'I'll be right with you after I've ordered some champagne.'

Dumbfounded, Connie watched him talk to the barman, produce a wad of notes and point to her table. She had to stop him because this was crazy. Too late, though. As she stood up he was already heading back towards her.

'Dorothy, I can't apologise enough!'

'I'M NOT DOROTHY!'

'What?'

'I'm not Dorothy.'

'You're not? Who are you then?'

'I'm Connie.'

'Connie?'

This whole conversation was becoming ridiculous.

'Yes.' She was aware of the waiter approaching with a bottle of Bollinger, two glasses and a dish of olives. They sat in awkward silence while he deposited everything on the table and opened the champagne. 'Will that be all, sir?'

Her new companion looked bewildered. 'Yes, yes, thank you,' he stuttered. Then, after the waiter was out of earshot, he said, 'You're *not* from MMM?'

'What or who is MMM?'

'Oh God.' He clapped his hand to his forehead and Connie wondered briefly which of them was the more confused.

Recovering his composure, he said, 'You must think I'm mad. I'm *so* sorry. You see, I'm supposed to meet a lady called Dorothy here, from MMM, and I'm forty minutes late. She said she'd be wearing a black top and white trousers. You're *definitely* not from MMM? Perhaps I got the name wrong?'

'I'm not from MMM, whatever it is,' Connie replied, wondering if you could get a refund on an opened bottle of Bolly. 'I'm Connie.' She drained the remainder of her gin and tonic, anxious to be gone. 'But I did see a lady wearing white trousers walking out of the bar about ten minutes ago.'

'Oh God! Poor Dorothy! I don't suppose she'll risk MMM again.' He smiled apologetically and Connie found herself smiling back.

'What is this MMM anyway?'

'MMM's just an agency,' he said. 'Well, never mind, we mustn't waste this bottle, must we? I'm Martin, by the way.' He stood up, hand outstretched. 'I should have introduced myself before this. I'm so sorry!'

'Do stop apologising!' Connie laughed as she shook his hand. 'But I can't possibly drink your champagne!'

'Why ever not?'

'Because I'm not Dorothy.'

'No, you're Connie! But I'm being thoughtless and you are probably waiting for someone?'

'No, I'm on my own, but—'

'Well, in that case, let's drink the champagne.'

With that he filled their glasses and raised his, grinning at her. 'Cheers!'

Connie raised her glass to him, studying his profile, which reminded her a little of Robert De Niro; lived-in, craggy, interesting. She took a sip of the Bollinger. Delicious.

'Are you here for business or pleasure, Connie?'

'Now that's a difficult question,' she said. 'Not business, though. And this, I think, is definitely pleasure, unexpected pleasure.'

'Well,' said Martin, 'here's to a great evening!' He refilled their glasses and popped an olive in his mouth. 'And I've booked a table for two at the Italian round the corner. I hope you like Italian?'

'This,' Connie said, champagne bubbles tickling her nose, 'is all quite ridiculous.'

He leaned towards her. 'You know what? I'm glad you're not Dorothy. She'd probably have been a dull old bird.'

Connie felt momentarily uplifted at not being considered a dull old bird. Not yet, anyway. And Martin was rather nice. This was the first time she'd been treated as an attractive woman (well, passable anyway) in decades and she was enjoying the sensation. Or was he just being dutiful, and feeling sorry for her? Well, she'd pay her way in the Italian restaurant.

'You must tell me about Dorothy and MMM,' she said.

He was a little reluctant at first to explain these mysterious initials, then finally admitted to them standing for 'Meetings for the More Mature'. Heavens, Connie thought, it's a dating agency for oldies!

Why would he need to use such an agency? Here was an attractive man, nice hazel eyes, well-cut short grey hair, well suited (sartorially at least) and clearly successful.

'I work very long hours,' he explained, as if reading her thoughts. 'It's difficult to meet anyone in the first place, and then it's even more difficult to get to an appointment on time. Tonight is a typical example.' His gaze was direct. 'I really don't think MMM is going to work for me.'

One of the things Connie liked about him was that he looked *at* her, not *through* her, or, worse, over her shoulder. In fact, he was quite the opposite of Roger. Connie McColl, she chided herself, what the hell are you *thinking* of! Are you so starved emotionally that you go soft on the first man who pays you any attention? And you haven't even been away from home twenty-four hours yet!

A couple of hours later, tucking into her tiramisu, Connie had told Martin all about her escape from a disinterested husband, demanding offspring and the bungalow. She made special mention of the plastic windows in particular. 'They're all plastic, the whole bloody place is plastic!' She wondered if she was enunciating her words clearly, knowing she shouldn't have let him top up her glass again.

'That's a pity, Connie, because there's nothing wrong with plastic, you know. It's made me a lot of money.'

He was the director of a company that made plastic containers of every shape and size. And the business was doing well. She didn't feel nearly so bad about the champagne and three slap-up Italian courses now. His wife had left him, he informed her. 'Took off with some Spanish waiter,' he said, 'and went to live in the Canaries.'

'Tweet, tweet!' Connie said, and they both dissolved into giggles.

'At last I can laugh about it,' he said, 'but I was devastated at the time. Fortunately the children were grown up.'

Perhaps they couldn't agree on the plastic, but they discovered they shared a love of Italian opera, Shiraz wines, Bruce Springsteen and cauliflower cheese. 'I could eat it all day long,' said Connie.

'Me too,' he said. He was rapidly becoming a soulmate. 'And, just because a person's getting on a bit,' he continued, 'it doesn't mean that you can't have some fun – companionship, sex, marriage even.'

'Oh, quite,' agreed Connie, hoping he wasn't planning to rip her knickers off. This was not a problem she'd encountered in many a year. She had to make it clear that she was *not* looking for another man.

'I'm not looking for another man,' she informed him, downing her espresso. 'I'm just trying to get away from the one I've got for a while.'

'Well,' Martin said, 'if you are ever looking for a replacement, MMM's as good a place as any to start looking.'

'I'll bear it in mind,' said Connie.

Martin was a nice man, as well as being attractive – really quite fanciable – but she wasn't sure she was ever going to be ready to fancy anyone. But she loved the fact that he appeared to be interested in *her*! How many men ever listened to what you had to say? I could count them on my fingers, she thought, and still have half a dozen to spare.

Their conversation never faltered; they talked for hours. She told him things she'd never talked to Roger about as he'd never seemed interested. She told him, among other things, how much she would have liked to study art, but her parents had been killed when she was just five and their financial legacy had all been used up by the time she was fifteen. Her uncle and aunt, having provided further education for their own brood, couldn't afford university or art school fees for her too. So she'd trained as a florist. She told him how much she loved flowers, and drawing.

'So, you're artistic,' he said.

'No,' Connie replied. 'But I like sketching. My mother apparently designed and put together costumes for theatrical productions just before the war, prior to meeting my dad, so perhaps I've inherited a little of her creativity.' For a moment she thought of Stratford, remembering that her mother had worked on a production there. And Stratford wasn't so very far away.

'Your mother sounds like a very talented lady.'

'Yes, I think she must have been,' Connie replied.

'And are you also a talented lady?'

'Oh, no, not really. But I am good with flowers. I love growing them and arranging them and, at one time when I was doing floristry, I had two greenhouses of exotic plants. We had a big garden then.'

'And you don't now?'

'No, I don't now.' Connie sighed. 'We downsized because the house and garden were too big – so said my husband anyway.'

'And you don't like this new place with its plastic windows much?'

'I've tried hard but the bungalow isn't exactly lovable. And it's got a tiny square garden; everyone in the cul-de-sac has a tiny square garden, packed with twee pots and twee borders full of dahlias and begonias. They last all summer, begonias do, which is why so many councils pack them into their public flowerbeds. God, how I *hate* begonias!'

Connie was surprised at her own outburst. Well, she *did* hate begonias and she wasn't that wild about dahlias either.

'I think I might head for Stratford next because my mother once designed the costumes for a production of *King Lear* – before the war, that is. Her brother, my Uncle Bill, said that everyone thought she'd marry someone creative – a thespian perhaps. But Dad was just an ordinary bloke and they fell in love.'

'And what did your ordinary dad do?'

'Dad was a policeman; he worked for the Met, in London. But he was a Geordie. I headed up north once, many years ago, to see where he was born. I've always meant to go back but, what with marriage and kids and everything, it's just never happened.'

'Well, you have the opportunity now. Perhaps you should go.'

Quite suddenly Connie felt light-headed, and it wasn't the champagne; it was an unexpected sense of freedom. 'Yes, I think I will.'

He smiled. 'Getting back to your flowers,' he said, 'I have a book which I think you might like. It has the most beautiful drawings and watercolour prints of flowers. And, if I remember correctly, it doesn't feature a single begonia or dahlia! I bought it for my wife as an early birthday present, but she'd bolted by then. Why don't I send it to you? That's if you wouldn't be offended?'

'Oh, that is so sweet of you, but I really have no idea when I'll be getting home.'

'It doesn't matter, Connie, I'll just stick it in the post sometime in the next few weeks. You'll have it when you eventually get back.'

'Thanks so much,' she said, delving into the depths of her shoulder bag for one of her cards. She hadn't planned to let anyone make contact with her at home, and here she was, doing just that, on her very first night away! Well, rules are made to be broken, she thought. And he's a true gentleman.

'Keep in touch, Connie. Let me know what you decide and how you get on. I rather envy people who take life by the scruff of the neck and really jolly well live it!'

Gosh, is he referring to me? Connie wondered. Have I changed already?

He insisted on walking her home and seeing her to her hotel door. 'I've enjoyed my evening with you enormously,' Martin said. 'How about I come in and we order some coffee, or a nightcap or something?'

She took a deep breath: payment time! I don't want to spoil this beautiful friendship, she thought, but I don't want him to kiss me, attractive though he is. She could feel the beginnings of panic rising in her breast as he leaned towards her.

'I don't think so,' said Connie. 'I'm *so* tired, Martin. It's been a long day.' This was going to be difficult because he had insisted on paying for the dinner. And she was really beginning to warm to him.

'No hanky-panky, I promise!'

She laughed. 'I'd really prefer not; I just want to get to sleep. But thanks for the offer. And thanks for a lovely, lovely and totally unexpected evening.'

As she braced herself for his reply, he very slowly lifted a stray tendril of hair, which had fallen over one eye, and placed it gently behind her ear.

'Goodnight, Connie,' he said, and pecked her on the cheek. 'Please keep in touch.'

'I will,' she said, as she watched him walk a little unsteadily down the corridor. 'I will.'

CHAPTER THREE

ESCAPE ROUTE

In spite of her exhaustion, Connie couldn't sleep. Martin must have fancied her a *little*, or at least fancied her enough to want to take things further, and she was flattered, no doubt about that. She felt elated. She'd forgotten what it felt like to be desired by a man. She was almost regretting warding him off. She'd never once in her marriage been unfaithful or even thought about being unfaithful. Was it fear, or was it faithfulness to Roger? And had *he* always been faithful? There were times when Connie wondered about those golfing weekends in Scotland, Ireland and Spain. It was difficult to think of Roger as a womaniser, though. Connie spent most of the night trying to analyse her feelings. She finally woke at nearly nine o'clock, not having got to sleep until four.

She'd had a lovely evening with far too much to eat and drink and now she couldn't face a big breakfast. Which was a pity, because you could fill up for the day on a big breakfast, and that was exactly what she was going to have to do from now on. There was no sign of Martin downstairs and Connie found, to her surprise, that she was slightly disappointed as she tackled a solitary croissant.

Well, of course he wouldn't be around at this time in the morning! He must live locally, after all, and at this very moment would probably be busily churning out his plastic bowls and boxes.

But, she'd had a date last night! OK, so it wasn't a *real* date, not a prearranged meeting because you fancied someone. But he hadn't fled in horror when he realised she wasn't Dorothy, had he? He must have thought she was *all right*.

Afterwards, when she'd eaten all she could manage, she drifted into the reception area and noticed the computer in the corner. Intrigued to know more about the agency behind her 'date' the previous evening, she sat down and googled MMM, and there it was! 'Meetings for the More Mature! Find your friend or partner with us! You're never too old!' There followed countless pictures of impossibly glamorous oldies gazing at each other in awe or, arm in arm, beaming at the camera. 'Only *some* of our success stories,' it warbled on. 'Just fill in your details, join us and we guarantee to introduce you to new friends!' In return for typing in her name, age, occupation and general interests, she would receive a list of 'friends' who might be compatible. And it appeared to be a free service. Connie giggled to herself. The last thing she needed right now was a list of needy men. She'd bear it in mind if she ever became needy herself, God forbid.

Connie bought a newspaper and sat reading it for a little while, before edging out of Oxford through the mid-morning traffic. She was heading for Stratford-upon-Avon, not least because of the connection with her mother, but also because she'd only been there once before, briefly, with Roger. She'd wanted to look around but Roger hadn't been impressed. It had been raining, he didn't fancy

Romeo and Juliet, and they were meeting his cousin in Evesham. For golf. She'd always wanted to come back.

The minor road would have been delightful had it not been for the enormous milk tanker that had positioned itself in front of her, mile after mile, with no opportunity to overtake, and which afforded her a view only of its huge shiny steel derrière.

The road twisted its way through picturesque villages of golden Cotswold stone, most with a pub, a church and roadside cottages, their gardens overflowing with summer flowers; sometimes a petrol station, a Spar and occasional flashing signs informing both her and the tanker that they were exceeding the speed limit. She'd only taken her eye off the speedometer for a minute but Kermit still had amazing oomph. Finally the tanker turned off to the right and headed down a narrow lane to collect its cargo from some unseen farm, signposted 'Stitfield' (some comedian had changed the first T into an H), and at last Connie had a view of the rolling countryside and the road ahead where, with half a ton of stuff on his back, a hitchhiker thumbed hopefully.

'Never, *ever* pick up anyone thumbing a lift,' Roger had instructed her shortly after they were married and when she'd started to brake, having passed two girls on the A29 waving a sign that said 'Bognor'. Connie wondered at the time why these two, with all the destinations on the planet at their disposal, would choose Bognor. Not that there was anything *wrong* with Bognor. Perhaps they lived there? But she never did find out because common sense had prevailed. These girls could be *anybody*, Roger had said, and they could be armed with knives, or even guns. Probably druggies as well. Otherwise why didn't they just get on a bus when there was a perfectly good service to Bognor half a dozen times a day? Roger knew this because he'd always lived in Sussex, and always would. And he was most definitely not the type to have ever hitch-hiked, not even in his youth. Perhaps she should have realised then how their future might be.

As she passed the hitchhiking boy she was immediately aware of his dejected appearance as he plodded along, being constantly ignored. There was a layby ahead and it seemed like fate was guiding her decision, so Connie decided to pull in. She studied him in the rear-view mirror and thought that he didn't look too menacing. This escape was, after all, an opportunity to do what she wanted and not what Roger would have done. Now that he was level with her, she could see that he couldn't be more than nineteen or twenty, clad in the usual attire of T-shirt, jeans and trainers. She wound down the window and the boy looked in.

'Hey!' he said.

'Where are you going?' Connie asked.

'Stratford-upon-Avon.'

Connie smiled. 'Stratford's just where I'm going. Dump that rucksack on the back seat.'

'Jeez, that's great.' He humped the rucksack off his back and stuffed it into Kermit's rear.

As he eased his long frame into the passenger seat she studied his freckled face, sandy hair and long, skinny legs in their faded denims.

'I'm Harry,' he said, holding out his hand. He made it sound like a question. Aussie? New Zealander?

Connie shook his hand. 'I'm Connie and, as soon as I can pull out of here, we'll be on our way to Stratford.'

'Cool. I didn't think you'd stop – a woman on her own, and all that.'

'I don't usually,' Connie said, 'but you just looked so dejected somehow.'

'Rejected, more like. It's not easy getting lifts. Truck drivers stop occasionally.'

'So, where have you come from today?'

'Last night I stayed in Oxford. Oxford was cool; I met a really nice girl there.'

'And…'

'And nothing. Nah, just ships that pass in the night, as they say. She was older than me anyhow, and cleverer.'

'Clever folk in Oxford. And lots of ships that pass in the night.' Connie grinned to herself. 'And where do you hail from originally?'

'I'm from Australia, near Sydney.'

'And now you're going to brush up on your Shakespeare?'

'Yeah, I might meet up with a buddy of mine there, and then we'll probably head north together. You live round here?'

'No,' said Connie. 'I live in Sussex. That's on the south coast.'

'So, you going on holiday then?'

'Something like that. Are you a student?'

'Yeah, I'm on a gap year, doing Europe. And, hey, your weather's beautiful; everyone back home said I'd either freeze or drown in the British summer.'

Connie laughed. 'They have a point; we do get some awful ones. But this year's an exception, so far anyway. What are you studying?'

'Law. My dad's a lawyer too, in Sydney.'

'Sydney. Lovely.'

'You been there?'

'Some years ago, when we went to visit my husband's sister.' And God knows why, she thought, because Roger had never got on with his sister.

'That's cool! Did you see much of Australia?'

'Well, we did do all the touristy things in Sydney, and even got up to the Blue Mountains on one occasion. And we went to Melbourne and Brisbane too.'

They drove along in silence for some miles. Connie thought about the Australian trip. She'd liked Roger's sister; in fact, truth be known, she liked her better than Roger.

Then she thought about her mother, who'd made the costumes for that Shakespeare play all those years ago. How gifted she must have been! After all, you couldn't just sew a few sheets together for a production in Stratford; it was no school play. She'd probably have to have had some knowledge of history as well as sewing skills. Connie had an old notebook of her mother's showing the sketches for *Lear* and lots of notes and, taped inside, the actual programme of the performance with her mother's name there under 'Costumes'. She had plainly been proud of her participation, and Connie was too. As a youngster, she and her cousin Joyce, who was a year older, had decided they too were destined to become costume designers or, better still, fashion designers. Until, that is, they produced some oddly shaped dolls' outfits, which had caused great mirth among the older cousins. Connie hadn't been very hot on history or needlework at school, but she'd been good at art and, years later, had won prizes for her floral displays, so perhaps she'd inherited a tiny bit of her mother's flair. She often longed for contact with the mother she barely remembered. How would they get on now? And what would her mother, and her father for that matter, think of her taking to the road like this and leaving her family behind?

'Are you visiting someone in Stratford?' Harry asked.

'No, not really. My late mother was a costume designer and did some work for the Shakespeare Memorial Theatre in the days before there was an RSC. She loved the town, so I'd like to get to know it a little.'

'So you've got no definite plans?'

'Well, just a trip to the theatre.'

Connie knew he was curious and was aware of his surreptitious sideways glances. No wonder, she thought: an elderly woman driving alone in an elderly car.

She smiled to herself. I think I'm going to like being an object of mystery!

'If my husband had been with me I wouldn't have been allowed to pick you up. He'd have had you down as an axe-murderer or something.'

'But I haven't got an axe. Why would he think that?' Harry sounded confused.

'Because that's the way he is – careful…'

'And you're not?'

'I'm trying not to be. Do you fancy a Mars bar? Help yourself – glove compartment.'

'Yeah, great. Jeez, how many Mars you got in there? You an addict or something?'

'Special offer. Tell me, have you eaten lately?'

'Not really. A slice of toast for breakfast.'

'I only had a croissant and I'm becoming peckish now. I've just seen a sign advertising an All Day Breakfast one mile ahead. Do you like All Day Breakfasts?'

'Love 'em!' said Harry, through a mouthful of Mars.

'Come on then,' she said. 'My treat.'

Connie, still feeling a little full from last night's Italian, settled for an omelette, and Harry had chosen the most enormous breakfast on the menu. 'You sure it's OK?' he'd asked. Later, as he wiped the last of his toast round the now empty plate, he said, 'That was awesome.'

'You remind me of my son, the way you demolished that lot,' Connie laughed.

'So, you got kids then?'

'Yes. Well, they're hardly kids of course. Diana, my eldest, is forty.'

He whistled. 'Jeez – I wouldn't have put you at more than fifty, fifty-five maybe.'

'You flatterer, you! And I have a son of thirty-two and another daughter of thirty. And three grandchildren.'

He was looking longingly at the slice of toast she'd left on her side plate.

She pushed it towards him. 'Go on, then.'

'Hey, thanks! You're a real angel, Connie. Hope your family appreciate you.'

'Sometimes they do, sometimes they don't.'

'So, where's the husband that doesn't let you pick up axe-murderers?'

Connie consulted her watch. 'Heading towards the eighteenth hole, probably.'

'Aw, right. So, you leaving him there then?'

'That's exactly what I'm doing.'

'You said that with feeling! How long you planning to be away for?'

'I've no idea. I'm free as a bird – a newly uncaged bird, though, and trying to remember how to stretch my wings and fly.'

'Well, looks like you're on your way, Connie.'

'Yes, I'm on my way. Now, do you want some tea, and a doughnut maybe?'

'That would be brilliant.'

When they arrived in Stratford-upon-Avon and she eventually found a parking space, Connie helped Harry heave his rucksack out from the back seat.

'I've really enjoyed your company,' she said.

'You've been a star, Connie.' He'd hoisted the rucksack onto his back and was trying to regain his balance. 'Wherever you're going, I hope you have a great time. And learn to fly again.' He gave her a clumsy hug.

'Thank you, Harry. You, too.'

'And don't you go picking up any axe-murderers now.'

CHAPTER FOUR

FIRST REACTIONS

Roger had read Connie's message. And then he'd read it again. And again.

Dear Roger,

By the time you read this I'll be on my way to who-knows-where, geographically at least, but hopefully on the way to finding myself emotionally. If I don't do it now I never will! Because all my life it seems that I've been told by everyone around me what to do. That probably began when I was dumped on poor Aunt Lorna as a newly orphaned five-year-old. With four of her own I was naturally at the very bottom of the pecking order. So I became a dutiful niece, and I like to think I've been a dutiful wife, mother and grandmother, because I've tried hard to please you all. But, do you know what? Being dutiful isn't enough any more!

I'm now going to spend some time pleasing no one but myself, finding out who I really am, and what I might like to do with the rest of my life, before it's too damn late. My senses need awakening and my wings need stretching. I'm not sure you'll understand but I don't know how else to explain it.

Last, but far from least, every single one of you forgot the anniversary of Ben's death. Everyone, that is, except my dear friend, Wendy, in Scotland...

I love you all very, very much but I just need some time for myself. I promise to come home when I'm ready, but not before.

xxxx

Diana McColl read her mother's email twice.

'Yesss! Go for it, Mum!' She clapped her hands with glee. And not before time, she thought.

Diana was the only one of Connie's children who had been even remotely interested in her mother's childhood. Di found it very difficult and quite heart-breaking to imagine losing your parents in a car accident when you were so young. It wasn't as if Aunt Lorna was 'blood' either. Uncle Bill was 'blood', of course, but he had been in Africa – something to do with oil – most of the time.

And Di was also aware that *she* was the real, and unplanned, reason her parents had married in the first place. It's what you did back then if the man hung around long enough. Two dutiful people! She also knew, much as she loved them both, that her parents weren't compatible at all – probably never had been. Well, no way was *she*, Diana McColl, going to get tied down with *anybody*, compatible or not.

She poured herself a glass of wine, knowing that her father would doubtless be on the phone any minute now asking if her mother was there. Hopefully her mother would be well on the way to wherever she was going. Good for Mum! It was the kind of thing that lots of married women would dream of doing, but didn't have the guts for.

Di raised her glass. 'Here's to you, Mum!'

❋

'What the hell's got into her – that's what I'd like to know!' Roger ranted at no one in particular as he downed a large gin and tonic in Nick and Tess's laboratory-like kitchen, which came complete with a sofa. Roger couldn't for the life of him fathom why anyone would want a sofa in their kitchen. He would have much preferred to be cosily ensconced in their sitting room, with olives and cashews in little dishes on the coffee table, and countryside views. Instead, here he was in this clinical place with only a view of Tess's overweight backside as she bent to shove things in and out of the oven. Still, at least they were feeding him. And thankfully the boys were in bed; that would have been the final straw. Lovely though they were, when they were around he had to watch his language.

'The thing is, Dad,' Nick said as he filled up his father's glass again, 'she's not exactly *left* us. She just said in her email that she needs some time for herself.'

'And why would she need that? She's got plenty of time to herself. I mean, what the hell's *wrong* with her?' Roger took a large gulp and sniffed. He'd noticed Nick and Tess occasionally exchanging glances; this whole thing was making him look like an idiot.

'This doesn't just affect you,' Tess snapped. 'What am *I* going to do on Friday if she's not here to look after Thomas and Joshua?'

As if that was all that mattered, Roger thought. What was it this time: Pilates, yoga, stained-glass-window making? Why the hell couldn't Tess look after her own kids like Connie had had to do? Perhaps it was no wonder Connie got fed up sometimes.

Roger couldn't come round here every night, he supposed, but hopefully Lou might feed him tomorrow and then Connie was *bound* to be back. Di, of course, was no good to anyone.

'Well,' his elder daughter had said on the phone, 'maybe she just wants a bit of "me" time.'

'What the hell's that?' he'd hollered. 'She gets plenty of that. Life of Riley. Everything paid for. Nice new house, nice enough car, nice family. What's she *playing* at?' Restless indeed! *Senses needing awakening and wings needing stretching!* What the hell was that all about? Just where did she get all this drivel? Probably from reading far too much soppy women's fiction. What was it with these women? he wondered. *Never* damn well happy.

※

Louise Morrison checked her mobile again but still nothing further from Mum; only yesterday's email, to which she'd added some kisses and a smiley face. Huh.

'We'd better ask your dad round for dinner, I suppose,' said Andy, as he uncorked the Sauvignon Blanc. 'I shouldn't think he knows how to boil an egg.'

'Time he learned then,' snapped Lou. 'Anyway, I expect she'll be home in a day or two.'

'Don't underestimate your mother,' said Andy. 'But I'd really just like to know what's brought this on. She never complains. You don't think your dad's playing around, do you?'

'Playing around? *Dad?* You must be joking. The only playing around he does is on the golf course.'

'Don't be too sure. He's still a good-looking man, and what about this new organic diet and the fancy haircut? Are there women members at this golf club of his?'

Her father's trendy, short haircut had taken years off him. For the first time Lou felt some stirrings of doubt.

'But he's coming up to *seventy*! Oh, I know, I *know*, that doesn't stop them. But *Dad...*' Lou shook her head. 'It's not as if they had a row or anything, Dad says. Mind you, he wasn't too thrilled at being marooned at the golf club last night. No reply when he rang Mum, and then he had to get a taxi home, and there was her note beside the kettle saying exactly the same as the emails we all got.'

'Well,' said Andy, 'we'll feed him tomorrow night, and after that he'll have to trawl the aisles in M&S like everyone else. Is that the baby I'm hearing?'

'Damn, damn, *damn*! I thought she'd gone down. Too good to be true – who would have a colicky baby?'

As she headed towards the door, sighing, Andy handed her a glass of wine. 'Here, get that down you first.'

<hr />

Roger McColl, home again, kicked off his shoes in the bedroom, which overlooked the garden and got the evening sunshine. He liked this room, although Connie didn't because of her crankiness about bungalows in general and having to sleep on the ground floor. What was wrong with *that*?

Roger surveyed himself in the full-length mirror. He wasn't bad looking, really. Slight paunch, of course, but he was working on it. He hadn't told anyone, including Connie, that he'd sent away for one of those gadgets he'd seen advertised in the newspaper. It was a kind of rowing machine that guaranteed (*or money fully refunded*) to tighten up the tum, bum and anywhere else in need. The paunch had to go. Connie might laugh, but she wasn't here, and he planned to start using it from tomorrow morning. It was all part of his rejuvenation, along with the haircut and the attention to his diet. He peered at his face in the mirror and already he thought he could perceive an improvement in his skin. Women, including Connie, spent a small fortune on so-called miracle creams but they all failed to grasp the fact that it was what you put *into* your body that mattered, not what you plastered on top of it. Well, he might be sixty-eight, but his skin was in damn good condition – better than hers, in fact. He'd been letting himself go, no doubt about it. Simon Barker's remark at the ninth hole the other day – something about 'old, overweight has-beens like us' – had really got to him. He did not want to be an old, overweight has-been. He thought he was looking better already.

So *why* had Connie done a runner? Had she met someone else? Connie? No, of course not. But he needed to know.

He hadn't told anyone that he'd actually gone to the local police station, because he'd wondered how to trace a missing person.

'But she isn't missing,' the policeman had explained patiently. 'She's gone away of her own accord and she's perfectly entitled to do that.'

Well, *he* certainly didn't know where she'd gone. In their forty-one years together he'd never had to face such uncertainty. They'd gone off separately before; he for his golfing weekends and she for her so-called 'girly' get-togethers. ('Girly' – ha ha, he thought, and not one of them under sixty!) But she'd always left a well-stocked fridge and freezer, and he was a dab hand with the microwave.

He would eat out often at the golf club, that's what he'd do. The food there was top notch, and there was the added bonus of being served by the beautiful Andrea.

CHAPTER FIVE

CULTURE VULTURE

What Connie really wanted was a glass of wine and an early night. But first she needed to find some accommodation and Stratford was bulging with tourists of every nationality; she recognised half a dozen different languages even as she walked the length of Henley Street.

The tourist information lady shook her head sadly. 'Very few rooms left anywhere, Mrs McColl.' She sighed. 'There's always the Cedars, I suppose. It's not exactly the Ritz but it's clean.'

Connie's back ached after the drive. 'Can you try them for me?'

'Yes,' said the tourist information lady a few minutes later, 'they have a single room. Let me give you directions.'

'Thank you.' Armed with the information, she headed back to where she'd parked Kermit, stopping at a small off-licence called Wise to Wines (but not so wise that they stocked corkscrews), where she bought a bottle of red wine with a screw top. She would have to buy a corkscrew on her travels – and soon. Then she spent twenty minutes circling the outskirts of the town (she'd always been hopeless at following directions) before she came across a tall, narrow terraced house sporting a 'Vacancies' sign although, for the life of her, Connie couldn't see anything remotely resembling a cedar.

'You're lucky,' said the fat, balding owner, whose name was Len. She could read the words 'I love' tattooed in blue up his left arm, but the object of his love was hidden by the rolled-up sleeve of his purple shirt. 'Not many travelling on their own, you see.' He gave her an appraising look before leading the way across the violently patterned brown and orange carpet, which stretched along the narrow hall.

'This is the residents' lounge,' Len continued proudly, opening a door on the right. What little she could see of it reminded her of the nursing home where she visited Aunt Lorna from time to time. Upright chairs round the walls, an enormous television screen and an elderly couple gazing vacantly at some noisy quiz show. The same carpet was fitted there and also up two flights of narrow stairs. Connie, dizzied by the decor, finally arrived at Room 5.

'Full English breakfast, seven-thirty to nine,' Len announced as he handed her the key. 'We don't do dinner –' he sidled slightly closer – 'but I could bring you up a few sandwiches.'

'No, thank you, I'm going to the theatre tonight,' said Connie with as much dignity as she could muster. She'd planned a two-night stay in Stratford before arriving at the Cedars. Now she was convinced that one night here would be quite sufficient.

'I'll give you a key for the outside door then,' said Len, plainly disappointed.

The room was one of the smallest Connie had ever seen. Into it was squashed a single bed with a tiny table alongside, an equally tiny wall-mounted TV and a narrow, ancient wardrobe with a time-blemished mirror on the door. Next to it was the en-suite, which had obviously once been part of the room and was the size of a cupboard. A preformed pink plastic shell with moulded loo, basin and shower had been fitted inside. The pink shower curtain hung sadly from three metal hooks, and stopped six inches short of the floor. Still, it was clean and it was cheap, and Len had even supplied the obligatory tray, overhanging the table alarmingly, on which were positioned a cup and saucer, two tea bags, two Nescafé sachets and four pots of long-life milk. No biscuits. No teaspoon. At least there was a plastic glass on the sink for her wine. And to think that last night she'd had that gorgeous room in the Randolph!

Connie sat on the bed and turned on her phone: seven missed calls and eight texts, three from Roger, all singing from the same hymn-sheet. Not to mention countless emails.

Roger: *Where are you? Why aren't you answering your phone? When are you coming home?* (Connie noted that in not one of Roger's emails or texts did he ask her if she was OK, or say that he loved her.

Nick: *Look after yourself, Mum, and come home soon.*

Lou: *Can't believe you could just up and leave! We all miss you.*

Diana: *Had enough of them all, Mum? Take care, keep in touch. Mauritius is fantastic!*

Mauritius! Roger had said Diana was in Malawi. Connie sent the same brief text to them all, switched off her phone again, and decided to shower.

At least the water was hot, even if the shower curtain kept wrapping itself around her body. After she'd dried herself, Connie took in her surroundings; she most definitely wouldn't be spending the evening in this dismal room.

Connie had never been to a theatre, or even a cinema, on her own. The thought of it was scary but here it was, a new challenge to her self-confidence, the first hurdle of independent womanhood. She reminded herself that women were assertive these days; they ran their own businesses and headed whole companies, even governed countries, so surely she could manage to park her solo bottom on a theatre seat. Nevertheless, she felt quite frightened and she probably wouldn't understand a word of the play anyway. But she was damned if she was going to slink into the theatre, hoping for invisibility. This was not why she'd left home, to cower around in other people's shadows! She'd left to become her own person again, to do new things, meet new people, have new experiences. She'd wear her best dress – her *only* dress – spray herself liberally with Chanel No. 5, and walk into the theatre with her head held high. That's what she'd try to do. She'd like to think her mum would be proud of her.

Connie stood outside the Royal Shakespeare Theatre in awe. As far as Shakespeare was concerned she only knew *A Midsummer Night's Dream*, because she'd done that for her A-Level English.

The lady in the box office was friendly. 'Tonight,' she said, 'it's *Richard II*. Beautiful production! Did you not check the Internet to see what was on?'

'Until this morning I wasn't too sure I was even coming here.'

'Really! A spur of the moment impulse, was it? How exciting! And we've just had some returns so I can find you a really good seat.' Exciting it might be, but Connie knew nothing whatsoever about Richard the Second, the Third, or any of them. She bought a ticket and, in a rash moment, spent £4 on a programme, which she hoped would help her decipher the story, just in case.

As she took her seat, Connie gazed around, looking hopefully for Harry and his friend. It would have been nice to join them for a drink at the bar in the interval. But there was no sign of them, so she concentrated instead on her surroundings. It was all plainly quite different from her mother's day. She'd read somewhere that it had had a three-year transformation, but that it had retained many of the Art Deco features of the original Shakespeare Memorial Theatre. Not inside the auditorium it hadn't, that much was certain. It looked half finished, with so much ironwork exposed and its stage jutting out into the audience. It was different from any theatre she'd been to before, but she liked it. Now she hoped she'd enjoy *Richard II* too.

It was easy to get lost in the play because it was so beautifully produced. The days of wobbly cardboard sets were long gone. Instead, much of the scenery was projected onto chiffon drapes, which must have been fifty feet tall. They served as cathedral columns, a forest, palace walls, or anything else the story required. The acting was excellent too, though Connie got confused between the dukes of Hereford and Norfolk, and who was killing who, and why.

By the end of the first act Connie realised she hadn't thought to pre-order a drink for the interval – as Roger would have done, of course. There was so much pushing and shoving at the bar it was like being in one of the skirmishes she'd just seen on stage. While she tried to decide whether a glass of wine was worth the fight, she studied the rear view of the tall man with the close-cropped white hair who was directly in front of her in the queue. Pity about the tartan jacket though. She was somewhat thrown when he turned round and said casually, 'We should have ordered these earlier, shouldn't we?'

'Yes, we should,' said Connie.

American accent. His tanned face and crinkly blue eyes afforded a more attractive front view. 'Good elevations' as Nick, the architect, would say. And he definitely had a good front elevation. Expensive teeth; so, definitely American.

'Say, you on your own?'

'Er, yes, I am,' said Connie.

'Me too. Please don't take this the wrong way, but may I buy you a drink?' He'd arrived at the bar.

'Well, I…'

'I'd be real glad if you would. I really like company to drink with.'

Right now, thought Connie, so do I. 'A glass of red wine would be lovely.'

A few minutes later they strolled out, clutching their glasses, to watch the river flow by. It wasn't yet fully dark and there were still a few people on the recreation ground across the water, walking their dogs or simply meandering beside the river. The waterfowl were enjoying the last of the light too, and several swans had collected around one of the narrowboats moored opposite, begging for a share of the alfresco supper a young couple was sharing.

'I sure like these trees, what d'you call them?' The American pointed to a willow whose foliage was caressing the Avon's lazy shallows.

'Weeping willows.'

'Such a sad name for something so pretty. Talking of names –' he held out his free hand – 'Aaron Forrest the Third. But I know you folks don't say it like that.'

She shook his hand. 'Connie McColl the First. And we *do* say it like that when it comes to our kings, as you'll have noticed.'

'I gotta admit I'm not too knowledgeable about either your kings or the great Bard himself. Forgive the cliché, but do you come here often?'

Connie laughed. 'First time, Aaron.'

'You too then? You enjoying it? I thought this play would be right over my head but, know what, I'm kinda liking it.'

'Me too. Is this your first visit to England?'

'Yeah, it is. We always planned to come to Europe but then Hannah, my late wife, got sick and we had years of not going anywhere.'

Connie sipped her wine. 'I'm really sorry.'

'Yeah, she was a wonderful woman. The kids clubbed together to send me over here, so I'm doing Europe on my own, which wasn't really the idea.'

Connie took another sip. 'Well, I'm not that used to being on my own either but I must admit I'm rather relishing it.'

'Say, Connie, you widowed too? Divorced?' He was genuinely interested.

'No, I'm still married. Just having some time to myself.'

Aaron looked quite shocked. 'Your husband's on his *own* at home?'

'Well,' she said, consulting her watch, 'I wouldn't count on that.'

'You know,' her new friend went on, 'Hannah and I never spent one day apart in forty years of marriage, except when she was in hospital of course. Not a single day.' He sighed. 'So why did you choose to come to Stratford?'

'My late mother did the costumes for a production of *King Lear* here before the war, and apparently she loved Stratford. And it *is* lovely, isn't it?'

'Sure is.'

'Thanks so much for the wine,' Connie said, relieved to hear the bell summoning them back to their seats. 'And I hope you enjoy the rest of your trip.'

'I only wish Hannah was with me. Say,' he went on, 'would you like to meet up tomorrow for some sightseeing, some lunch maybe?'

'Well, that's sweet of you, Aaron. But I'm hoping to get together with some friends.'

'Gee, that's a shame. It's been nice to meet you.'

'Thank you, Aaron. It's been most interesting.'

Connie smiled to herself as she returned to her seat. That poor guy is lonely, she thought, already looking for a replacement for the sainted Hannah. They'd probably been one of those couples joined at the hip. Not that I ever wanted that, which is just as well because I didn't get It. And Aaron Forrest the Third should really have gone on a cruise. He'd have met many willing replacements there.

Aaron was a nice guy but next time, she decided, she wouldn't mind at all drinking her glass of wine on her own, although she could recall a time when she had so wanted to be one of a couple

– a long time ago now, of course – and when to be on her own somewhere like this would have been social suicide. That thought had been uppermost in her mind when she'd first arrived at the theatre this evening. But she'd straightened her shoulders, taken a deep breath and, with her head held high, strolled inside, hoping that this show of outer confidence – which she did not feel inside her churning tummy – would make her appear more interesting and mysterious. Plainly Aaron Forrest the Third had thought so. As she settled back in her seat, Connie smiled beatifically at everyone who looked in her direction. And they all smiled back.

By the end of the play, Connie felt as if Shakespeare had stepped inside her mind and helped to move things round a bit. She'd never considered that anything the Bard wrote could possibly apply to her and was therefore astounded to find that his turn of phrase could sum up her feelings so completely: 'Thus play I in one person many people, and none contented...' It might have been *written* for her! There she was, pulled in every direction, and definitely not contented. That Bard knew a thing or two.

The bed at the Cedars was surprisingly comfortable and Connie slept well. She woke early to the rhythmic sound of a bed creaking against the wall behind her. The creaking got faster and faster, making it impossible to get back to sleep, and making her wonder if she herself would ever like sex again, not having given it much thought for a long while. Because she and Roger hadn't indulged for years; was that normal? She'd read somewhere about septuagenarians and even octogenarians still shagging away happily and regularly, apparently age being no barrier; in fact, it could even be nicer in old age. Oh, *really?*

Perhaps if she still fancied Roger she might feel like that, but presumably he didn't much fancy her either because she couldn't remember when he'd last made any overtures in her direction. In fact, his attitude to sex was dutiful at best. So she didn't think he had ever been unfaithful – although one could never be sure. The wife was always the last to know and you read such mind-boggling stories in the newspapers. No, not Roger though. Of course, she wasn't aware of what he'd got up to during his working days but it seemed highly unlikely. Apart from anything else, an affair wouldn't fit in to his strict routine.

At seven-thirty, when Connie ventured downstairs, she found Len seated at his desk in the hall, still wearing yesterday's purple shirt. Or perhaps he'd bought a job lot.

Len looked at his watch. 'You're early! The missus is just starting breakfast.'

The missus, who was called Mary, loomed large at the door of the dining room, enveloped in a voluminous red kaftan, with a great deal of gold embroidery for good measure across her enormous bosoms. Connie doubted health and safety would ever have recommended such apparel for the serving of breakfast. They were indeed a colourful couple. The tables wobbled noisily as Mary bounced around the room setting down cutlery, little pots of red and orange jam and miniature blocks of butter.

'I like things to be nice,' she informed Connie. 'Do you want your egg poached or fried?'

Connie considered for a moment. She might as well start as she meant to continue and have the full works, which should keep her going until the evening.

'Poached, please.'

She was glad that the dining room was still empty as she didn't want to engage in the usual banal conversation and, fortunately, Mary did not appear to be in a talkative mood. Which was just as well for Connie, because she had plenty to occupy her mind. She'd seen the main tourist spots in Stratford, albeit briefly, on her previous visit with Roger, so now she decided to head for the Cotswolds as it was such a lovely day and she adored the pretty villages.

But her decision was mainly because of Freddy. *Who* could forget Freddy Barclay? Their friendship had developed from the summer they had spent as tour guides in Athens for a holiday company, forty-odd years before. She was supposed to have been accompanied by a Greek-speaking girl, who failed to turn up and, at the last moment, was replaced by Freddy. ('Here I am, darling, to help you hurl the plates!') He was the funniest man she had ever met; camp as a row of tents and didn't care who knew it. They frequently fell in love with the same guy. Neither of them spoke a word of Greek but they were popular with the tourists. Back then homosexuality was kept firmly in the closet and the holidaymakers loved the jokes, the innuendo, the pure theatricality. And Freddy still lived in one of those Cotswold villages.

When Connie checked out Len asked in a not-very-interested voice, 'And where are you heading today, Mrs McColl?'

'The Cotswolds, I think.'

As he lifted up his money-box to give her some change, Len's purple sleeve rode up a few centimetres, and she was able to decipher 'I love An—'. *Who* could it be? Anne? Anita? Angela? It certainly wasn't Mary.

Connie laughed out loud at the very idea of Roger having her name tattooed on his arm. Or wearing a purple shirt.

CHAPTER SIX

FOREVER FRIENDS

It was another beautiful morning, the sun high in the sky, the swans idly gliding along the Avon, as Connie got into her car.

She rooted in her handbag for her address book because she knew Freddy's number wasn't on her phone. They'd kept in touch over the years and always exchanged Christmas cards. And he'd even come to stay a couple of times after she'd got married, when Roger had endured Freddy for Connie's sake, but admitted afterwards that Freddy's sexuality made him feel uncomfortable. And Roger's sense of humour did not extend to Freddy's risqué jokes and never-ending innuendoes. Nevertheless, Connie and Freddy had still met up occasionally, but it struck her now that she hadn't seen him for years, far too long in fact. However, according to last year's Christmas card note, Freddy and his partner, Basil, had opened up an antique shop in Chipping-Somewhere-or-Other. She studied the address book for his phone number, and then, ridiculously pleased to find it, Connie realised just how much she missed the Freddies of this world. He might be a tad outrageous, but at least he was *fun*. And she needed to laugh, very badly.

She was delighted when Freddy himself answered the phone.

'Connie, *darling*, how wonderful to hear from you! How's life down there in Sussex-by-the-Sea?'

'I'm not in Sussex-by-the-Sea, Freddy, I'm in Stratford-on-the-Avon! And I'm about to head for Stow-on-the-Wold and Some-where-or-Other-on-the-Hill!'

'That is just fantastic! But these villages are *heaving* with tourists at the moment, darling, so come to see us as soon as you can. I'll be here from mid-afternoon. Is The Roger with you?'

'No, Roger isn't. Just me…'

'Even *better*! No offence, darling, but he's not really my cup of tea. Oh, this is *so* exciting – just wait until I tell Baz! Now, here's how to find us…'

'I'll be with you later,' she assured Freddy after she jotted down the somewhat vague instructions.

'And you'll stay the night, I hope? Oh, *please* say yes!'

'Yes, please,' replied Connie.

With time to kill, and in spite of the tourists, Connie decided to visit some of the pretty villages on the way: Moreton-in-Marsh, Bourton-on-the-Water, Chipping Campden. Once she'd found somewhere to park Kermit, she strolled round one honey-coloured village after another, admiring the chocolate-box cottages, their steeply pitched roofs and mullioned windows, their gardens bursting with roses and geraniums. And the inevitable begonias. The larger houses, set further back from the road, had impressive drives leading up to oak front doors and wisteria-laden porches. She explored the teashops, the boutiques, the antique shops. (Roger would have classed the lot as twee, but very pretty nonetheless.)

Connie had a bowl of soup in Tilda's Tea Shoppe (*snacks and light lunches a speciality*), where she was served by a tall, elegant, Boden-clad, white-haired lady. Could this be Tilda herself? Whoever she was, she was as far removed from Mary-of-the-kaftan as it was possible to get. Tilda's had white lilies in tall vases, and scones with cream and homemade strawberry jam in pretty, flowery dishes. None of Mary's nasty little pots in here.

Connie got lost several times trying to find Freddy's hideout. 'You'll see a sign for a pottery, darling,' he'd said, 'just outside the village. Then first left, just up the hill and past the field with the llamas. Easy-peasy.'

Easy-peasy it was *not*, but she found it eventually, having had to ask for directions several times. Finally, there in front of her was a large barn conversion, which was not at all what she had expected, having pictured him in the archetypal country cottage with the roses and the geraniums.

Freddy's hair had gone from salt and pepper to sugar-white since she'd seen him last. He was about the same age as she was, of course, and obviously didn't indulge in highlights and lowlights – although she wouldn't have put it past him – but he looked very dapper, slim and tanned in white shirt and tight jeans.

'Darling! This is *such* a surprise! You're looking fab – not a day older! Come in, come in! Do you *like*? Isn't it *wonderful*? Baz and

I did the conversion; well, we did the *designing*, not the digging, darling – didn't get our hands too dirty.'

Connie stood awestruck inside the building. It was beautiful indeed with its soaring, vaulted ceilings, exposed stone, oak beams and walls of glass overlooking the countryside. She hadn't expected anything as modern as this, although there were a few strategically placed antiques dotted around. There were also several enormous red sofas, positioned with care to take in the stunning views, and sumptuous oriental rugs on the acres of polished floorboards.

'Wow!' Connie said.

'Tea?' he asked. 'Coffee? Something stronger?' He glanced at his watch. 'Is it wine o'clock yet? Sun must be over the yardarm *somewhere.*'

Connie laughed. 'Tea would be lovely for now. And I've brought you some wine.'

'Naughty girl, no need! Now, I'm longing for you to meet Baz – he'll be home any minute; he's been minding the shop today.'

Connie followed him into the equally impressive kitchen area with its granite worktops and red accessories, climbing onto a red-cushioned stool at the breakfast bar while Freddy fussed around the red Aga, made the tea – proper tea, with tea leaves – in a large red pot. Not a tea bag in sight.

'Now, why are you up here on your own? Tell me all.'

'Nothing to tell, really. I just decided to take off.'

'From The Roger?'

'Well, yes, but from them all really. I'd got settled in a sort of domestic rut, cooking, chauffeuring, endless babysitting while Roger's permanently golfing, and I just need a change of scenery.'

'Good idea – make them appreciate you. What did The Roger have to say about this idea?'

Connie cleared her throat. 'Well, the thing is, I didn't exactly tell him I was going.'

'*Exactly* tell him?'

'I didn't tell him at all. I just decided to do it and departed, all within two days. I left him a note.'

'My God, Connie, whatever brought that on? Is he having an affair? Are *you* having an affair?'

'I'm not and I don't think Roger is either, Freddy, but we lead such separate lives now. I mean, quite apart from the golf, he's always organising things: the district newsletter, the Rotary Club, the church fund-raising, the Masons.'

'*E-nough*, darling!' Freddy rolled his eyes.

'The thing is,' Connie continued, 'I'm not much of a joiner. I've probably become a bit of a loner. It was different when the children were young because I didn't have time to think, and their needs came first. You remember I trained as a florist after I left school? And that I had the florist's shop in our village until the lease ran out a few years back? Well, since then I've felt somewhat superfluous to requirements except for becoming the family dogs-body. It sounds clichéd, but I'm hoping to find myself.'

'Darling, you're *independent* – you don't need to be forever joining things. Ah, here's Baz!'

Basil Braden-Smith wasn't at all like Connie had imagined, having envisaged some sort of older, aristocratic, tweedy, dusty type – not this good-looking, shaven-headed, be-jeaned guy, at least twenty years younger than Freddy, who further surprised her by speaking in what could only be described as an Estuary accent.

'Hi, Connie – great to meet you at last. Christ, Fred, haven't you got anything stronger than tea on the go?'

Shortly afterwards, comfortably settled at one end of an over-sized red sofa, gazing out at the rolling Gloucestershire country-side with an enormous glass of Shiraz by her side, Connie felt supremely happy and relaxed. Her hosts insisted on waiting on her, in between popping in and out of the kitchen to stir this and sauté that. She realised she was ravenous, and looking forward to whatever it was they were concocting, which turned out to be slow-cooked shoulder of lamb – the best she'd ever tasted – accompanied by an inexhaustible supply of wine. They regaled her with stories of how they'd met, how difficult it had been to get their shop up and running, and peppered the conversation with oodles of hilarious local gossip. Neither Freddy nor Baz questioned her further until they were back on the red sofas later with coffee and liqueurs.

'Nobody drinks liqueurs these days except us,' announced Freddy, as he proceeded to half fill a wine glass with chilled Limoncello, to which Connie had admitted to being very partial. 'We brought this back from Amalfi, didn't we, Baz?'

'Yes,' said Baz as he set the glass down beside Connie. 'We did. In *my* suitcase. And we could have bought it in the bloody super-market here. But never mind. As you can see, Fred doesn't believe in those teeny-weeny glasses.'

Connie was beginning to wonder if she'd ever make it to the bedroom, as she was already feeling decidedly squiffy. The Limoncello might be chilled, but it was producing a nice, warm feeling somewhere deep inside her.

'Now,' said Freddy. 'I'm curious. If The Roger is leading his own life, and you're leading yours, why do you feel the need to get away?'

'I don't know. I sometimes feel like I'm disappearing into everyone's lives, being put upon and not much appreciated. I suppose I'm loved, but I don't feel it. And I'm under-stimulated, too. Maybe now they might all be more aware of my existence or, at least, my absence. Does that make sense? My two youngest live locally, both with infants who need constantly looking after. Don't get me wrong, I love them all to bits, but…'

'But they take you completely for granted?' Baz suggested.

'I suppose they do. I think I'm too eager to please, and so I seem to have lost all sense of who I am. Of being Connie, who had a job, and who met people every day and had something interesting to talk about. All I've done for years now is what everyone else wants. I've forgotten how to make my own decisions, to stand up for myself. Do you follow me?'

'I think I do, darling.' Freddy was waving the Limoncello bottle with raised eyebrows. 'Refill?'

She shook her head vehemently. 'I'm ninety-nine per cent pickled already.'

'Make it the hundred; it'll do you good. You must have a lovely time and do all the sorts of things you wouldn't do at home. Mind you, you're a bit long in the tooth to be having a mid-life crisis, so what should we call this? A *Saga* saga?' They both dissolved into gales of laughter. 'Now, do tell us why you were in Stratford in the first place. I hardly had you down as a culture vulture.'

'I wasn't in Stratford in the first place. I started in Oxford.'

She told them about Oxford and her first love, leading to the nostalgic visit. And she told them about Martin, and his quest to meet 'a Dorothy', and about MMM.

'MMM?'

'Apparently it's "Meetings for the More Mature".'

'Mmm!' exclaimed Baz, and then they all dissolved into further gales of laughter.

Connie didn't remember getting into bed, but must have done so because she woke up in the middle of a king sized modern four-poster, with only the faintest trace of a hangover, having slept for nearly ten hours. She looked around. Everything was cream and calm and countrified, a gentle breeze ruffling the filmy curtain. She felt she wanted to stay there forever; safe, cosseted, entertained. But she knew she must be on her way; the urge to keep travelling north was stronger. When she'd set out from Sussex she felt she was getting away from something; now she felt she was moving towards something, and it lay in the north, of that much she was certain. But quite what it was, she wasn't so sure.

Freddy and Baz insisted that she have a 'teeny-weeny bacon butty', which was the perfect antidote to any hangover, they promised.

'You keep in touch, darling. Let us know where you are. It could get lonely sometimes, and we don't want you rushing back to The Roger for all the wrong reasons. And are you absolutely *sure* we can't persuade you to stay another night?' Freddy asked anxiously. 'No? Well, you know where we are, so come back anytime at all. Now, let's check your oil and things. Are you sure that old banger's going to get you to wherever you're going? Now, promise you'll come to see us again? *Promise?* We want to hear about everything you get up to! *Everything!* Now, off you go! *Where* did you say you were going today?'

'I didn't,' said Connie. 'But northwards – possibly Manchester.'

'Manchester? Why on earth Manchester?'

Connie recalled her one and only visit to Manchester at Sally Parker's wedding over forty years previously. She and Sally had shared a damp flat in Hammersmith around the time of the Greek summer. And it was there, in Manchester, watching a beaming Sally head up the aisle, that she made her decision to marry Roger. Manchester was also the place where she decided to accept the fact that she was pregnant, having missed two periods. A decision-making place, perhaps. A location that had changed her life.

'I think it owes me,' she replied.

As she got into the car Connie realised that she envied Freddy and Baz for their easy relationship, their hands touching as they passed each other, their banter, their teasing, their laughter. OK, so they hadn't been together for as long as she and Roger had, but she couldn't recall Roger ever squeezing her arm as they passed, or howling with laughter at a ridiculous joke. But, of course, every rela-tionship was different. She just wished hers hadn't been *so* different.

❋

Freddy watched the little green car head down the driveway and then turn into the lane. Connie gave a final toot of the horn and waved out of the window just before she disappeared from view.

'Do you think she'll be back?' Baz asked as he came up from behind and slid his arm round Freddy's waist.

'I really don't know, darling. *Anything* could happen. How many women of sixty-something are swanning about out there with little idea of where they're going, for God's sake?'

'What's the husband *really* like?' Baz asked as they wandered back into the house.

'Well, I'd say he's probably good enough husband material, if somewhat boring, and predictable and… well, you know he was a *chartered accountant*? Nothing wrong with that, of course, but they're not generally a terribly exciting species. I *did* point this out to her when she introduced me to him shortly before they were due to be married.'

'But you didn't like him, did you?'

'Not a great deal. And he certainly didn't care much for me – or any of her Megatour friends for that matter. Of course, Middle England didn't like gays to come out openly back then.'

'So, why did she marry him, I wonder?'

'Well, he was tall, good-looking and I think she craved security, because he had enough money for a house, which was very im-portant to Connie. And he put her in the pudding club, to boot.

Would you believe she met him on a return flight from Athens where he was attending some sort of *mathematical* convention? How boring is that!'

'She should have known then,' sighed Baz.

'Indeed she should,' said Freddy. 'And, somewhere deep inside, I think she probably did.'

CHAPTER SEVEN

THE BOND

Connie was somewhere near Derby when she saw the sign for Barney's Cafe – one mile ahead. Judging by the line-up of heavy goods vehicles parked outside, Barney's was a favourite with truck drivers, and just the sort of place where Roger wouldn't dream of eating. With this in mind, and aware that her tummy had been rumbling and grumbling for some miles, Connie turned in and parked Kermit alongside one of the biggest articulated monsters she had ever seen. Inside the cafe she was greeted with the noisy babble of male voices and laughter, the clicking of knives and forks, and the almost imperceptible sound of Frank Sinatra trying to make himself heard somewhere in the background. There was just one table free – for two – by the window, where Connie sat down and regarded her surroundings. The clientele consisted mainly of drivers, one or two youngsters and an elderly couple. The red Formica tabletop was spotlessly clean, as was the row of hefty sauce bottles.

'You had a look at the menu yet, love?' She pronounced it 'loov', so Connie knew she'd hit the north. The waitress, who looked about sixteen, was encased in metal-ware from her pierced, ringed eyebrows to her studded nose and lip, and then sideways to her multi-pierced ears, which jangled as she bent down.

'I'm starving,' Connie remarked, picking up the menu.

'How about a Barney's Bonanza, then? Comes with the lot – black pudding, sausages, chips.'

'Oh, all right then,' Connie grinned. 'Bring it on!' Then she wondered what size she would be by the time she got home, eating all this stodge. *If* she went home. Well, *of course* she'd go home – where else would she go?

She was aware that one of the drivers at the table opposite was openly staring at her. Connie felt flustered. She supposed a woman on her own might look out of place in here. Then he winked and grinned. Cheeky bugger! While she awaited Barney's Bonanza she tried to avoid eye contact with her new admirer. Meanwhile Sinatra laboured on, against the din, with 'Strangers in the Night'.

'Mind if I share your table?' Without waiting for an answer, a large woman with cyclamen-coloured hair plonked herself down on the seat opposite. She wore a matching cyclamen-coloured low-cut top, from which her two enormous boobs bounced, perilously close to escape. She had some pink roses tattooed up her arm but, unlike Len in Stratford, they didn't appear to profess her love for anybody.

'Innit hot?' Her new companion wiped her upper lip with the back of her hand.

'Yes,' agreed Connie. At least the woman blocked her view of the driver. Now, she thought, *please* don't start talking. Increasingly suffering the after-effects of Freddy's hospitality, she now craved some peace and quiet.

'I just got off the bus from London,' the woman went on. 'Sweltering in there it was, like a bleedin' oven. I was sweatin' like a pig. That bus goes on to Leeds,' she added, as if Connie cared. 'But there's another one comes along in about an hour or so which gets me right the way home. You live round here?'

'No,' said Connie. 'Sussex.'

'Blimey, you're a long way from home then! You on your own?'

'Yes.'

'Aw, nice to have company then. I'm Kath.'

'Connie.'

Just then the waitress jangled up with Connie's Bonanza, which she served with a flourish.

'Blimey, Connie, you gonna get on the outside of all that lot?' Kath looked impressed.

'I'm going to try,' said Connie. Please let her shut up now.

'Hey!' Kath yelled at the waitress, pointing at Connie's plate. 'Bring me one of them, please – and some bread and butter.' She turned her attention back to Connie. 'You on holiday then?'

'Yes,' said Connie, as she swallowed her first mouthful. It seemed the simplest thing to say.

'So, where are you going?' That inevitable question.

'Oh, here and there,' Connie replied, after she'd swallowed some more. 'Where the fancy takes me.'

'The *fancy*! Get *you*!' Much raucous laughter.

Connie continued eating but Kath was not about to give up the conversation.

'I always eat here when I change buses. Ever so clean it is.'

Connie swallowed and nodded. 'The food is delicious,' she admitted as she speared a chip. The chips were the best she'd ever eaten; chunky, golden and tasty. None of those thin sticks that were only good for dipping in something.

'Yeah, the food's good. But didn't think I'd see a posh lady like yourself in a transport caff though.'

'*Posh?* I'm not posh!'

Kath looked around and guffawed. 'Well, you're a damn sight posher than most of this bloody lot.'

Just then Kath's Bonanza arrived and Connie hoped it might keep her quiet, but no such luck.

'I eat here, see, 'cos it's late by the time I get 'ome and it saves me cooking.'

Connie nodded. After she'd swallowed another mouthful she asked, out of politeness, 'Have you much further to go?'

'Just to Manchester, love. I'm a Londoner though. I expect you can tell that from the way I speak? I've been livin' up here for bleedin' years. Could've got a train from London, of course, but I get a freebie on the buses 'cos me youngest works for the bus company. But it means I gotta keep changing buses, so it's a long day.'

'Do you go back to London often then?' Connie asked, as it was obvious that Barney's Bonanza was not going to stop Kath rabbiting on.

'Every couple of months, usually. Go to see me son. *Another* son, that is.'

'Does he live there?'

'At Her Majesty's pleasure, Connie! At Her Majesty's pleasure! Three years he got. Not his fault though; always got in with the wrong crowd, Wayne did.'

Connie digested this information along with her next mouthful. 'I'm sorry to hear that.'

'Yeah, well, it happens. You got kids?'

'Three.'

'Well, I got five and two of them turned out to be real pains in the arse.' She had the remarkable ability to talk and eat at the same time without it distorting her speech in any way. 'I expect your three have all done well for themselves, 'ave they?'

'Yes, quite well. I've been lucky.'

'I had me first when I was sixteen, at home in West Ham. Me dad chucked me out, so I came up to Manchester with the baby's father, 'cos he came from up here, see. We stayed with his parents for a bit but it didn't work out – not after the baby was born, like. Then I met Trev. He didn't mind me having a baby, but he couldn't marry me, see, 'cos 'e was still married to someone else who wouldn't divorce 'im. I think they was Catholic.'

'Oh,' said Connie.

'Trev and me had twins. We was together five years before he scarpered. You've just had the one bloke, I suppose?'

'Well, yes, I've only been married once.' Connie realised that this statement didn't fill her with as much pleasure or pride as she would have liked.

'So, is he still around? You widowed? Divorced?'

'He's still around and I'm still married to him.'

'I got married too after that, though. Joe took me on with the three kids; he was a good bloke, and we had three more. Joe died a couple of years ago.'

'So you've had *six* children?' Connie said as she scraped her plate.

'Yeah, but I lost one. Billy – one of me twins. Only seventeen he was, on that bloody motorbike. Awful it was, worst thing that ever happened to me. You can't bleedin' imagine.'

Connie pushed her plate to the side and leaned forwards. 'Oh yes, I can. I lost a son, too, twenty-three years ago.'

Kath stopped chewing, and laid a hand over Connie's.

Connie was strangely moved by this gesture. 'It's a long time ago.'

'Yeah, maybe it is, but it still hurts like buggery, don't it?'

'Yes, it does. If he'd lived he'd be thirty-five now. And no one in the family remembered the anniversary of his death last week.'

'That's bleedin' awful.'

'He was only twelve. He was on his bike too.' Connie smiled. 'His was a push bike, of course. Got hit by a speeding car mounting the pavement in a thirty limit while he was cycling down the road. The driver only got a few years.'

In spite of herself, Connie felt her eyes welling up. Ben, so long ago now but always, *always* there in her thoughts. (She could still see the policeman on the doorstep. 'Mrs McColl?' he'd asked solemnly. She'd known straight away it was one of her children.) And none of them had remembered the other day. They hadn't even noticed she'd gone alone to the grave; she was damned if she was going to remind any of them.

Kath withdrew her hand. 'I tried religion for a while, but it didn't last. Didn't help at all.'

'Roger, my husband, he turned to religion too, but it didn't do it for me either. In fact, I blamed God, if he exists, for taking Ben. I still do. I tried séances as well, as I was so desperate, but they all seemed to be a bit of a con. Perhaps I didn't meet a genuine spiritualist.'

Connie recalled sitting round a table with four others while Zena (if that was her real name) called out 'to those beyond the grave'. Judging by the reactions of two of the others she had had some success. With Connie it was 'someone who died when you were a child', and that person was all right and happy among the angels, and 'watching over her'. If that was supposed to be one of her parents, he or she was not doing a very good job, letting her boy be taken from her.

'All I wanted to do was shut myself away,' she told Kath, remembering the unbearable grief.

But Connie had three other children. Children are more resilient; they grieve and cry for a bit and then they get on with it. Life is for living, after all. In the meantime Roger worked twelve hours a day and went to church on Sundays. That was his way of dealing with it. But she'd so wanted him there. She remembered not only the grief, but also the loneliness; she'd only wanted to curl up with her husband and weep until she could weep no more. But Roger wasn't that kind of husband.

'Séances! Lotta mumbo-jumbo, if you ask me.' Kath had finished her Bonanza and was looking at her watch.

'What time's your bus?' Connie asked.

'I got about fifteen minutes yet,' Kath said as she drained the dregs of her tea. 'But I'm really sorry to be going 'cos I'd really like to talk to you more about, you know…'

'Maybe I could give you a lift?' Connie heard herself say. She suddenly realised that she didn't want to stop chatting to Kath.

'You going to Manchester then?'

Connie grinned. 'It just so happens I am! But you'll have to give me directions to your place.'

'You're a bleedin' angel, Connie.'

As Connie unlocked Kermit, Kath said, 'And here's me thinkin' you'd have a posh car!'

'Don't you want a lift in this then?'

'Course I do! I just thought—'

'You just thought I'd have a smart BMW or something,' Connie cut in. 'Well, our family car is a bit grander than this, but Kermit is my little run-around and I love him.'

'*Him?* I thought cars were supposed to be female?'

'Not this one. Kermit's his name because he's green and noisy. Now, sling your bag on the back seat.'

As Kath settled herself in the front Connie wondered how many more waifs and strays she might collect on her travels. If he could see any of her travelling companions, Roger would have an apoplectic fit.

She found herself relaxing with Kath. Sometimes she desperately needed to talk about Ben, but people – even Roger most of the time – shied away from the subject. Such a loss was unimaginable to most, and they had no idea what to say, so they coped by avoiding the subject altogether, careful not to even mention his name.

Kath had no such reservations and was eager to talk about Billy and 'that bleedin' bike' which, apparently, he'd insisted on riding at breakneck speed 'all over the bleedin' place'. In turn, Connie spoke about Ben's accident, and how it had almost killed their marriage as well. But they'd come through it, and soldiered on for the sake of Diana, Nick and Lou.

As they headed towards Salford, Connie asked, 'Do you live on your own?'

'Yeah, I do now. Two-bedroom terrace I got, straight out of *Corrie*. You watch *Corrie*? No? Well, they're threatenin' to knock us all down in Packingham Street, 'cos Salford's gone posh now, what with having the BBC and all up here.' Kath was squinting through the window. 'Here, you need to take the next left! Where are you going after you've dropped me off?'

'I was planning to spend the night in Manchester. A cheap B&B or something.'

'Have you booked a B&B, then?'

'Not yet, but I'm sure I'll find somewhere.'

'You can stay with me if you like. I got a spare room – nothing fancy, mind. *Fancy*, ha ha, here we go again!'

Connie felt quite choked. 'I wouldn't want to put you to any trouble—'

'No bleedin' trouble!' Kath interrupted. 'I wouldn't have asked you if it was, would I?'

Kath's house was tiny, but immaculate. The front room into which Connie was ushered had countless knick-knacks on every available surface, along with at least thirty framed photographs of her considerable brood.

'That was Billy,' said Kath, removing one of the larger photographs and polishing it with the hem of the purple cardigan she'd just put on.

'He looks like you,' Connie said softly.

'Yeah, he did. Everyone said that. He was a twin, you know; the other one was a girl. Mandy.'

'How did she take it?'

'Not too bad. They wasn't that close. She's in Canada now, nursing, married, two kids, done all right for herself.'

'Did it affect your marriage?'

'Joe was great; I think it made us close. Don't forget he wasn't Billy's father either. What about you?'

'No. It didn't bring us closer.'

'No? Well, if that don't bring you together then nothing will. He sounds a bit starchy, your old man. Why d'you marry him in the first place?'

Connie thought for a minute. 'At the time I thought he was the bee's knees. Good-looking, good job. I was a bit short of relatives and security, you see. Then, believe it or not, he got me pregnant the first time we slept together, and that clinched it. I wanted the baby, and to settle down, so that's what I did. Forty-one years ago.'

'And you've never wanted to leave him?'

'At times, of course, but I wouldn't even have considered it when the children were at home. It's only lately that I've felt restless – yes, that's the word: *restless*. After all these years I think I'd like to feel insecure and free again. For a while, anyway.'

Kath was silent for a moment. 'You might get addicted to all that,' she said. 'You might enjoy the freedom.'

'I suppose I might,' said Connie. She told Kath she'd been a florist but had retired a couple of years previously. 'I love flowers,' she said. 'Particularly roses.'

'Yeah, me too,' said Kath, tapping her tattoo. 'See, this way I can have them all the year round!'

Connie laughed. 'Do you work at all, Kath?'

'Well, I did. I was a carer at the local nursing home, the Haven, just down the road. I couldn't give it up altogether though, so I still do the odd shift when they're short. Keeps me in gin! You get so involved with them old folk, especially them ones that don't have no one to come and see them. It must be bleedin' awful to die all on your own, but I sit and hold their hands and that. If I had me time over again I'd train to be a nurse, like my Mandy did. It'd be nice to do the thing properly instead of just running around with bedpans and things.'

'Good for you, Kath. It can't be an easy job at times.'

'Well, at least I've booked my place in there for when I go doolally myself!'

Later Connie drank some instant coffee, having refused Kath's offer of gin.

'I had a session with some friends last night,' she explained. 'Drank far too much.'

'Don't mind if I do then?' Kath poured herself a generous measure and topped it up with orange juice from a carton. It was years since Connie had met anyone who drank gin and orange.

'Don't like them bitter drinks,' Kath said. The more gin she imbibed, the funnier she became. And the fruitier her language became too. But she doesn't offend me, Connie thought, and I don't know why, because some people who swear like troopers can be awful. In fact, I really *like* her. Which just goes to show that the old cliché is so right: you can't always judge a book by its cover. Even a cyclamen-coloured one.

It wasn't the most comfortable bed in the world, but nevertheless Connie slept well for nearly six hours in the flowery, frilly bedroom that looked out over a builder's yard at the back. After a cup of tea and a slice of white toast (delicious – she'd forgotten how tasty white bread was; Roger would only eat granary or wholemeal or seeded), Connie prepared to take her leave. She felt quite sad; their shared tragedy had brought them close for a short time. And, underneath her colourful exterior, Kath was a kind, caring woman.

'It was so good to be able to talk about Ben again,' Connie said.

'Yeah, and Billy.'

Connie smiled. 'Bill and Ben, our Flowerpot Men!' She wondered if Kath had been a fan of *Watch with Mother* back in the sixties.

'Blimey, that was a long time ago!' said Kath. Then she added, 'You can stay another night if you like.' She sounded hopeful, and Connie wondered if she was lonely now.

'You're more than kind, Kath, but I must be on my way.'

'And where might the *fancy* take you today, may I ask?'

'Well, I'm going to take a look round the city centre.' She thought of Sally's wedding and her own major decision all those years ago. 'And then I might head towards the Lakes. All this talk of Ben has made me think of his last holiday there.'

He'd had that special holiday in the Lake District, only a year before he died, with his friend Peter. Peter's parents had rented a holiday cottage somewhere near Windermere (she wished she could remember where) and he'd begged to go. He'd never been away from home before and Connie worried about him every single day. He'd loved it all – the climbing, cycling, sailing, even the rain – and didn't want to come home. She remembered him saying, 'Can I go again next year, Mum?' Connie dearly wished he had been able to.

'Well, it's been great meeting you,' said Kath. 'You know where I am if you ever need a bed again. Fifty-four Packingham Street, if they haven't knocked us down by then. I got your phone number and you keep in touch now! I just hope that bleedin' car of yours keeps goin', and that you sort yourself out.'

'Thanks so much for everything, Kath. I will keep in touch. I'm really glad to have met you,' Connie said truthfully as they hugged and then, as she drove away, she was surprised to find that her vision was blurred with tears. She blinked them away and started to look for a 'City Centre' sign.

❈

Kath watched as the little green car made its way along the street, before it turned onto the main road and out of sight.

She'd often wondered what made middle-class women like Connie tick, and she still didn't know but, underneath that ladylike exterior, there seemed to beat a heart much like her own.

But what exactly was Connie running away from? It was plainly what she was doing, even though she didn't seem to know it herself. Kath tried to imagine having the same husband for forty-one years, an ordinary family, a nice house near the seaside (what was wrong with a bungalow anyway?) and a car of her own. Her own life might have been turbulent, but it had certainly never been dull.

Kath made herself a mug of tea and carried it into the front room. She decided she must use this room more often; what was the point of keeping it for best? She straightened Billy's photograph on the wall and wondered what sort of man he might have been. She'd spoken about him a lot last night; more than ever before, because Connie had *understood*. Where bereavement like this was concerned, everyone hurt much the same.

CHAPTER EIGHT

MORE REACTIONS

Connie parked Kermit on the second floor of a multi-storey car park right next to an Audi identical to Roger's. That made her feel guilty at not having given Roger much thought recently, and she supposed she should check for emails to make sure that the family were OK. As she dug her phone out from her bag she wondered if there would be any signal in this vast concrete edifice, but fortunately there was. And there were four emails waiting to be read.

From: Roger McColl

To: Connie McColl

Dear Connie,

Heaven only knows if you'll pick up this email or not but I can't keep on texting and you won't answer your phone. Where are you and what on earth are you playing at? We're all worried stiff. Can you at least give us some idea of when you plan to come back? Mrs Henderson next door remarked she hadn't seen you for days, so even the neighbours are noticing now. I've had to say that you've gone off to see some friends for a week or so, so make sure you're back by then as it's becoming embarrassing. I can't imagine why you feel the need for all this freedom. Surely you've got enough freedom round here? Perhaps you've been reading too many soppy novels or watching too many late-night films!

Everyone here's OK – if you're interested. Tess moaning about babysitting as usual. Lou moaning about her crying infant. So, as you'll gather, nothing new.

Please reply if you ever read this.

Roger

Connie clicked 'Reply':

Yes, Roger, I am picking up emails now; I've discovered I can read them on my iPhone. Sorry you find the situation so embarrassing, but I've no intention of returning any time soon. I need some time for myself. Please don't worry about me – I'm absolutely fine. And I'm sure you'll all cope.

Love to all,

Connie xx

Typical Roger, she thought, worried about what the neighbours think. She would like to have been told that he missed her.

From: Diana McColl

To: Connie McColl

Hello, Mum – wherever you are!

I can well imagine the reactions you're going to be getting from them all, but I want you to know that I'm with you, metaphorically speaking, every inch of the way. Let them all get on with it, enjoy your freedom – please no one but yourself for a change. I can't tell you how much I admire your decision – and your guts to carry it out!

And I can only apologise for forgetting Ben's anniversary. My only excuse is that I was in Crete being shown round by a particularly obnoxious local tourist official. But I should have remembered and emailed or something. So sorry, Mum.

Now, if you need cash – and I'm sure you may at some point – I can forward money online to your account, if you just let me have the details. I really mean that – please don't worry about money.

And please, Mum, don't take any risks either. Stay safe and keep in touch.

I love you lots and lots and lots!

Di xxx

Connie clicked 'Reply':

Dear Di,

Thanks so much for your very encouraging email; I had a feeling you might understand! Knowing that one of you at least is on my side is very reassuring and given me the strength to open up the rest of my mail! And thanks, too, for your generous offer of cash, but I'm hoping to be able to manage.

I promise to be careful and not take any risks although a few little adventures might be nice of course. I just need to sort myself out and decide what I want from the rest of my life, even at this late stage. And I promise to keep in touch.

Lots of love,

Mum xxxx

From: Nick McColl

To: Connie McColl

Hi Mum,

I've no idea where you are but Dad says you're coping with emails on your iPhone now so here we go! It would be good to know where you are. Dad reckons you're on the Continent because he says you've taken your passport. If so, drive carefully, Mum, and remember to stay on the right!

Tess is wondering if you've found another bloke but somehow or other I don't think that's it. She's a bit fed up about the child-minding – you know how she is. I can't help much because we're still so busy at the office and I've been working overtime. We've got a new architect joining us, so that might lessen the load. He's from that place with the long, long unpronounceable name in Wales originally, but he's been working up in Scotland for a couple of years. Nice chap.

Dad seems to be resigned to your absence and eats at the golf club most evenings. I think he's trying to escape the neighbours, particularly that Mrs Henderson who keeps asking about you, he says.

The boys are fine. But they miss you, as do we all. Are you OK, Mum? The boys keep asking when is Nana coming back? What do we tell them?

Look after yourself,

Much love,

Nick xx

Connie clicked 'Reply':

Good to hear from you, Nick. I'm having a very interesting time, looking up old friends and making some new ones.

Sorry about the babysitting. I do miss the little ones – and yourselves, of course – but I won't be ready to come back for some time yet.

Love to you all,

Mum xxxx

From: Louise Morrison

To: Connie McColl

Dear Mum,

Where are you and why don't you answer your phone? I'm worried sick about you – we all are, particularly Dad. He is as devastated and mystified by your behaviour as I am.

Why, Mum, why? Surely we can't put it down to a mid-life crisis at your age!!! And, as for 'finding yourself', well, surely you know by now who you are!

And I can't imagine somehow that there's someone else! Not many wrinkly romances go undetected round here! Needless to say Andy finds the whole thing a huge joke but then he's always had a weird sense of humour. And of course he's never here during the day when I have to struggle with Charlotte all on my own.

What have I done to deserve such a bad-tempered baby? She still rarely sleeps at all during the day and not much at night, so I am tired out all the time. I don't suppose you gave us a thought when you decided to take off on your holiday or whatever you'd call it.

Not only that, Dad expects me to do some shopping and cleaning for him as well! I notice he doesn't ask Tess although he'd be lucky to catch her with all her classes and stuff. She even had the gall to ask me to look after Thomas and Joshua the other day – can you imagine?

So, as you can see, you're sorely missed and we all think it's high time you came home.

Love from us all,

Lou xxx

From: Connie McColl

To: Louise Morrison

Dear Lou,

What a tale of woe! Who'd have thought that my absence would have caused so much inconvenience? And mirth! Good old Andy – I've always rather liked his sense of humour.

You've always been very close to your father so I can understand your concern for his feelings. In fact, you seem to be a lot more concerned than he is. And, as for Charlotte, you're not the first to have a colicky baby, darling. Di was an absolute nightmare but the rest of you were fine, so don't let it put you off having more! (Although you probably don't want to think of it at the moment!) It will pass, I promise you. And surely your health visitor can suggest something?

I'm seeing some interesting places and people. In doing so I'm hoping to rediscover some of the emotions I'd forgotten I had and, although I miss you all, I really need to be on my own at present. And the reason I didn't inform you all of my impending departure was because you would have attempted to talk me out of it, and I badly need to do this.

Rest assured I'm fine and will be back eventually.

Much love to you, Andy and Charlotte,

Mum xx

Connie switched her phone off. It was good to hear from them all. She appreciated the positive comments from Di and Nick, but was not altogether surprised that Lou's thoughts were on a par with Roger's.

CHAPTER NINE

CITY SLICKER

The city centre was greatly changed since Connie had attended the fateful wedding reception, but then that *was* more than forty years ago. Come to think of it, wedding receptions had changed as well. She recalled outfits in sweet-pea colours: pale blue, mauve, pink, cream, with frothy hats and shoes to match. And gloves, of course. She'd worn a pale yellow dress, and had kept running her hand over the bump that was barely there, while wondering if she should marry Roger or not.

Now the quality of the shops, the appearance of the buildings and the sophistication of the whole place rivalled London. And she'd forgotten about the warmth and friendliness of the Mancunians. That hadn't changed at all. After she'd bought some knickers in M&S she went in search of a florist. When she eventually located Blooming Marvellous, she ordered a bunch of pink roses to be sent to Packingham Street.

'Is there any chance,' Connie asked the assistant, 'that you could deliver a bottle of gin along with the flowers?' (Was it possible this woman was *really* named Marigold, as the badge pinned to her bosom pronounced?)

'A bottle of *gin!*' Marigold's neatly pencilled eyebrows nearly hit her hairline. 'We're florists, loov, not a gin palace! Mind you, if you go and get the gin and bring it here, there's no reason really why not, I suppose.'

'You're a star! And can I write the card, please?'

Marigold produced the card and Connie wrote: *With many thanks, and in fond memory of our Flowerpot Men.*

By the time she'd found a mini-market, bought a bottle of Gordon's, and then found her way back to Blooming Marvellous, Connie felt peckish. She took herself across to Piccadilly Gardens with an M&S sandwich and a cold drink, then examined the map of Great Britain she'd stopped off to buy in WH-Smith, because she felt it was the normal thing to do, to have some idea of where you might be going and how to get there. In the end she decided to look out for names beginning with Bs, like Bolton or Blackburn, which led in the general direction of the Lake District.

'Do you mind if I share your bench?' A pretty auburn-haired girl, clutching a cardboard cup of coffee, smiled shyly at Connie, who nodded and smiled back before continuing to study her map.

When she looked up a minute later, Connie noticed the girl lifting the cup to her lips with trembling hands. She looked almost frightened. It was none of her business, of course, but Connie couldn't help herself... 'Are you OK?'

The girl nodded, then took another shaky gulp. 'Yes, I'm OK – just had some earth-shattering news.'

'Oh, I'm sorry,' Connie said, unsure whether or not to pursue the conversation.

The girl looked around as if afraid of prying eyes or ears, then, in a lowered voice said, 'I've just found out I'm pregnant.'

'Well, congratulations!' Connie's response was spontaneous and only after the words were out did she stop to think they might be insensitive. 'Are you pleased?'

The girl had the most enormous, black-lashed green eyes. 'I don't know,' she whispered.

Connie noted her ringless fingers. 'Not exactly planned, then?'

'Not exactly.'

'And will that be a problem?' Connie kept her voice low.

'I don't know. I've not had a chance to tell him yet.' She gripped her cardboard cup tightly and a coffee fountain spouted and splashed, narrowly missing her coat.

'Can I get you another drink, er – what's your name?'

'Hannah.'

'Well, Hannah, I'm Connie! Now, would you like another coffee, since you're spilling most of that one?'

Hannah grinned. 'You're very kind. Yes, please. No sugar.'

Pregnant! As she headed towards the coffee vendor Connie vividly recalled being in the same situation. How *could* she have become pregnant after only that one weekend with Roger? She remembered little about Sally's wedding, only her own turbulent thoughts. What should she do? Should she marry Roger? Would he ask her?

Roger hadn't seemed unduly concerned; on the contrary he seemed rather pleased with himself. 'Well, we can get married, Connie. We'd probably be doing that anyway, so let's just bring it forward a little.' This was Roger's idea of a proposal and she could only recall feeling grateful at the time.

When Connie returned with two coffees she found Hannah fiddling with her mobile.

'He's not answering,' she said.

Connie handed her a coffee. 'You weren't going to tell him on the phone, were you?'

'No, just wanted to arrange to see him later, to tell him then.'

Connie took a sip. 'Believe it or not, many years ago, on my only previous visit to Manchester, I too discovered I was pregnant.'

'But you were married?'

'No, I wasn't.'

'But he married you though?'

'Yes, he did. Back then, Hannah, you usually got married if you could, because the disgrace of having a baby if you didn't was too awful to contemplate. Families turned their backs on you; babies usually had to be adopted. Such a hoo-ha. You wouldn't believe it. Not now.'

Hannah leaned forwards. 'If it *was* now, would you have married him?'

Connie thought for a moment. 'I really don't know, and that's the truth.'

Had she *really* loved Roger or had she been looking for security, stability and to be able to keep her baby? Life was very different then. She could remember poor Barbara Collins who'd been in her class in school. 'Her mother isn't *married*,' Connie was informed in shocked, hushed whispers. It wasn't Barbara's fault, but she'd had to endure the boys shouting 'Barbara is a bastard!' again and again. Thank goodness times had changed.

Connie took another sip. 'How old are you, Hannah?'

'Eighteen. And I'm at college because I want to become a teacher. Little ones, you know, infants.'

'You might need to postpone that for a bit then. What about your guy? Would you like to marry him?'

'I'm not sure. Don't think he'd want to get tied down 'cos he keeps going on about going to Australia for a couple of years.'

'That's tough.'

Hannah sighed. 'I fancy him, but that's not the same, is it?'

'No,' Connie replied, 'it isn't. What about your mum? Would she help?'

'She'll go ballistic. She's a single mum herself.'

As if on cue, a toddler with a chocolate-smeared face tottered up and gazed, unblinking, at the two of them until his mother, muttering apologies, snatched him away.

Hannah laughed. 'The thing is, I love little kids.'

Connie watched the toddler escape his mother's clutches yet again, colliding with a coffee-carrying elderly woman, who was not pleased.

'They can be a handful,' said Connie, 'but it's *so* worth it.'

Hannah patted her tummy. 'There's just no way I'd want to get rid of it – I know that already.'

'I'm glad to hear it because each life is so miraculous, so precious. I think so anyway. And you'll make a lovely mum.'

She would too; there was something about the girl – a dignity, an independence. She'd be a survivor.

Hannah drained her cup. 'Thanks so much for listening, and for the drink, Connie. You've really helped, you know.'

'You just follow your heart, Hannah.'

As they stood up, Connie gave her a quick hug. 'I wish you all the luck in the world, but I'm sure you're going to be just fine. And, do you know what? If it happened to me now, I wouldn't bother getting married. I'd go it alone.' And that, Connie found to her surprise, was the truth.

She'd loved Roger, but was that different from being 'in love', which was such a hackneyed expression? Was she beginning to sound like Prince Charles? Perhaps she was a romantic at heart though and would have liked more passion, more heart-thumping, violins playing? And could she have managed to bring up little Diana on her own? Would she have been a social pariah like poor Barbara's mother? And, if she hadn't married Roger, she might never have had more children. No Nick, Lou, or Ben.

It was almost rush hour by the time Connie located the car park where she'd positioned Kermit and crawled into the snarl-up of traffic. Connie was unaware of which direction she was heading in. She seemed to be going in slow-moving circles for what seemed like hours. Could that possibly be the same Odeon cinema on her left that she'd passed twice already? Yes, it was. She needed to change lanes; she knew that, otherwise she'd be passing the Odeon for a fourth time. She was almost ready to head back to Kath's, if she only knew how to get there. Finally a van driver let her out and she was able to move in a different direction – not necessarily the correct one – and at last found a sign that promised 'Bolton – 10 miles'. Hallelujah!

Feeling very weary, Connie saw a Travelodge sign ahead. 'Rooms at bargain prices', it said. Well, hang the expense, she thought, although she'd had no intention of spending another night in Manchester, and she pulled into the car park.

The room was as she expected: neutral, functional and reasonably priced. She lugged in her bags, washed her dirty clothes and hung them up in the shower room where, she hoped, they would dry overnight. Then she needed to do nothing except loll on the bed, watch whatever was on TV and see how much wine was left in her bottle. There was a good half and, as she sipped it, she thought about Hannah, hoping that both her boyfriend and her mother would be supportive if nothing else.

That night Connie had her recurring dream again. There was Aunt Lorna peering down at her five-year-old self and saying, crossly, 'Do we *have* to have her?' And there was Uncle Bill saying something soothing like, 'Of course we do…' just as her aunt metamorphosed into a crocodile. This caused her to shout out as usual, which woke her up, also as usual.

CHAPTER TEN

THE GETAWAY GAL

The clothes had dried overnight. Connie decided to resist the Travelodge breakfast, and settled for a cup of do-it-yourself coffee in the bedroom, along with some digestive biscuits she'd bought in the mini-market. In spite of the nightmare, Connie felt refreshed and ready to leave the city sprawl behind, with every intention of avoiding all built-up areas in future. She'd worked out a route to bypass Bolton and then, eventually, arrive at the Lakes.

She'd filled up with petrol and driven several miles when it happened. Kermit gave a slight jolt, followed by the dreaded sound of metal scraping on tarmac, which signalled the death rattle of a punctured nearside tyre. The traffic was heavy and Connie knew she had to get off the main road, even though it would completely ruin the tyre by driving on it. She should have taken Nick's advice. Mercifully there was a road just a few yards ahead on her left. Without having time to signal, she coaxed Kermit round the corner and parked noisily. Brandon Street had lots of parking spaces, but the terraced houses here were shabby, some with boarded-up windows, all with overgrown gardens. Connie pulled into the first available parking spot, outside a house whose front garden had an old washing machine sitting forlornly amidst the long grass.

She jumped as someone hammered on the window. She wound it down cautiously to find herself face to spotty face with a tall, gangly youth wearing a grey hoodie and dirty low-slung jeans.

'You can't park that here!' he yelled. 'Me brother and me mate will be here in a minute and that's *their* space.'

Connie got out of the car to survey her deflated tyre. 'Well, I'm very sorry but I can't go any further because I have a puncture. As you can see.'

He looked down at her wheel. 'Yeah, so you have,' he said.

'I'm about to phone for help,' Connie continued, as she withdrew her mobile from her bag, 'and then I'll be out of here, I assure you. Pronto.'

'Nice phone,' remarked the youth. The comment suddenly made Connie aware of her vulnerability. She must have looked terrified because the guy said, 'I weren't planning to nick the bloody thing!'

'I didn't think you were,' Connie lied.

'Christ, they're 'ere!' He turned his attention to where a noisy black Sierra had rolled up and parked behind. 'Hi, Marco!' he said reverently.

'What's that bloody thing doing parked there, Gary?' asked the large black youngster who emerged from the driving seat. A round-faced, long-haired boy got out from the passenger seat, and both of them glared at Connie.

'She's got a fucking puncture,' replied Gary. 'Sorry, Marco, I couldn't do nothing about it – she's only just got here.'

Marco kicked at the offending tyre as Connie stood awkwardly on the pavement. He and the other boy bent to examine the tyre, exposing varying degrees of builders' cracks.

'I was just going to phone for help…' Connie began nervously.

'Foxy'll fix it,' said the good-looking black boy, indicating his companion. 'Won't you, Foxy?'

Foxy looked like he knew which side his bread was buttered. 'Yeah, OK, Marco. Have you got a jack in your boot, missus? And I'll need the spare.'

Connie opened the boot with some trepidation. 'But *really*, you don't need to do this. I can easily get the AA.'

'They'll take all bloody day to get here,' said Marco, standing back in a supervisory fashion while Foxy wrestled with the wheel. 'Foxy'll do it. He used to work in a garage – didn't you, Foxy?'

'Yeah.' Foxy seemed to know what he was doing, loosening the nuts, jacking up the car and removing the wheel.

Foxy didn't look at all fox-like, so perhaps Fox was his surname. Connie stared at him for a moment; there was *something* about him… Perhaps it was the way his hair grew upwards and refused to lie flat. Perhaps it was his cheeky grin. Something, *something* reminded her of Ben. Yes, yes, *that* was it, the way he grinned.

'This is really kind of you,' Connie said, wondering how much she should pay him.

'It's 'cos you're buggering up our parking space,' said Gary.

'Shut up, Gary,' ordered Marco. 'She can't help it, can she? And don't just stand there, give your brother a hand.'

Gary also did as he was told.

Marco was obviously used to being obeyed. He was a nice-looking lad, his T-shirt and jeans immaculate, gold watch, gold earrings and signet ring. And he certainly didn't believe in getting himself dirty.

After much swearing, Foxy replaced the wheel with the spare and lowered the car.

'Take that across to Dick's and see if you can get it fixed,' Marco went on. 'Though it's a right bloody mess. You're gonna need a new one, lady.'

'Oh no, please, don't go to any trouble!' she protested. 'I can get that done at the next garage I come to – *really*.'

'Foxy'll get it at *cost* for you.'

The three stood murmuring together for a moment before Foxy stuck the offending wheel in the back of the Sierra and drove off.

'You wanna cup of tea?' asked Gary as he replaced her case in the boot.

'Well, that's very kind of you but—'

'Of course she does!' Marco said. 'And I can't keep calling you "lady" – so what do we call you?'

'I'm Connie, but—'

'I'm Marco, that there's Gary, and his brother's Foxy, the one that's doing your tyre. He'll be half an hour at least so you might as well have the tea. Get the bleeding kettle on, Gary.'

Connie locked her car and followed Gary up the overgrown path, past the washing machine and into a dark hall with ancient cracked linoleum on the floor, Marco bringing up the rear. She was led into a grubby and untidy kitchen, the sink jammed with dirty dishes and glasses.

'Bloody tip,' observed Marco.

'Well, me mam's away,' Gary explained, as he cleared a path through the dishes in order to fill up the kettle.

'Perhaps I could do some washing-up for you?' Connie offered, feeling duty-bound to do something, anything. Not that she could see a sponge or a dishcloth or anything resembling washing-up liquid.

'Don't matter,' muttered Gary.

'I wouldn't go anywhere near that lot if I were you,' said Marco. 'You could pick up a nasty infection. How can you live in all this shit, Gary? Sit down, Connie.'

He moved a pile of newspapers from one of the kitchen chairs positioned round the Formica-topped table, which was loaded with even more dirty crockery and an open carton of milk. He turned his attention back to Gary. 'Where am I supposed to look for a clean mug for Connie here?'

'Dunno,' said Gary as he lit the gas ring under the kettle.

'Connie here's a lady who'd like a cup and saucer, I expect, wouldn't you, Connie? Ain't your mum got no cups and saucers, Gary?'

Gary looked bewildered. 'Only them fancy ones in the cabinet in the front room.'

'Well, go and get one then!'

Connie started to protest again but Marco was shepherding Gary into the adjoining room from where, with much swearing and clattering, they returned with Gary bearing a china cup adorned with blue and yellow butterflies.

'Me mam would kill me if she knew...' Gary began.

'And I'll kill you if you don't get us a bloody cup of tea,' said Marco as he found an open box of PG Tips. He rinsed out a couple of mugs in cold water and lined them up next to the cup and saucer, then stuck a tea bag in each. While Gary filled them up from the kettle, Marco picked up the carton of milk and sniffed it suspiciously.

'It's OK, I think,' he informed Connie. 'You take milk?'

'Just a dash, please.' The cup was very dainty, and emptied after a few sips, exposing a deep dark crack in the bottom. She wouldn't let herself think about how many germs might have been harbouring there, or for how long.

Gary produced a packet of tobacco and some Rizlas from the pocket of his hoodie and began to construct a roll-up. 'Where you heading for then?' he asked as he sat down opposite her and slurped his tea.

'Oh, the Lake District,' said Connie.

'Nice up there, innit,' Gary remarked without much interest.

'Don't suppose he's ever *been* up there,' said Marco. He was standing at the sink, gazing out through the dirty window. He turned to Connie. 'Excuse us for a minute.' He then shepherded Gary, in the process of lighting up his cigarette, out into the hall. 'Connie don't want to inhale your evil bleedin' smoke.'

She could hear them talking in low voices and wondered what was going on. Then she heard Foxy return and further conversation ensued before all three re-entered the kitchen.

'Foxy's brought back your wheel with the new tyre fitted,' Marco informed her.

The amount was less than half what Connie had expected to pay and, as she fished around in her purse among the diminishing wad of notes, she said, 'I just can't thank you all enough. I only wish I could think of some way to repay my gratitude.'

Connie was aware of some exchanged glances before Marco said, 'Well, actually, Connie, there *is* something you could do for us.'

She wondered what was coming and if this tyre was really going to be such a bargain.

'It's like this, see…' Marco began.

'We need a driver,' said Foxy.

'This lunchtime,' added Gary, puffing on his cigarette.

'A *driver?*' Connie looked from one to the other. 'Don't you all drive?'

'Well, yeah, we do,' said Marco. 'It's just that we have this appointment, see. We need to pick some stuff up from a mate and he needs to see us *all*.'

'And it's all double yellow lines round there,' said Gary. 'And there's one bastard of a traffic warden who's got it in for us.'

'So,' continued Marco, 'we wondered if you could just drive us there, park on the yellows and, if the law comes round, say you're delivering something.'

This wasn't making much sense to Connie. 'Couldn't one of you drive and the other two collect whatever it is?'

'No, no, Connie. Our mate definitely needs to see the three of us together, see. If it wasn't for these bloody yellows it wouldn't be a problem, but last time we got a ticket. And you can't park anywhere round there – no car parks, nothing. And we'll be in a bit of a hurry 'cos we've all got appointments afterwards. The dentist and all that. It would be doing us a great favour, Connie.'

This didn't feel right somehow. 'But I've never driven a Sierra before,' Connie said.

'No *need*, Connie!' said Marco. 'We'll use yours! See, the reason we keep getting done for parking is 'cos they see this car coming a mile off. But they won't know you, nice respectable lady and all that.'

'I don't know,' said Connie.

'Aw, come on, Connie!' said Foxy. 'We done you a favour.'

'And it'll only take a few minutes,' Gary added.

'And, after you've collected us and dropped us off, Connie,' Marco said, 'you can be on your way to the Lake District with that *bargain* tyre.'

Ten minutes later, the wheel replaced, the spare back in the boot and her case and belongings reloaded, Connie got into Kermit's driving seat with Marco alongside. As the other two clambered into the back, she felt even more apprehensive; something was definitely wrong. She longed to be rid of them, and the whole area, once and for all.

Marco consulted his watch. 'Off we go!' he said cheerfully.

Connie must have driven only half a mile or so into the high street, before she was instructed to park – 'just there, beside Dorothy Perkins' – on the dreaded yellow lines in what seemed to be a normal shopping area.

Marco got out first and scanned the horizon. 'You should be OK; can't see any wardens. We'll only be a few minutes, Connie, and then we'll want to be away *quick*. I've got this appointment with the dentist, see, so keep the engine running.'

Connie was so busy looking around for any sign of police or wardens that she didn't notice which doorway they'd entered. She drummed her fingers on the steering wheel, hoping fervently that they wouldn't be long.

Foxy wasn't. After what could only have been a couple of minutes Connie was aware of uproar behind her and, looking in the mirror, saw a frantic Foxy running towards the car, carrying a bag. There was no sign of the other two but bells were ringing and sirens were blaring in the jeweller's shop just behind. Foxy burst into the front seat and dropped his bag on the floor.

'Go! Go! Go!' he yelled at Connie.

She fumbled with the gears. 'What's going on? Where are the other two?'

'Go, for Christ's sake! They've been nabbed!'

Dear God, what have I done now? Connie wondered.

'What the hell were you *doing*?' she asked as she pulled away from the commotion. 'Surely you weren't robbing the jeweller's? I cannot believe this!'

'That was the idea,' admitted Foxy, hood up, looking round anxiously to make sure they weren't being followed. 'The bloody owner was supposed to be at lunch, just the girl in the shop looking after things. But the bugger was there and grabbed Marco, and set off the bloody alarms. Then this great big bloke came in and landed Gary on the floor, and all hell broke loose. Keep *going*, for God's sake!'

Foxy not only resembled Ben but she noticed he'd even got some of his mannerisms; the pull of his earlobe and the picking of his fingernails when he was nervous or scared, which was what Foxy was doing now. How old was he? Nineteen? Twenty?

She turned down a side street. 'I can't let you do this, Foxy.'

'Connie, for God's sake…'

Connie parked and turned off the engine.

'Just get the hell out of here, will you,' Foxy yelled. 'There's a bloody police station down the end of this road!'

The boy was shaking visibly. Connie put her hand on his arm. 'Whose bright idea was this?'

'Not mine,' he said, reaching for the door handle.

'Don't go for a minute,' Connie said, still holding his arm. 'No one's looking for you here. Was it Marco who dreamed this up?'

'Yeah, and every bloody thing he does gets fucked up. Gary too.'

'What about *you?*'

'Me? I keep out of it. Well, not this time, 'cos Marco said they needed three of us. And I was short of cash 'cos the garage where I was working has just laid half of us off. Just when I found something I liked doing.' He no longer looked as if he was about to bolt.

'How old are you, Foxy?'

'Seventeen.'

God, seventeen, and the poor kid probably on the brink of a lifetime of petty crime.

Connie sighed. 'What's in the bag?'

'Notes, from the till. I only got a handful before the bloke got hold of Marco. Him and Gary were after the jewellery, see.'

'Look, Foxy.' Connie prayed she was saying the right thing. 'If you hand that money in right now, tell them you got talked into doing this…'

'You must be bloody mad!' Once again he had a hold on the door handle and once again she grabbed his arm. Firmly.

'I probably am,' she said with a grin. 'And I can't stop you running away. But, if you were to hand that cash in right now, and – yes – apologise for having been persuaded to rob the jeweller's in the first place, they'll probably let you off very lightly. A reprimand or something. But you start spending that money and you're sunk.'

'Why should *you* care?' Foxy still had his hand on the door handle but he wasn't moving.

'You remind me of my son, and I'm doing the same for you as I would have done for him. And I want you to find another job in another garage, and you aren't going to be able to do that with a criminal record hanging over you.'

Foxy thought for a moment. 'I ain't going inside no police station.'

Connie thought quickly. 'Leave the bag then, and I'll take it in there.'

He hesitated, fingering the handle of the canvas bag.

'Please!' Connie said. 'Please! It's important.'

He shrugged and then nodded.

'Now, where's the police station?'

Again he hesitated. Then replied, 'A couple of hundred yards down on the right.'

Connie took the bag from him. 'Can you walk home from here?'

'Yeah, it's only ten minutes.'

'Be off with you then.' She took the bag and started to look round for a scrap of paper to write on. When she looked up again Foxy had gone.

Police Constable Trevor Wainwright didn't like being on the front desk, but the sergeant was in the office having his tea and his ham sandwich.

Trevor had joined the police to catch criminals, not listen to hysterical women bawling about their bags being snatched, or dotty pensioners wittering on about missing cats. He stifled a yawn as a woman in a green dress came through the door, clutching a canvas bag. *Now* what?

'Can I leave this with you, officer?' she asked, laying the bag and a piece of paper on the counter.

'What exactly have we here?' he asked in what he hoped was his most authoritative voice, while fishing around under the desk for an appropriate form.

'It's money,' the woman said, and then added with the glimmer of a smile, 'I haven't counted it, but I've left a note to go with it.'

'Found it on the street, did you, madam?' Damn, where *were* the wretched forms? 'Can you hang on a minute while I get the correct paperwork?'

Trevor headed into the office alongside, and found the sergeant had now started on a packet of custard creams while slurping his tea. After some searching he finally found the forms he was looking for and returned to find the office empty. She'd gone! But the bag and the paper were still there on the counter.

'Shit!' he said.

'What's up?' The sergeant peered round the door, wiping crumbs from his mouth.

'The woman's gone! She's just left this…' He waved at the countertop.

'I've told you before; you're supposed to make sure you've got all your paperwork at the beginning of a shift. Anyway, she must be around somewhere. Check the CCTV – she's probably in the car park.'

But there was no sign whatsoever of a woman in a green dress.

'So, what's in the bag?' The sergeant peered in warily before withdrawing a bundle of notes. He counted them carefully. 'Three hundred quid. All twenties. Perhaps it's a donation. What's the note say then?'

The piece of paper had plainly been pulled out of a small notebook. The writing was neat and legible.

Trevor read:

I haven't looked in this bag but I believe it contains cash stolen from the till of a local jeweller's a short time ago. I inadvertently gave a lift to the young man who took this money. His two companions are probably in custody by now.
He very much regrets doing this, and has asked me to hand it in. Please be lenient with him. They were all kind to me and seem like good lads who need a bit of guidance.

CHAPTER ELEVEN

HONEYMOON HUNTING

Roger McColl feverishly opened and shut drawer after drawer as he searched in vain for the tin opener. How was a man supposed to have a bowl of soup if he couldn't open the bloody tin? Where had Connie put it? Finally he calmed down sufficiently to look in the top drawer again and there it was, exactly where it should be. In fact, she'd left the kitchen immaculate, so he supposed he couldn't complain about that.

Had she been planning this for long? And was he to blame? Everyone would, of course, point the finger at him. And he hadn't done a damn thing! He knew that he was considered to be an upright citizen, responsible, dutiful, conscientious, irreproachable. He'd been told this many times. It was just the way he was, and always had been. Unlike Connie, who didn't get involved in anything much. God knows, he'd tried often enough to get her interested in golf. Other fellows' wives practised regularly and some became jolly good players. Clive Hemming's wife even got a hole-in-one a couple of years back.

But not Connie. Always prattling on about it being cliquey. So what? If she was a member she'd be one of the crowd. Instead of pottering around in that bloody great garden they used to have. Gardens weren't really his thing, apart from occasionally mowing the grass. Now, with this beautiful new bungalow, the builders had given everyone a sensible-sized patch at the back and a communal lawn at the front. His only complaint would be that the newness of it all, and the lack of shrubbery, meant that he had no escape from that nosy old biddy next door who kept trying to make conversation with him.

'Haven't seen your wife around lately,' she'd called out just this morning when he ventured outdoors to chase away a neighbour's cat, which was about to squat on the flowerbed. Neither have I, he thought.

'She's away for a few days,' he'd muttered. Damn the woman. Get inside before she asks any more stupid questions.

Well, *he'd* done nothing wrong, so heaven only knows what was going on in Connie's mind. He'd always found the workings of her brain a puzzle. And she didn't seem to care one bit that he might be starving to death. She need hardly blame him if his eye had wandered elsewhere occasionally.

※

While Roger was hunting for the tin opener, Connie was heading north, and toying with the idea of revisiting their honeymoon spot. When she'd studied the map a few days earlier she'd wondered if she should go – just for a day. Then she changed her mind. Then she changed it back again. She *would* go to Harrogate.

'We'll have a few days in Harrogate,' Roger had announced when they'd set the date for the registry office.

It was January, it was cold, and Connie was pregnant. She hadn't considered any kind of honeymoon since she'd spent much of the previous weeks throwing up copiously each morning, and any dreams of romantic Caribbean idylls or the like had rapidly been dispersed. Anyway they'd only had a week and very little money. But *Harrogate*? She wasn't even too sure where it was. Yorkshire?

Roger had been sent to boarding school a few miles from Harrogate. His father, an irascible major stationed with the Royal Tank Regiment in West Germany, had insisted on his only son having a proper English education but could find nothing either available or affordable in Sussex. He'd finally dispatched Roger to Arrodale, on the edge of the Yorkshire Moors, where they offered a concessionary rate for the sons of officers serving abroad, and where they still believed in cold showers, corporal punishment and bracing ten-mile hikes in all weathers. Roger said he'd hated it. But he'd become fond of Harrogate, where boys escaped on special occasions for genteel afternoon teas, thanks to visiting relatives. And his schoolfriend, 'Dicky' Dixon, just happened to live there.

'I'd rather like to see the old place again,' Roger had said. 'And we'll find a nice cosy hotel with log fires and cream teas.'

As it hadn't been *too* cold, Roger had suggested a walk on the moors and was then horrified to discover Connie's lack of appropriate footwear or outerwear. Thus the first day of their honeymoon was spent in pursuit of walking boots and a 'proper' anorak for Connie, who would have been perfectly happy strolling round the Harlow Carr gardens, winter or not. And the hotel did indeed have log fires and afternoon tea with tiered plates of dainty sandwiches, scones and tiny cakes coated in lurid pink and green icing.

Now she struggled to remember the name of the place. Was it the Huntsman's Horn, or the Huntsman's Return, or the Huntsman's Something-or-Other? A sturdy, grey, stone building, probably Victorian. And, forty-one years later, what would be the chances of it still being a hotel? But you could never be sure. And she had to find Harrogate first, never mind the Huntsman's anything.

Thus Connie was relieved, and not a little surprised, to reach Harrogate without taking any wrong turnings. And she was delighted to see a pleasant-looking B&B, with vacancies and a car park, on her way to the town centre. She'd treat herself to one night and have a look round tomorrow.

'I spent my honeymoon here,' Connie informed Ellie, the amiable young landlady, as she was shown to her room.

'What, right here?' Ellie pointed towards the floor.

'No, no, not right here, but in Harrogate. Somewhere called the Huntsman or the Hunter or something like that. Nice old building opposite a park. My husband would probably remember.' Knowing Roger, he'd probably still got the receipt.

'He's not with you?'

'No.' Connie, eager to avoid awkward questions, added, 'I'll have to call him.'

But of course she wouldn't ask him. She'd look around for some likely landmarks and find the place herself.

Now, because it was late, Connie had a stroll around, then opted for a pub lasagne and a couple of glasses of Merlot before heading back to the B&B for an early night.

But sleep eluded her. First of all she thought about Foxy, and what might become of him. And whether she'd been seen; were the police on the lookout for a little green Ford? And then she re-called her honeymoon. She'd never dreamed she'd come back here alone, out of choice, so many years later. What did that say about her marriage? she wondered.

Connie tossed and turned. Why ever had she come here? Had she really thought that Harrogate might provide an answer to the slow deterioration of her marriage? Well, she was here now so she might as well have a look round in the hope of being able to recon-nect with the way she'd felt about her marriage then.

Connie clearly remembered the large park opposite the hotel, which had had ornate wrought-iron gates, and several tennis courts. Not that anyone had been playing tennis in January.

'My husband can't remember the name either,' she lied ruefully to Ellie at breakfast in the morning. However, Ellie had kindly marked out some possible locations on a map of the town, and Connie decided to try them all, particularly as they were within walking distance.

It was a case of third time lucky. She spotted the elaborate gates first, and then the tennis courts, but nobody was playing today ei-ther. The gates, recently painted a glossy dark green, creaked as she entered. Remembering that the hotel would have been some way along on her left, she skirted the path on the inner perimeter for several yards until, across the busy road, she espied an ugly concrete edifice with 'Hunter's Lodge' emblazoned in flashing orange lights across the front. And, in case she missed that, they flashed down the sides as well. Whatever had happened to the old building? Horrified, she sat down on a bench facing the road and stared across at Hunter's Lodge. It looked exactly the same as countless other overnight stops, and doubtless the rooms would also look exactly the same as the one she'd occupied in Manchester a couple of nights before. She felt sure Roger would be equally horrified. If he knew. If she decided to tell him.

Connie continued to stare at the flashing orange lettering through four lanes of heavy traffic. It had been a quiet, two-lane road back then. She took a picture with her phone, in case she ever did decide to tell her husband. And then she recalled the room in the old-fashioned hotel, with its four-poster bed and the bathroom down the corridor. Nobody expected en-suites then.

Due to her pregnancy it hadn't been a wildly romantic honeymoon, but Roger had been caring and considerate. Even during that hike on the moors he'd insisted that she sat down periodically on any suitable boulder. It had been cold and windy and Connie could still remember how icy those boulders had felt under her bottom. And the newly bought boots had hurt like hell.

Roger had been adamant that Connie must meet Dicky Dixon, who still lived in Harrogate with his overbearing wife, Sonia. Sonia was one of those women who knew everything. And everybody. And, as she'd given birth some months previously, she'd been an expert on that as well.

Roger and Dicky had reminisced continuously throughout that long, tedious evening, with much guffawing and back-slapping. Dicky had an endless repertoire of smutty schoolboy jokes at which Roger laughed uproariously. Connie had willed the evening away but recalled Roger still chortling hours later as he collapsed onto the four-poster.

Had they had anything in common even then, except an embryo? she wondered. She'd been fond enough of Roger to have three more children and stick with him all these years. And, in his younger days, he was a very good-looking man. But when had the indifference really set in…? Perhaps her children, the floristry and, in summer, her garden had occupied too much of her time. Then Roger's newly set up accountancy firm, plus golf, of course, had occupied most of his. Their shared time had centred mainly on birthdays and Christmases and holidays. But weren't all marriages like that? Connie wasn't sure. She had several friends who still openly adored their husbands and did everything as a twosome.

In retrospect Roger had been, and was, a dutiful husband. And I'm a dutiful wife, Connie thought. But is being dutiful the recipe for a happy marriage? she considered. Probably not.

Connie crossed the road with difficulty, dodging between cars and trucks, and entered the deserted lobby of Hunter's Lodge. A bored-looking youth glanced up momentarily from his laptop and said, 'Sorry, love, we're full.'

'I don't want a room,' Connie said. 'I just wondered if you might know what happened to the nice old hotel that used to be here?'

He looked at her blankly. 'Nah,' he replied. 'I only been here a couple of months.'

'Well, is there anyone around who *might* know?'

He sighed and yelled into an inner office, '*Glad-ys!*'

Gladys, hefty and hennaed, emerged with much tut-tutting at being disturbed from whatever it was she'd been doing. 'What is it *now*, Kevin?'

Kevin pointed mutely at Connie, who repeated her request. 'I spent my honeymoon here, you see,' she added.

Gladys, beneath the henna and many layers of make-up, appeared to be around sixty.

'Yeah, I remember, dear,' she said. 'Nice old place it was. Must have been twenty-odd years ago they knocked it down. Think they had a few problems and, anyway, they needed to widen the road. Progress and all.'

'Progress,' Connie repeated, looking around at the check-yourself-in machine and the coffee machine and the soft-drinks dispenser, and the plastic-framed windows. 'And they did such lovely afternoon teas!' she added.

Gladys snorted. 'You'll need to go to Bettys for that, dear.'

Connie was fortunate enough to get a window table at Bettys Tea Rooms, from where she could admire the stunning flower plantings in The Stray opposite. She remembered now that it was called The Stray, the area of grassland that wrapped itself round the Old Town of Harrogate and linked the most popular landmarks. As she nibbled her smoked salmon sandwiches, Connie recalled their visit to the old Turkish Baths and Roger's lean, toned body. She'd looked good then too, even in early pregnancy. Years of being slumped over columns of figures hadn't done much for Roger's, which now sported a considerable paunch. And she had also increased considerably in girth due, in part at least, to four pregnancies and too much wine.

Connie tackled the sultana scones with strawberry conserve and clotted cream next, none of which was likely to improve matters. She must try to walk some more. But, never mind, she thought, there'd be no dinner tonight after this lot, and she should get to the Lakes before it gets too late. There would be plenty of opportunity for walking there. She poured herself another cup of tea and selected a lemon macaroon.

Was it kids that held marriages together? she wondered. We adored our kids; they dominated our conversation, our everything. Lou had been the last to leave home. Was that when she realised she and Roger had so little in common?

Hunter's Lodge had certainly provided no answers. Neither had Gladys. Nor Betty. But at least the tea was delicious.

CHAPTER TWELVE

MERE MEMORIES

Blue sky, continuous sunshine and a warm breeze; could this incredible summer weather continue for much longer? The surface of Lake Windermere shimmered in the afternoon heat as a boatload of sightseers made its lazy way westward, and Connie stretched herself out on the hillside above. She wondered if Ben had ever been here, in this very spot. Perhaps he'd walked up this hill. She knew he'd sailed on the lake because he'd mentioned it in his postcard. She could still see the untidily scrawled words: 'Sailing is the best – Peter fell in the water!' He and Peter had been inseparable. The family had moved away not long after Ben was killed. The last she heard of Peter he was a naval officer, and she only knew that because he was interviewed on TV once when his ship came back to Portsmouth from the Middle East or somewhere.

Connie stared at the lake, trying to imagine her Ben at the tiller of a dinghy. She surveyed the surrounding countryside wondering if she might be seeing the place where he had stayed. She'd had his holiday address at one time, but that had been chucked away when he got home. If only she could remember...

She got out a drawing pad and some pencils she'd bought in Kendal; she'd always enjoyed sketching and this had seemed an ideal opportunity to rediscover her drawing skills. As her pencil wrestled with the lake and the hills and the boatloads of tourists, she pondered why she'd had to travel all these miles to recapture this long-forgotten urge. She examined her effort. She'd got the perspective pretty well, the trees were good, but the lake was disappointing. It needed colour and light to do justice to the sparkling water. Perhaps she should stick to people. She'd bought the pad and pencils in case she might feel like sketching people she met along the way. But where to start? Perhaps she could recall enough of Martin's Robert De Niro looks to achieve a reasonable likeness?

But, for now, she'd concentrate on Kath. She'd start with the pink hair, although she couldn't portray that without buying some pastels or crayons. But she could at least recreate the spiky hair, the broad forehead and the pale eyes that were almost the colour of silver. And that long nose with the slight bend in the middle. Had it ever been broken? Getting the contours of the double chin was a challenge too. An hour later she had a reasonable head-and-shoulders likeness of Kath.

Pleased with her work, Connie laid her sketchpad aside, leaned back and stretched her legs out in the sun. She hadn't worn shorts for years, not since she'd first noticed the ripples and wrinkles rolling down from her thighs towards her knees. She'd bought the shorts in Kendal too, emboldened by the fact that people older and fatter than her were all exposing their lower limbs to the elements. And why not; who *cared*? Her own legs were in reasonable shape, but would look a great deal better if bronzed. She might even have to buy some spray-tan! Roger would be aghast at the very idea, which pleased her even more.

'Would you just look at these *orange* people!' he'd ranted while viewing a popular programme featuring some minor celebrities. For sure, some of them had overdone the spraying, but Connie didn't think they looked that bad; a touch of orange as opposed to winter-white: no contest. And surely, with minimum finger pressure on the nozzle, plus some natural colour of her own, the effect might be quite acceptable?

Connie stretched and sighed and went back to her drawing of Kath.

It might take all afternoon to get the sketch completely right, but she didn't care. For the first time since Manchester she'd stopped looking over her shoulder. She couldn't be completely sure that she hadn't been seen outside the jeweller's, or that someone hadn't seen Foxy getting into her car. Or that the police hadn't seen her drive off after she handed in the bag, although she'd left Kermit parked at least a couple of hundred yards away. Now she felt reassured by the remoteness of the B&B she'd found. No one would find her there, she hoped.

'Will you be hill-walking? Would you like a packed lunch?' the B&B landlady at the Retreat had asked.

'No, no thank you.'

'Call me Pam,' she'd said, as she shepherded Connie upstairs to the pristine single room. It was the whitest space Connie had ever seen, with its pale dove-grey walls, cream carpeting, snow-white

bedding and milky coffee-coloured armchair. Countless shades of
pale. ('A Whiter Shade of Pale' by Procol Harum: they'd played
that at Sally's wedding. She'd always loved that song.) Better be
careful, though, with slurping red wine up here. She wondered at
her wisdom in booking for three nights.

'So, are you on holiday, Mrs McColl?'

'Something like that,' Connie replied, looking round in the
hope of finding somewhere to lay her less-than-pristine bag.

'I always use Farrow & Ball,' Pam wittered on. 'Their colours
are so soothing and I like my guests to feel they've come somewhere relaxing and calm.'

As she sat down to Pam's full English breakfast the following morning, Connie struggled to remember something, anything, about
the address where Ben had stayed on that last holiday. It was a
farm and its name was somehow connected with the weather. Was
it 'storm' or 'rain' or something? *Wind!* That was it! 'Something
Wind'? North, South, East, West – yes, *West!* West Wind Farm!
Surely she should be able to find that, because she knew it was
close to Windermere and perhaps the post office could help, or the
police. No, on second thoughts, perhaps not the police; better to
avoid the police, just in case. She'd ask Pam's advice.

Pam hadn't heard of it but she had a friend who used to work
in the local council offices and she would know for sure. And
she did.

And so Connie, armed with a map and some very detailed
directions, set off along a network of country lanes, mostly sin-

gle-track with few passing places, and prayed she'd meet nothing larger than a bicycle.

West Wind Farm, a solid grey stone construction, was perched on top of a hill, overlooking the lake. As she emerged from the car, Connie scanned the panorama before her and reckoned you could probably walk directly down to the lake in five to ten minutes, whereas it had taken her at least fifteen minutes weaving her way up here in the car. Not for the first time did she wonder at the British propensity for twisting and turning their roads round every field and tree, whereas the French, for instance, would probably have bulldozed theirs in a nice straight line from A to B. Well, I suppose that's what makes us quaint, she thought.

The gate was closed and Connie wondered if she dare open it. There was a yard and a cluster of outbuildings surrounding the farmhouse, where countless chickens were roaming around two tractors and an ancient Morris Minor. Somewhere a dog began to bark hysterically and Connie hesitated. Perhaps she shouldn't investigate any further. After all, this must have been where Ben had stayed, and this was the view he'd have had, and that was the walk he and Peter would have taken down to the lake. And, let's face it, nobody was going to remember anything now, after all these years, so she'd just enjoy the view for a minute, imagine Ben running down the slope, and be on her way.

She was about to leave when a man emerged from one of the outbuildings, two Collies leaping at his Wellington-booted heels, barking furiously.

'Can I help you?'

He sounded friendly enough so Connie decided to come clean.

'Oh, I do hope you don't think I'm snooping, but I just wanted to see the farm where my son and his friend once came on holiday.'

As he leaned on the gate Connie noted he was fortyish, with a farmer's ruddy face and a nice smile.

'Ah,' he said, 'we haven't had holidaymakers staying here for a very long time. Sure you've got the right place?'

'I'm pretty certain this is it,' Connie replied, 'but I'm talking about twenty-four years ago.'

'That's a long time back! Can't help you there, I'm afraid. I've only been here fifteen years, since I married Tilly.'

'Oh well, never mind.' What did I expect? Connie wondered. But, nevertheless, she experienced a little wave of disappointment.

'Why is it so important after all this time?'

The dogs were jumping up at the gate, tails wagging, tongues lolling, desperate to meet their visitor.

Connie considered for a moment. 'My son enjoyed his holiday here so much and…' She hesitated. 'He died the following year.'

'Oh, I'm sorry to hear that.' The farmer looked uncomfortable.

'I wanted to come years ago,' Connie continued, 'but my husband wouldn't agree; thought it would be too upsetting.'

'Look,' he said, opening the gate after ordering the dogs back to where they'd come from, 'why don't you come in and meet Tilly? She grew up on this farm, you see, and she just might remember some of the visitors they had back then.'

'If you're sure…'

'Please, come in.' He held out his hand. 'Will Hartley's the name.'

'Connie McColl.' He had a nice firm handshake.

He led her up to the door of the farmhouse and ushered her in to a large kitchen, where the mouth-watering aroma of spices was emanating from a huge pot on an ancient Aga. A large boy was stretched out on a battered old sofa, engrossed in his phone.

'Where's your mother?' Will asked.

Without taking his eyes from the screen, the boy pointed mutely towards what was obviously a walk-in pantry, from which emerged a short woman with glorious red hair, bearing a tray of empty jars.

'Tilly, this is Connie, er…'

'McColl,' Connie prompted.

'Yes, Connie McColl. Her son –' he glanced at Connie 'her *late* son had a great holiday here twenty years ago.'

'Twenty-*four* years ago,' Connie corrected.

Tilly laid the tray of jars down carefully on the table. 'Just making some chutney,' she explained. 'Why don't you sit down while I make a cup of tea?' She didn't speak again until she handed Connie the mug. 'So your son died, did he?'

'Yes,' Connie said.

She nodded in sympathy. 'Mam and Dad used to let this house out every summer. We had to move into the old dairy out the back there, and we'd be right fed up of it by the end of the season, I can tell you!'

Connie laughed. 'I can well imagine! And I certainly don't expect you to remember but Ben, my son, came here with his friend Peter, and Peter's family, twenty-four years ago this very month.'

Tilly stared hard at her. 'What was his name again?'

'Ben. Ben McColl. And Peter Portman.'

'This rings a bell,' she said. 'Ben and Pete. Yeah, of course, just before we all went back to school. You know why I remember? Because we'd had a whole summer of old fuddy-duddies staying here. "Keep quiet!" "Don't make a noise!", etc., etc. That's all we heard all summer long. And then, right near the end of the season, here were two kids I could play with! We were all about the same age, I think.'

Connie could scarcely believe what she was hearing.

'Oh, Tilly, I'm so glad you remembered. He'd had such a great time here and wanted to come back, but he was killed the following summer.'

Tilly nodded. 'I'm so sorry.'

'It just helps sometimes to retrace his steps,' Connie said. 'But I can't *believe* that you actually remember him!'

Tilly removed a large black cat from the table, and headed towards the Aga. 'And I'll tell you why I remember him and his friend – because they were so naughty! We were forbidden to go down to the lake with other kids unless we had a grown-up with us, but we'd sneak out anyway and swim around for hours. And we used to play a kind of glorified hide-and-seek around the farm, and I thought I was very clever because I knew all kinds of places to hide that they didn't.' She stopped to pour more tea. 'Anyway, on this occasion I climbed up the ladder into the hayloft, which was also forbidden because Dad said there were rats up there. But one of the boys had seen me, and the little buggers came along and took away the ladder so I couldn't get down! And they left me to it! I yelled and yelled for ages until eventually my sister heard me and went to tell Dad. I can't tell you the walloping I got!'

'The naughty little devils!' Connie laughed as she sipped her mug of tea.

'Well, of course, I shouldn't have been up there in the first place. But they were such fun! Great lads.'

'Thank you so much for telling me,' Connie said, 'because he certainly didn't tell me *that* when he got home!'

'Now I come to think of it,' Tilly went on, 'I'm sure there's a photo somewhere if I can only find it. Jason – get up, and let this lady have a seat!'

Without moving his eyes or his thumbs from the screen, Jason eased himself up and sauntered out of the door.

'He's glued to that bloody thing from morning to night,' Will sighed, as Tilly went off in search of the photo. 'He'll forget how to talk soon.'

Connie laughed. 'They're all the same. But I'm just so thrilled Tilly remembered Ben. And I only hope I'm not interfering with your plans for this afternoon.' She lowered herself into the sofa and drained her tea.

'Plans? We've got no plans. It's just nice to have a visitor.'

Then Tilly came back into the kitchen clutching a photo album. 'I'm sure it's in here somewhere,' she said, laying it on the table alongside the jars, and flicking through countless pages until she was almost at the end. 'Ah, here we are!'

There were three photos neatly glued onto the black page. There was a young Tilly riding a horse, a young Tilly with two mischievous-looking boys, and another one of just the two boys. Ben and Peter. And it was a particularly good one of Ben.

'Oh, I *love* this one!' Connie exclaimed.

'Then you must have it,' Tilly said, removing it from the page with difficulty.

'Oh, I didn't mean for you to remove it…'

'I know you didn't,' Tilly said. 'But I want you to have it. I've got the other one.'

'Thank you, Tilly.' Connie knew her voice was wobbly. 'Thank you so much.'

'And any time you're up this way, you just come in and see us,' Will added.

'If you hang on a bit,' Tilly said, 'you can have a jar of my bean chutney.'

Later, sitting in the evening sunshine in the garden of the Dog and Duck, Connie ate her crab salad and refilled her glass from the bottle of Merlot.

'And I'll have the cork, please,' she'd instructed the barmaid, 'so I can take it away with me. That's if I don't drink it all here.'

Perhaps she should drink it all here, because she shuddered at the prospect of spilling one drop on Pam's pristine white bed linen or cream carpeting. All that beige, bone and buttermilk. There was definitely something to be said for some colourful curls and whirls at times. She'd certainly had no need for such concerns in Stratford-upon-Avon.

Connie considered her finances. She'd been away from home for a week now, spending money like water. Bed and breakfasts were expensive, petrol even more so. But it had been worth every penny she'd spent just to get that photograph of Ben.

There was money in her personal account, of course, but at present it was going out a great deal faster than she expected. It was vital to be independent and there was no way she was going to use their joint account because, for one thing, Roger would probably be able to trace her whereabouts each time she withdrew cash. Or, heaven forbid, he might even be able to put a block on it. She liked to think that he hadn't got the faintest idea where she was; no landline calls that could be traced, no postage marks. She could be in France or Spain or Timbuktu. And, much as she appreciated Di's offer, no way was she going to be subsidised by her daughter.

At some point, Connie realised, she would probably have to turn round and head back south, but not yet. It would have to be a turning point in every sense. But her wings had only just begun to unfold and, in the meantime, she needed to escape Pam's waxen decor. This would be her last night at the Retreat.

Since yesterday, she'd felt rejuvenated. Discovering a small part of Ben's life she'd never known about before had somehow nourished her soul, and made her feel as if he wasn't entirely gone from the world. It was as if she'd found a lost piece of a jigsaw and the picture was now just a little more complete. And that photo! She kept taking it out to have a peek. And Connie felt prepared now to seek out more missing bits of her life, and of herself. She was ready to move on.

That final morning Pam hovered over the breakfast table. 'Will you be having the full breakfast today, Mrs McColl?'

'Yes please,' said Connie, wondering where and when she might be having her next meal.

Pam was obviously curious. She already knew the life stories of the retired couple from Denver, Colorado, the middle-aged couple from Christchurch, New Zealand, and the Scottish couple from somewhere unpronounceable near Perth.

'Well, Mrs McColl, and where might you be heading when you leave us today?' she asked with a fixed smile as she delivered Connie's breakfast.

'Do you know what, Pam, I might just head north.' Then she couldn't help adding with a smile, 'Or wherever the fancy takes me.'

'Oh well, at least the weather's holding,' Pam added lamely before heading off to the American couple, who would doubtless provide her with a detailed itinerary of their day ahead.

Martin from MMM's suggestion had taken root and Connie knew exactly where she was going: Newcastle. She could still recall her father's Geordie accent, and his height. She'd remembered him as being very tall but then, of course, she'd been very small. And she remembered clearly that he'd lost the tip of one of his fingers – the little one, she thought. How had he done that? A police incident? A schoolboy prank? She'd never know.

She'd kept meaning to visit Newcastle during her teenage years, but somehow the pull of holidays in the sun had won over until she was twenty-one, when she'd finally come up to trace his birthplace, and found the tiny terraced house where he'd been born in Boxwood Close. Now she longed to see it again, and also the little church on the corner with the wonky spire and the tiny churchyard where her grandparents were buried. She'd taken photos at the time and wished now she'd brought them with her. For the first time Connie felt a little homesick; probably something to do with looking into her family background. She opened up her emails in the hope that one of the family might have been in touch. There was nothing from any of them but there was a message from her friend Sue.

Sue, of course, was beside herself with curiosity. Surely Connie didn't have a lover?

Or surely she'd have told Sue if she did! She was *so* envious! Perhaps she could come along too? She could join up with Connie somewhere on the way? Perhaps Connie was lonely?

No, Connie thought, definitely not. I am not at all lonely. And, fond as I am of Sue, this is one time when I very much need to be on my own.

CHAPTER THIRTEEN

A LOVE OF ROSES

Connie was becoming addicted to the excitement of being on the move, of never staying anywhere long enough to get bored, and never knowing when and where she might go next or who she might meet along the way. Of being impulsive again, defying the conventions of forty-one years spent playing by the rules.

Perhaps, had the weather been unsettled, she might have felt differently, but one warm day followed another and Connie began to wonder why she needed to seek accommodation at all. Why not buy a sleeping bag and bed down under the stars? A memory stirred somewhere deep inside her. *What?* And be awakened by the dawn chorus, the lowing of cattle, the bleating of sheep? Then washing in a nearby stream and perhaps picking wild berries for breakfast? Connie considered this rural idyll for some miles without really concentrating on signposts, fairly confident that she was heading towards Newcastle. Even so, she was gobsmacked when she drove past the iconic, awe-inspiring Angel of the North, standing tall over Newcastle and Gateshead – so much so that she nearly veered off the road.

After her experiences in Manchester, she decided to avoid city centres at all costs, but she did need to find somewhere to withdraw cash, and perhaps visit a shop that sold tents and sleeping bags. And Primus stoves? Well, that might be taking things a bit *too* far, but a sleeping bag for sure. And she could ask around if anyone knew where Boxwood Close was, because she certainly couldn't remember.

A few miles further on, Connie turned into a multi-storey car park attached to what seemed to be a sizeable out-of-town shopping area, and decided to have a look around. Luck was with her and there was a camping shop nearby.

'This,' enthused the young sales assistant, whose name was Brian, according to his badge, 'is the Miracle, so-called because it always keeps you at just the right temperature; warm when it's cold, and cool when it's hot. They don't call it the Miracle for nothing. And you'll need a nice self-inflating sleeping mat to go with it.'

It all sounded good to Connie, who was fascinated by the way Brian's Adam's apple bounced around as he extolled the further virtues of the bedding. She reckoned it might be quite possible to sleep al fresco so long as it didn't rain, and she could always try stretching out in the car when it did. And no, he'd never heard of Boxwood Close. He pointed out, not unreasonably, that Newcastle was an enormous place and hadn't she best check with the post office or the library or something? Or, better still, buy a map or use her phone to access a street map? Brian was full of useful tips.

She was about to emerge from the shop with her purchases when she heard a scream from outside on the pavement. Dumping her packages with Brian, she rushed out of the door to find a tiny elderly lady struggling to get to her feet, and the rear view of a hooded youth as he sprinted away towards the end of the street.

'Dear God!' exclaimed Connie, as she bent down to help. 'Are you all right? What happened?'

'It's my bag,' said the little lady plaintively, 'he's taken my handbag!'

A small crowd had gathered by now, with much tut-tutting.

'That's the second mugging round here in as many weeks,' one man said.

'Which way did the bastard go, pet?' asked another. Nobody made any move.

'You won't catch him now,' said the first man cheerfully. 'He'll be miles away.'

'Can you manage to stand?' Connie asked as she bent down.

'Perhaps in a minute or two, dear.' The old lady rubbed her head. 'He tripped me, you see. And he's got my purse, all my money.'

'I'm so sorry,' said Connie. 'Is there anyone I can contact for you?' She turned towards the onlookers. 'Do you think we should call an ambulance?'

'*No, no!*' protested the lady. 'I'll be fine in a minute. Really. Just a bit dizzy.'

'Somebody should be with her,' said a woman with bright green hair.

'I'll stay with her,' Connie said as she helped her to her feet.

Brian, from the shop, had produced a chair from within and positioned it in the doorway. 'Here, get her to sit on this,' he said, patting the seat.

She tottered slightly for a moment and then sat down gratefully. 'I'm sorry to be such a nuisance,' she said. She was so tiny and bird-like.

'What's your name?' Connie asked as Brian reappeared, on instruction, with a glass of water.

'I'm Jeannie,' she said as she took the glass from Connie. Her hand was shaking so much that water was spilling everywhere.

Connie steadied the glass for her. 'I'm Connie. Just take it easy, Jeannie. Do you have far to go home?'

Jeannie shook her head. 'No, not far, but I need to get the bus. And he's got my bus pass and all my money.'

The onlookers were now dispersing, one by one, clutching their bags more tightly and relieved that someone else appeared to be taking over. 'Tsk, tsk,' they said to each other. 'And in broad daylight too! It didn't used to be like this round here, did it, pet?'

'We should call the police,' Connie said. 'And would you like me to take you to the hospital, just to get checked over? You've had a nasty fall, quite apart from the shock of what's happened.'

'You're very kind, dear, but really I'm fine. I'm tough as old boots. It's just my pension, you see, and he probably saw me coming out of the post office.' A tear rolled down her wrinkled cheek.

Connie wished she could get her hands on the mugger. What sort of rat would do something like this to a pensioner?

'I'm eighty-nine,' said Jeannie, 'so it takes me a minute or two.' She chuckled, but Connie could see that she was still quite shaky.

Jeannie must have been a beauty in her day, Connie thought, as she noted her straight little nose, chiselled cheekbones, large brown eyes, and thick white hair tied up in a chignon.

'Tell you what, Jeannie, do you see that cafe across the street? If you lean on my arm do you think we could get across there for a cup of tea? And then, when you feel strong enough, I can drive you home.'

'That's so kind of you.' Jeannie stood up slowly.

Connie noted she was wearing mascara, lipstick and some trendy cut-offs too. A youthful old lady. I want to be like that, she thought.

The cafe owner, who was elderly, bald and, judging by his T-shirt, a Newcastle supporter, had witnessed the event and fussed about, pulling out chairs and refusing Connie's offer of payment for the teas.

'It says something when you can't walk down the street in broad daylight,' he ranted. 'And who would rob a pensioner?' With that he produced a plate of cream cakes. 'And I've already rung the police,' he added importantly. 'Apparently there's a copper just a street or two away and he should be along any minute.'

The young policeman, when he arrived five minutes later, found Jeannie on her second cream cake and looking surprisingly perky. He was polite, concerned and took copious notes before adding, 'I'm really sorry to say it, madam, but the chances of retrieving your money are virtually nil.' That, of course, was hardly a surprise.

'Are you related to this lady?' he asked Connie.

'No,' Connie replied, 'but I'm happy to take her home and make sure she's OK.'

The policeman seemed satisfied with this and departed, having promised to let Jeannie know if there were any further developments.

'There won't be,' Jeannie said sadly after he left. 'Nobody got a proper look at him and he'll have spent the cash by now – probably bought himself a raspberry, or something like that.'

'A *raspberry*?' Connie asked.

'Yes, it's a sort of phone, you know, which does all sorts of things.'

'Oh, a BlackBerry!' Connie laughed.

'Whatever, dear.' Jeannie was looking much recovered after the cream cakes.

'Now,' said Connie as they finished their tea. 'Do you think you're steady enough to accompany me to the car park? But first I must collect my packages from the camping shop over there.'

Fifteen minutes later, weighed down with her parcelled-up sleeping equipment under her left arm and Jeannie leaning on her right, Connie was reunited with Kermit in the car park. Jeannie had regained her composure and was proving to be remarkably light on her feet, but quite frail. She was also extremely lucid and gave Connie precise directions to where she lived, which turned out to be a one-bedroom ground-floor flat in a large, converted Victorian house on a tree-lined avenue.

'This is lovely!' Connie remarked as she took in her surroundings, having parked and helped Jeannie out of the car. Well-maintained houses, glossy front doors, shiny brass knobs and knockers. Jeannie's front door was painted black, the polished-brass number ten positioned at eye level, just like Downing Street.

'Oh, I like it here,' said Jeannie. 'It's so important to live in as nice an area as you can afford. Where do *you* live, dear?'

'Sussex.'

'Sussex!' The old lady stopped in her tracks. 'My word, you're a long way from home! Are you up here on business?'

'No,' said Connie. 'It's a long story, but basically I just felt I needed to get away from things for a while and, since I found myself heading north, I thought I'd revisit my roots, or my father's roots at least. He lived in Boxwood Close. I don't suppose you know where that is, do you?'

'No, dear, I don't think I've ever heard of it.'

'No matter, I'll get directions tomorrow from somewhere. I know it's near the docks because I came up once before, but that was over forty years ago.'

'Newcastle's changed a lot in that time…'

Jeannie asked no further questions but led Connie into a large hallway, withdrew a key from her pocket ('Thank goodness this wasn't in my bag, dear!') and opened a door on the left which was labelled 'Flat 2'. The first thing Connie noticed in the tiny hallway was a chandelier, and then the ornately framed posters and photographs all over the magenta-painted walls.

'Come in, Connie, come in!'

The sitting room had much more of the same. The chandelier was larger and more ornate, and the framed posters and programmes were larger too, with colourful displays of ballets, shows and revues. There were elaborate velvet curtains, silk shawls draped across the sofa and an enormous bowl of red roses positioned on an intricately carved mahogany table. This certainly bore no resemblance to any old lady's flat Connie had ever visited.

'Jeannie, this is amazing!' Connie looked around in fascination.

'Well,' said Jeannie, 'I know there's rather too much stuff in here, but I love it all, you see. It's my history and I can't quite bring myself to part with any of it. Now, sit down, dear. Would you like a drink?'

'Coffee's fine,' Connie said absently as she took in her surroundings, particularly the posters of dancers and events from all over the globe. Paris, Athens, Cairo, Singapore, Sydney, and one name predominating: Jeannie Jarman.

'Coffee's not fine,' Jeannie said firmly. 'I've had a shock and you've been diverted from where you were going and so we both need a brandy.' She was rummaging around in the base of a mahogany cabinet. 'Or Scotch? Or gin?'

'That's most kind but I'm driving, you see—'

'Tonight? Where to?' Jeannie interrupted.

'Um, well, I'm going to stay in Newcastle tonight so I can look for Boxwood Close tomorrow,' Connie said.

'But you've got nowhere booked?'

'Not really,' she said.

'Well, in that case, you can stay here and you can tell me *all* about this travelling you're doing. I'm pouring you a drink, and that's all there is to it.'

Connie wondered if she dared argue. 'Jeannie, you've just been robbed and—'

'And I have some delicious meals in my freezer which can be ready in minutes. Now, what's it to be? Perhaps you're a gin and tonic person, are you?'

'That would be lovely.'

As Connie wandered around admiring the posters, Jeannie touched her elbow.

'I was a dancer, as you can probably see; all my life, from when I started ballet lessons as a tiny wee girl in Gateshead. And then I went on to dance, sometimes solo, sometimes as part of a troupe, all over the world. America, even.'

'Jeannie, you're amazing!' Connie accepted her gin and tonic in its cut-glass tumbler, complete with ice and lemon. The ice sang as it clinked in the crystal.

'No, I'm not amazing. But I was very fit. I've always had to keep myself fit, you see, and I still try to exercise every day in spite of the fact that I've got a few medical problems at the moment. If I'd seen that wretched oaf coming for me today, my dear, I'd have kneed him in the balls, but he came up from behind and caught me unawares.'

Connie nearly dropped her drink. 'You know what, Jeannie? I believe you.'

Half an hour later, on her second gin, Connie had had a complete résumé of Jeannie's amazing career and the admirers and lovers she'd amassed over the years. 'Millionaires, my dear, and ambassadors, sheikhs – and thespians, of course.'

'And did you never marry, Jeannie?'

'No, my dear, I did not, although I had proposals from some very lovely men. There was only one I would have married – he was very famous but I couldn't marry him because he was already married, you see, and his wife flatly refused to divorce him, so it was all very clandestine. I still get roses from him every month. Are you married, Connie?'

'Oh yes, indeed I am.'

'And are you happy?'

Connie hesitated. 'I'm not sure, Jeannie, and that's the truth.'

Was she happy? Did *not being unhappy* mean the same thing? Was she merely bored, or just plain silly?

'I'm sixty-six, you know,' Connie continued, 'and here I am running around, trying to sort myself out like some rebellious teenager.'

'You could be my daughter! You've plenty of time to get sorted out. At your age I had a lover called Henry who wanted to marry me, but I could see he was about to become decrepit, and I'm really not cut out to be a nurse.'

'And the man who sends the roses?'

'Oh, he died thirty years ago.'

'But, the roses…?'

'In his will he left instructions that I was to receive a bouquet of a dozen red roses on the first day of each month for the rest of my life.' She indicated the bowl on the table. 'And they just keep on coming. Just as well he was rich because I don't suppose his executors expected me to live this long.' She laughed. 'He would have been delighted. His wife was not, but she could do nothing about it. She, too, died years ago.'

Connie felt a totally unjustified pang of envy. To receive flowers from *beyond* the grave! Roger rarely sent them from *this* side of the grave. What romantic memories would *she* have to sustain her through her dotage?

'Now, tell me about your husband,' Jeannie said, as if she was reading Connie's thoughts.

'He's a retired chartered accountant, Jeannie. He's reliable, methodical, a pillar of society. He's done absolutely nothing to upset me. I think my problems – my doubts, my demons – are all in my head. I seem to have lost myself somewhere along the line.'

'Well, at least you're doing *something* about it. There are so many bored, restless women out there just getting on with it. But I read recently that some women – and men too – are beginning to rebel. "Silver singles" or something, I believe they're called.'

Connie sighed. 'Lately, since I retired from my floristry business, I seem to be withering away; I just feel invisible. And I don't even know if I love Roger any more. He thinks I have too little to do and should join things – the golf club, the WI, things like that. He's probably right, he usually is. He's very sensible.'

'This Roger of yours is plainly trying to compartmentalise you into a bog standard, jam-making lady, and I can see you're not at all like that. Was he *ever* exciting?'

'Not exciting, no. But he loved me in his own way, and we had four children. I really didn't have the time or inclination to analyse our marriage. Now I have both.'

Over spaghetti carbonara and a bottle of the wine Connie had stocked up on in Kendal, she told Jeannie about the death of her parents, about being bundled off to live with Uncle Bill and Aunt Lorna. Uncle Bill, her mother's brother, spent most of his time in the oil business in Nigeria. Connie had known, even at five years old, that she was there on sufferance and never felt much loved except when her uncle came home, which wasn't often. She'd got on reasonably well with her cousins, the youngest of whom, Linda, was her own age and with whom she still kept in touch fairly regularly. She described her escape at sixteen to train in floristry, followed by her stint as a tour guide – and then Roger coming along.

'"A good catch", everyone said approvingly, and then, before I knew what I was doing, I was three months pregnant and there we were shivering in an unheated registry office one icy January day. But, enough about me,' Connie concluded. 'Right now I'm still more concerned with the fact that your money's been stolen.'

Jeannie shrugged and sighed. 'I won't pretend it's not a blow because I depend on my state pension – there were no company pensions in my line of work. And I don't have any savings because they all went on buying this flat, but I'll manage.'

Connie noticed that Jeannie picked at her food, but ate very little. And, on closer inspection she could see that the entire flat was slightly shabby, the carpet threadbare in places, a typical example of slightly faded grandeur. The furniture was old, and it was entirely due to Jeannie's innate sense of style that it gave the impression of opulence.

The mahogany table had been draped in an ancient, yellowing lace cloth, with silver cutlery and crystal wine glasses, along with a beautiful antique Crown Derby bowl containing the salad. 'It belonged to my mother,' Jeannie explained. 'I do like nice things, don't you?'

Afterwards, when she'd helped Jeannie clear up, Connie said, 'I really should go and not put you to any trouble.'

'Go? Go where?' Jeannie asked. 'You'll be done for drink-driving, my dear. Oh no, you are spending the night here. We've already decided that. I only have the one bedroom, but I can make up a bed for you on the sofa, if you wouldn't mind that.'

'Of course I wouldn't mind that. And I have my Miracle bedding in my car, which should do the job nicely and save you too much bother. Now, tell me more about your dancing.'

Jeannie's sofa was comfortable, but not quite long enough. The Miracle was warm and light, and Connie slept well but woke with a crick in her neck. She wondered if she'd have been more comfortable on the sleeping mat that Brian had persuaded her to buy.

As they sat down to coffee and toast for breakfast, Jeannie said, 'The thing is, you get used to being solitary. It's one of the reasons I never married. Some people are better on their own than with others and I wonder if you, too, aren't like that. Perhaps, when you were living with your uncle's family, you constructed an invisible wall around yourself?'

Connie nodded thoughtfully. 'Yes, you're right, I think I might have done. And yet it seems crazy to class myself as a loner when I've been married all these years with a family.'

'Well, they say you can feel very alone even when you're surrounded by people, and maybe you need to be on your own again now, to take stock. Don't give up on your marriage, Connie, but don't rush back either. Somewhere along the way you'll decide what you should do with the rest of your life – or perhaps the decision will be made for you. Believe me, I have a strong feeling about it. It's important to be on neutral territory and it's important to follow your instinct. Promise me you'll keep in touch and let me know what you decide?'

'I promise,' said Connie.

Later, while Connie was preparing to take her leave, and Jeannie was showering, she dug into her bag and found a sheet of paper on which she wrote, 'You've helped me so much, Jeannie. Please accept this for my bed and breakfast at one of the most delightful places I've stayed in!' She then folded two twenty-pound notes into the piece of paper and wedged it under the bowl of red roses on the table for her hostess to find later.

· ❀ ·

Jeannie found the note and the money when she sat down at the table at one o'clock, to tackle a bowl of soup, which she probably wouldn't finish. How kind Connie was! But there's a sense of sadness around her, Jeannie thought, and I hope she can find that part of herself that she's lost because she deserves to be complete and properly happy.

She thought about Paul again. All so long ago now, of course. Their affair had lasted twenty-four years, a well-known 'secret'. She kept his photo by her bedside. She'd be joining him soon. The surgeon couldn't be sure how long she'd got. 'Could be weeks, months,' he said, after she'd refused the last lot of treatment. Well, she'd had a good innings and there wasn't much to live for now.

'Wow!' Connie had said when she'd been shown round the little flat and had seen Paul's photo. 'Wasn't he handsome! Oh, Jeannie!'

And Connie had hugged her; a lovely, spontaneous gesture. What a nice woman she was, Jeannie thought, and so deserving of some passion in her life; memories to hold onto during the grey years ahead. You'll need your memories then, Connie, she thought, so get them before it's too late! And it was so kind of her to leave that money. It wasn't as if she was a rich person; she just couldn't be with that old car, and a sleeping bag in the boot. But

I've got her mobile number so I must thank her, and I do so need that money. Thank you, Connie, thank you.

That night Jeannie dreamt of Paul again. There she was, on that now famous stone seat in front of the Taj Mahal, having strayed from the rest of her group. No sign of them anywhere and she wondered briefly where they might all have gone. Well, they'd have a good idea where to find her, since everyone posed here when they come to the Taj.

She was suddenly aware of someone sitting beside her. She cast a sidelong glance, recognising his elegant feet, his long legs and lean body and those dark, smouldering eyes that were studying her intently. She stretched out her hand to take his, but he'd disappeared again. And she'd so wanted to hold him.

CHAPTER FOURTEEN

CLOSE CONNECTIONS

Connie found her way to the docklands in spite of the fact that Jeannie's instructions were somewhat vague, but at least she was able to work out in which direction she should be heading. It might, perhaps, help to have a more detailed map of the area, an Ordnance Survey or something and, with this thought in mind, she parked in front of what appeared to be a newsagent-cum-post-office-cum-general store. Connie found no detailed maps and so decided to ask the girl at the counter if she had any idea where Boxwood Close might have been. She was relieved there was no queue but the girl, unfortunately, had never heard of Boxwood Close. However, the little old man with the rheumy eyes and the bicycle clips behind her had. He nudged her to one side to allow the rapidly forming queue to proceed.

'Don't think it's there any more, pet,' he said, stroking his stubbly chin. 'Thirty years or so back they took down all them old terraces, y'know, and built all them flats and things. But Boxwood was only a few streets away from me mam's when we were little so I can tell ye where it *should* be. Now, the best thing ye could do would be to head for Cypress Avenue and have a walk down there because Boxwood would have been a turning off that.'

'Is that near here?' Connie asked.

'Not far at all. Just take a left out of here, down to the traffic lights and turn right. Down to the roundabout, or is it another traffic light? Can't rightly say, I'm on me bike y'see. No. I tell a lie, it's definitely a roundabout. So, ye take the third turning off the roundabout. The *second* roundabout. No, wait a minute, it *would* be the third roundabout…'

'Thanks so much,' Connie said. 'And now I've lost you your place in the queue.' And all sense of direction, she thought.

'Doesn't matter, dear, I'm in no hurry.' And with that he shuffled back to the end of what was now a long line.

What a gentleman, she thought, as she got back to Kermit and tried to make head or tail of his directions. She was relieved to hear Cypress Avenue wasn't too far away and, in her usual fashion – and by now thoroughly confused, having gone the wrong way down a one-way street and found none of the roundabouts he mentioned – found it entirely by accident. It was tree-lined and quite grand, and she couldn't for the life of her imagine terraced houses around here.

Connie pulled in opposite an imposing white Georgian-type structure with a shiny black door adorned with bay trees in little boxes on either side. Decidedly posh. It was then that she felt the bump from behind; someone had hit Kermit!

Connie leapt out to find herself face to face with a tall, very handsome Asian gentleman emerging from a sleek black Jaguar.

'I'm *so* sorry,' he said. 'I think I've just hit your bumper.'

Connie bent down to study the collection of dents on Kermit's rear bumper.

'Well, I did feel a little jolt,' she said, 'but I couldn't tell you which of these dents, if any, it might have made.'

'I definitely hit it,' the man said. 'And I can only apologise as this car is quite new, and considerably longer than my previous one. And I realise now I was trying to drive into far too tight a space. Luckily for me I don't seem to have done any damage to mine.'

'Oh, don't worry, please.'

'But I *do* worry! And I must give you my card.' With that he withdrew a card from the inner pocket of his immaculate, expensively cut grey suit. 'If there's any problem at all with your car you must contact me straight away.'

'Well, OK, just in case...'

'In the meantime, please come across to my office and have a cup of coffee to recover.'

'No, really, I'm OK—'

'I *insist*. Anyway, I need to give you the details of my insurance, just in case...' He held out his hand. 'I'm Rav Mukherjee. Please call me Rav.'

'Connie McColl.'

'Well, Connie McColl, now you come with me, please.'

Ignoring her protestations, he guided her across the road towards the black shiny door and the bay trees, where a gleaming brass plaque announced 'The September Lodge Clinic'. She glanced down at the card he'd given her. He was plainly a doctor of some kind, his name followed by a long line of initials, none of which meant a thing to Connie. Might he be a gynaecologist, or a heart specialist, or what? Looking at his offices, he was the real deal for sure. But whatever he was he sure as hell wasn't NHS, she thought, as she was ushered into a sumptuous reception area with deep-pile beige carpeting and lots of tall, exotic potted plants. The receptionist (or could she be a nurse? – no, on second thoughts, she definitely couldn't) was caramel-skinned, blonde and beige-clad – completely colour-coordinated with her surroundings. She bared a row of perfect teeth as they approached.

'Have a seat for a few minutes while I make some calls. And then Arabella will show you up to my office,' he said.

Connie sat down on a pale grey chair underneath the branches of some tall, silvery-leafed plant, feeling hot, bothered and completely out of place in her old jeans and T-shirt. The coffee table groaned beneath the weight of a ton of glossy magazines, which Connie noted were all up-to-date as well. No six-month-old *Hello!*s round here.

Whatever this man was, he must charge a fortune to afford a set-up like this. And a top-of-the-range Jaguar. And expensive suits. And Arabella.

Mr Mukherjee was talking with a client, said Arabella, but he wouldn't be long. Not a patient, a *client*. At this point a stunning-looking woman came in and spoke to the receptionist in dulcet tones before sitting herself down opposite. She bestowed a small, tight-lipped smile at Connie before immersing herself in *Vogue*. Connie, feeling scruffier by the minute, was tempted to sneak out of the door, but at least she was beginning to have a good idea what this doctor did for a living.

'Mrs McColl?'

Connie jumped.

'So sorry to have kept you waiting. Do come up to my office.' He glanced across at the *Vogue* lady. 'Oh, good morning, Mrs Middleton! Honey will see to you shortly. Just the usual, is it?' There was a 'Honey' as well!

He turned to Connie. 'This way.'

With his hand beneath her elbow, he shepherded her up a flight of stairs and into his office, which was very large and very white, adorned with framed certificates which Connie strained to read, but couldn't manage without her glasses.

'Please sit down and I'll order some coffee. What do you prefer: espresso, latte, cappuccino?'

'No, thank you. Really. I'm fine.'

'If you're sure? I have *never* hit another car before, Connie. May I call you Connie? I am *horrified* with myself. Now, let me have your address. Where do you live? Sussex! That's a long way from here. Are you in Newcastle on business?'

'Er, no. I'm on my way to try to find the street where my father was born, and then on to see some friends in Scotland. Just passing through. Would you know a Boxwood Close?'

'I think there's a Boxwood something-or-other round the corner. I'll show you in a minute.'

'So, I'm guessing you might be a plastic surgeon, Rav?' She studied his well- manicured, capable hands.

He leaned across the table. 'Well, dermatology's always been my thing. I'm fascinated by *skin*, Connie, it's the first thing I notice.'

'Oh, interesting,' said Connie, feeling increasingly uncomfortable. What was he going to say next?

'As long as there are women wanting to sweep away the years, there's plenty of work for me.' He laughed. 'Do you know what the worst thing about this job is? It's the panic on women's faces when I tell them what I do, and they think I'm sussing them out as prospective customers.'

'Is there panic on my face then?' Connie asked. Dear Lord, what must I look like?

'Not too much. You look fine. You've got a nice friendly face, just a few sun blemishes, which most fair-skinned ladies of your generation have. You weren't very savvy about sun protection back then, were you?'

'That's true. And surely your wrinkles are part of your personality,' said Connie. 'I certainly wouldn't want a stiff Botoxed face, or whatever it is you use. I want to be able to laugh.' She wondered if Mrs Middleton ever dared to laugh.

And, she thought, I want to laugh a lot more, because I'm learning to – and bugger the wrinkles.

'I've written my insurance details on here.' Rav tore off and handed her a sheet from his memo pad. 'Now, where did you say you were going?'

'After I've looked for Boxwood Close I'm heading for Edinburgh.'

'But are you *quite* sure I haven't damaged your car? Let me escort you across the road so I can be reassured that it's OK.'

In the reception area Mrs Middleton had disappeared and Arabella was engaged in deep conversation with a stick-thin woman wearing enormous sunglasses. Connie could only catch a smidgen of their conversation. 'The swelling will go down, Mrs De Vere, I promise.'

Outside Rav said, 'I've enjoyed meeting you, Connie. Can I interest you in a quick spray-tan before you go? I'm sure Honey could fit you in.'

'No, thanks,' Connie replied. 'I'm hoping to get the real thing.'

Rav raised one eyebrow. 'In *Edinburgh*?'

'Well, it seems to be a good summer all over the country. But I'm going to have a wander round Newcastle first in the hope of finding Boxwood Close.'

'OK, try taking that first left along there.' He pointed down the road. 'And are you *sure* this will get you all the way to Edinburgh?' He patted the roof.

'It's got me all the way from Sussex, so I'm certain it will.'

'Any problems with the car, Connie, you get in touch.'

She smiled to herself as she headed along Cypress Avenue. Who were women like Mrs Middleton trying to impress? She looked as fake as the buildings Connie was now passing. Endless neo-Georgian architecture and blocks of stylish low-rise flats (every one of them with plastic windows!) fronted with greenery-filled balconies. The whole area had plainly been gentrified beyond recognition. When she reached the turning Rav had indicated, her heart leapt. St Egbert's Way! St Egbert's, of course, had been the name of the church at the end of Boxwood Close. Relieved to see a name she recognised, she proceeded down St Egbert's Way, which was narrower than the avenue by far, and also full of mock-Georgian residences and smart cars. And silence. No kids playing around here, unlike the last time she visited, forty-five years ago. She walked on – and then she saw it: the little church with the wonky spire. And the tiny graveyard. It was still there and, as far as she could remember, looked exactly the same, only dwarfed by the larger buildings. She reckoned Boxwood Close would have been just a few yards further on, to the left, and then she saw the sign: 'BOXWOOD MEWS – RESIDENTS ONLY'.

Boxwood *Mews*! There had never been a mews here; the only horses around would have been pulling milk-carts and coal-carts along the terraced streets. When had they knocked them all down? And whose bright idea had it been to create a mews, of all things? It wasn't, of course, a real mews, just designed to look like one. So much pretence everywhere! She gazed at the subtly coloured shutters; Farrow & Ball having a field day again. Even with the sun high in the sky, as it was today, the occupants were highly unlikely ever to need these shutters, or to be dazzled by the sun in their smart open-plans, because you could see that it was still a dark, north-facing alley.

Oh, Dad! Connie was sure he'd be no more impressed than she was. And yet, who could deny that stylish interiors, en-suites and all, were preferable to tiny, dingy rooms with a privy at the foot of the garden. Correction: no garden – it would only have been a small *yard*.

Sadly she began to make her way back towards Cypress Avenue and, as she passed the little church, she hesitated. Would it be open? When she discovered it was, she entered the cool, dark interior with some trepidation, as she wasn't a churchgoer, never had been.

She slid into a pew and looked around. Her dad had probably attended this church and Sunday school, because children did then, and perhaps he had sat in this very spot in his Sunday best, where he sold groceries. An old neighbour, whom she'd met when she'd come up here so many years ago, had told her that he'd been a well-respected, hard-working man, and had been proud as punch of his policeman son 'down south'. He was fortunate, Connie thought, that he'd not lived long enough to have to bury his beloved son. But, she thought, enough nostalgia. It was time now to look ahead, make decisions, think about the future.

Time to move on.

boots polished. She didn't think she could pray but she closed h
eyes anyway and tried to imagine her father; would he have bee
the tallest boy in his class? Everyone who knew him said that he
been a kind man, and a polite one. From the few photographs sh
had, it seemed Di actually looked more like him than any of th
others. And then she wondered how life would have been if he
parents hadn't been killed in that accident. Would her father, in
particular, have approved of Roger? Would she have been a different kind of mother or wife if she'd been able to emulate her parents' lives? Would she have let Ben go out on his bike that fateful
day if her policeman father had constantly stressed the importance
of road safety?

A dog barked somewhere and she opened her eyes to see a little
printed tract lying on the floor, which had obviously dropped out
of a hymn book. It featured a child's drawing of a brightly coloured train, and beneath: 'Life is a one-way journey – no return
tickets available.'

No return to Boxwood Close, no return to Ben, no return to
her old life, perhaps? Or had she not yet passed that point of no
return? She left the church with the distinct feeling that her dad
would think she had.

As she made her way round the graves she wished she'd though
to bring some flowers. Her grandparents, who'd died around th
time of her birth, were among the last to be buried in the litt
graveyard. Robert and Maria – resting in peace, while all arour
had been bulldozed into the twenty-first century.

Connie knew little about them, only that Robert, her gran
father, had had a small shop or a stall down near the docks, fr

CHAPTER FIFTEEN

THE OASIS

Northumberland was truly beautiful and Connie had stopped several times to photograph the views. There was a vague familiarity about it all, although she couldn't remember ever having been up here before.

Some time later, Connie felt sure she must be in Scotland. There were only a few signs, of course, because she'd stuck to B roads or smaller (did C roads exist?) but, with occasional glimpses of sea to her right, she had no need to refer to maps. Nevertheless, even on this narrow road she'd encountered a diverse assortment of traffic; tractors being a speciality, plus a police car with sirens blaring and an Ikea delivery pantechnicon. She'd had to pull in at a farm gate to let it pass. There were few signs of habitation around and she wondered idly where someone might be about to come to grips with the assembly instructions of an Ikea flat-pack. Now she was seeing signposts leading to places with distinctly Scottish names. It must be The Borders.

Connie had been following a cattle truck for some miles, with little prospect of overtaking. She pulled over to take a swig of water when she spotted a river down to her right, with a fringe of trees on each bank. It looked peaceful and unspoilt. There was even a rough track leading down, which she thought Kermit could cope with. It seemed to offer peace, solitude and tranquillity – tantalising and inviting. She was well supplied with drinks, sandwiches and wine – not to mention some remaining gooey Mars bars.

Down and down she drove, Kermit brushed on both sides by cow parsley, foxgloves and nettles. At the river the lane widened into a flat grassy area, surrounded by alders, rowans, silver birch and ash. These trees stood tall and verdant, irrigated by their nearness to the river, and screened this little utopia from the road. Having parked Kermit, Connie got out, stretched and looked around. Complete privacy. The only sound was that of birdsong and the melody of rushing, gushing water, with the occasional faint hiss of a vehicle on the road above. This was what she'd had in mind when she'd bought the sleeping bag. As it was already evening she would soon be able to stretch out on her – as yet unused – sleeping mat, snuggle into the Miracle, and doze off to the lullaby of the river. Just for a moment she wished she'd bought a Primus stove because she fancied some tea. On the other hand that would mean lugging around tea bags and milk, which would sour and curdle in the warmth. Connie considered the alternatives: lukewarm orange juice or lukewarm wine? No brainer.

She managed to wedge the bottle of Sauvignon Blanc between two stones in the river, while she soaked her feet in the cool, blissful water. They appeared white and pulpy as the water swirled over them, like looking in one of those wonky mirrors at the funfair. And there were some minnows! She wished she had a jar; she and

her cousin Linda had tried to catch minnows on holiday once —
Cornwall, perhaps, or Wales? When she finally squelched her way
back to the bank she was relieved to see her feet looked normal
again.

Half an hour later, feet and bottle suitably cooled, Connie unearthed her old folding garden chair from the depths of the boot,
dusted off its faded flowery canvas (she'd just *known* this would
come in useful at some point), sat herself down with her plastic
glass, and contemplated the river. She wondered if it had a name.
It wasn't a very big river at the moment, but she could see from the
exposed rocks and boulders between the water and the banks that
this could be a formidable torrent at times. Connie felt supremely
happy as she breathed in the pure air deeply, watched quizzically
by a male blackbird from a branch above her head. The river, shad-
ed and dappled by overhanging branches, was catching the sun as
it splashed over the boulders, rippling and glittering as it made its
way to wherever it was going, presumably the North Sea.

Although the surrounding countryside was craggy and heathery, this little oasis was bright emerald green, like a newly mown
and manicured lawn. Hostas and irises and aquilegias would
all thrive here, Connie thought. Flowers brought Martin from
MMM to mind again; hadn't he said something about sending
her a book? She'd like that but he'd probably forgotten all about
it — and her, by now, particularly if he'd finally caught up with the
real Dorothy.

Then Connie spotted an eglantine. The wild rose was a poor
cousin of the luxuriant blooms Jeannie received each month, yet
the little flower's delicate toughness reminded her of Jeannie, and

she got out her sketchpad. It would be hard to capture Jeannie's joie de vivre, but she'd have a good try. The soothing scratch of her pencil strokes, aided by sips of wine, kindled thought and reflection. She'd carry on and head for Edinburgh, mainly to see her friend Wendy. But how much further north should she go after that? No decision about going back home needed to be made yet, which was just as well because she didn't think she was much closer to making one. Come to think of it, what exactly *was* there to decide? For, delightful though this nomadic existence might be, Connie was aware that she couldn't be on the move forever. But what were the alternatives? Going home? *Not* going home? Roger and his golf and his gin and his Audi? And did she still love him, did he still love her, and did it matter anyway at their late age? She had a nice enough home (albeit the hated bungalow), some great friends (if they were still talking to her) and a loving family (if a little ungrateful at times). Some women might kill to have her good fortune. She was patently experiencing some sort of late-life crisis, this last chance to change things before she became too doddery to do so, and far more important than the mid-life version when there were still decades of opportunity ahead.

Connie wondered how far north she would need to drive before she arrived at some solution and that turning point. If she hadn't decided by the time she got to the north of Scotland, would she just fall off the end at John o'Groats into the sea? What lay beyond – Orkney? Shetland? The North Pole? The whole thing was becoming farcical. Why hadn't she just stayed at home and got on with it, like other women of her age? What if I turn out to be one of Jeannie's 'silver singles'?

Connie refilled her glass, stretched out her legs and thought about Jeannie with her memories and her red roses. She consulted the photo on her camera for which she had persuaded Jeannie to pose. 'Why on earth would you want a photo of *me?*' Jeannie had asked. 'Because you're lovely, and I want to remember you,' Connie had replied. 'I might have been once,' said Jeannie, sounding wistful. But she was still lovely.

Connie settled down to try and depict a likeness of Jeannie, and just do some thinking. Think of red roses and forbidden love. Surely the very fact it was forbidden lent it an aura of intrigue and mystery that might soon have disintegrated with the everyday ups and downs of marriage. Let's face it, Connie thought, anything that's rationed or scarce becomes instantly desirable. We are a funny lot, we humans.

Then, as she glanced at her previous sketches, she thought about Kath, with the pink roses tattooed up her arm. Surely she, too, must have *some* passionate memories, after three husbands, or whatever they were. And she wondered yet again if she could remember Martin's features sufficiently to do him justice on paper.

She considered for a moment if she should check for further emails. No, definitely not – so she switched off her phone, dug out one of the sandwiches she'd bought at a petrol station ten miles back, ripped open its triangular wrapper and savoured the surprisingly good hoisin duck filling, washed down with cold(ish) Sauvignon Blanc.

The light was now fading fast and Connie was becoming increasingly weary. But would she be safe here, a woman on her own in the middle of nowhere? Perhaps that axe-murderer was waiting for this very moment? Should she try to sleep in the car? No, she thought, don't be such a wimp. And what had been the point of buying the Miracle and the mat if she was too afraid to use them? Silly woman, she thought, get on with it.

First she decided to tackle Brian's self-inflating sleeping mat. As she removed it from its wrappings she very much hoped it *would* self-inflate, as she doubted she'd have enough puff to get the thing into any kind of shape. She didn't like reading instructions; she'd never read the booklet that came with the washing machine, or the cooker or the microwave either; just found a programme that worked and stuck to it. So now she unscrewed the valve and – glory of glories – it worked! It lay there invitingly on the grass.

She unearthed an old cushion from the boot, which would have to do as a pillow, and laid the Miracle on the top. She'd sleep in her bra and pants, with a T-shirt at the ready, just in case. Just in case of what? What possible protection would a cotton T-shirt provide? No, she'd wear her nightie, that's what she'd do. She hauled her bed close to the car and, after a quick look around, stripped off, got into the nightie and slid into the Miracle. The mat felt a little hard but surprisingly comfortable.

Connie lay staring up at the stars as clouds floated across intermittently, blocking her view. It was silent except for the swoosh of a couple of vehicles on the road far above and then the distant hoot of an owl.

Connie awoke from a deep sleep just before seven. Yawning, she saw the early sun was already dancing through the overhead branches and forming a kaleidoscope of patterns on top of the Miracle. She had never slept in the open before. Or *had* she? Somewhere in the depths of her subconscious lay a distant memory of waking up in the open air, just like this, on a sunny morning. But not alone... sandwiched between two warm, loving bodies... The image disappeared as quickly as it had arrived. *Of course!* Uncle Bill had mentioned something about how her parents had loved camping. ('All the way up to Scotland in a dodgy old Hillman and a leaking tent,' was how he'd put it.) And she couldn't have been more than three or four! Perhaps they'd even been *here*, in this very spot! And then she recalled a red-coloured castle. She'd visualised that castle before but had no recollection of where she might have seen it – probably a picture in a book somewhere.

She climbed out of the Miracle, feeling invigorated, if a little stiff. The sleeping mat was adequate but hardly luxurious, and her sixty-six-year-old bones protested as she slowly straightened them all up. At least her neck seemed to be better. She knew exactly what she wanted to do, what she'd been dreaming of for days, and the setting was now perfect with not a soul around and the sun already pleasantly warm.

Connie whipped her nightie off over her head and burrowed into her overnight bag for some soap and a towel, which she considered would be large enough to wrap around the bits she thought should be covered, but then she thought what the hell, and proceeded towards the water waving the towel in the air. Dropping it on a large boulder and clutching her soap, Connie paddled cautiously over the slippery stones towards the deeper water in the middle of the river so that she could position herself in such a way as to comfortably allow the water to flow over her body. She was surprised at the strength and speed of the current as she carefully settled herself on a large rock, emitting squeals as her bottom and midriff made contact with the icy water and then shrieking some more as she splashed the water over her top half while soaping herself. Once she got used to the temperature, she laughed out loud. Years ago, in that misspent youth, she remembered skinny-dipping at night in the Mediterranean. Much warmer water, though – not like this. But there was no feeling quite like the freedom from clothing and inhibitions. Perhaps as a result of this, she might one day even consider joining a nudist colony! It would only be the prohibitive British climate that would make her reconsider. She giggled at the thought of Roger's reaction.

She lay down as much as she dared to allow the water to rinse off all the soap, then wondered about the fish in this river and how they would cope with these ripples of Palmolive. But how she loved the sensation of the cold water rushing over her skin! It was so therapeutic, as if her worries were washing away with the current. An unexpected wave of happiness flowed over her. Funny how that could happen when you least expected it. She would never forget this funny little place, although she had no idea where it might be. Finally she eased herself up and out of the water, and reached for her towel.

Then she saw it. The deer was standing stock still beside Kermit, staring in her direction. She froze, hoping it hadn't seen her so she could watch it for a while. It wasn't very big, so it was probably young, although Connie knew nothing about deer. She could only admire its proud and elegant stance, the monarch of her tiny glen. Beautiful, beautiful creature. It had seen her of course and turned, sprinting away with a speed that left her breathless. The deer had taken off in fear; fear for its life, fear of this unknown creature emerging from the water. Not like me, thought Connie. Fear didn't enter into my reasons for taking off; perhaps, on the contrary, she'd felt too safe. But, what a thrill! What a place!

She dressed and sat down on the old folding chair with her bottle of water and one of her remaining sandwiches. Strange how this place had brought back such distant memories. Perhaps it was that, being close to nature, she'd felt a stronger connection with her parents and even with Ben. She'd like to spend all day here, just watching and listening to the river and the birds, and the sighing of the leaves. It was solace for the soul.

It was late morning before Connie was able to tear herself away from the idyllic spot. She wanted to get to Edinburgh and find a B&B somewhere before all the 'No Vacancies' signs were displayed. Perhaps she'd come back here again one day; perhaps she might even return this way. Perhaps it would be cold, or raining, and she mightn't like it so much. Perhaps... perhaps... perhaps...

CHAPTER SIXTEEN

SUSPICIOUS MINDS

Nick was becoming increasingly concerned about his mother, not least because Tess kept going on and on and on about his father. He had to agree there was some cause for concern the way his father was preening himself. But could he possibly be having an affair at his age? Unlikely, of course, but anyway it was high time his mother came home and life got back to some form of normality.

From: Nick McColl
To: Connie McColl
Hi Mum,

Haven't heard from you for a bit so hope you're well and safe. We're all OK here, but missing you. The boys keep asking where you are and it's becoming increasingly difficult to give them a satisfactory reply.

We hardly see Dad these days. When you first left he was here every five minutes and he doesn't seem to be at home often either. I guess he feels lonely in the house on his own although Tess is still convinced he's up to something and I must admit I'm beginning to wonder. I popped round the other night to borrow his electric drill (mine's on the blink again) and he wasn't at all keen to ask me in after we came out of the shed. Normally he'd suggest a cup of tea or a beer, so it wasn't like him not to offer.

Maybe my imagination's running riot but I really think you should come home soon, Mum. If you and Dad have problems then you should be talking things over together. Tess agrees with me and we all send you...

... much love.

Nick xx

From: Connie McColl

To: Nick McColl

Hello Nick,

Good to hear from you. I'm fine, really, and having lots of adventures.

No, I don't think Dad and I have problems that need to be discussed and many marriages become mundane with time. The problem, Nick, is most likely all mine. I need some freedom, some space and to have a little fun before I become too old. I've been feeling restless for a while and need to get this thing out of my system.

So, has Dad something to hide? Well, according to reports, he's been acting strangely lately so who knows?

Tell the boys that their grandmother is off having adventures and, when she gets back, she'll tell them all about it! I'll probably be home before too long, and before autumn sets in properly. Right now I'm constantly on the move, and loving it.

I miss you all. Big hugs and kisses to my wee boys – and my big one, of course – and Tess too!

Much love,

Mum xxxx

Lou sighed as she put the phone down. Now her father wanted her to pick up a load of dry-cleaning. Whatever next? Wasn't it enough that she'd gone round and dusted and vacuumed – all these jobs her mother should be doing. It was high time somebody told her to come home.

From: Louise Morrison

To: Connie McColl

Hello, Mum, wherever you are,

We are now getting seriously worried. You've been gone for ten days and no one has any idea where you might be or even if you're ever planning to come back. Di and Nick may think it's a bit of a joke, but I certainly do not – on my own here all day with a screaming baby.

And what about poor old Dad, rattling around in that bungalow all by himself? Nick and Andy of course think he's up to no good, but that's men for you! We know Dad isn't that sort of person, although one could hardly blame him if he was, being left on his own like that and obviously beside himself with worry. And the place is in a bit of a mess, but I haven't time to go round there every five minutes.

Fortunately we're OK here and the little one is sleeping slightly better at night now so we're benefitting from some occasional uninterrupted shut-eye.

Well, Mum, I only hope you're OK and that you'll come home soon. We all miss you.

Love,

Lou xx

From: Connie McColl

To: Louise McColl

Dearest Lou,

There is absolutely no need for you to be worried. I'm constantly on the move and having some amazing adventures. I miss you all too, but am still not ready to come home.

As for your father, I haven't heard from him for days now, and Nick says he's rarely at home, so it doesn't seem to me that he's particularly heartbroken or worried.

It might be an idea for you to find a child-minder or a babysitter sometimes as it would be good for you to get out more. I'm not quite sure how I managed to bring up four children without any assistance from grandparents, or sisters-in-law or child-minders. Or anyone really. Somehow or the other I managed.

Give the little one a big kiss from me – Nana will be home eventually!!!

Love, Mum xxx

Connie worried about Lou more than the other two, who had always proved to be capable of looking after themselves. Little Lou, the baby of the family, was, without doubt, Roger's favourite. He and the other three had doted on this tiny, beautiful new arrival, who absorbed their attention and admiration like a miniature sponge from day one. Connie found her younger daughter an enigma, so different from the others. Loving and amenable when things went her way, sulky, moody and aloof when they didn't. Had Lou been so badly spoilt? She was sure she really loved all her children equally, but had never felt this was fully reciprocated with Lou, who gravitated towards her father at every minor crisis. She'd felt some relief when Andy came along, and joy at the arrival of Charlotte, until Lou had started complaining about sleepless nights, difficult feeds and 'why did I ever think having a baby would be a good idea?' Lou also made it clear that she considered her mother remiss in her grandmotherly duties. 'You spend far more time with Nick's two than my little one,' she'd whined. 'No I don't,' protested Connie, who religiously balanced her time between the two households. 'But there are *two* of them, so occasionally I have to be there more often.' She remembered babysitting Tom when Josh was rushed to the doctor with an ominous rash.

As she'd told Lou, she herself had had no mother to babysit, badger or blame. And what about Aunt Lorna, who brought up all her brood single-handed, with a husband who spent most of the year in Africa?

So, where had she gone wrong with Lou? *Had* she gone wrong with Lou?

CHAPTER SEVENTEEN

GOLDEN GIRLS

Connie was heading at last for Edinburgh, a city she'd always wanted to explore, but mainly to look up the Sinclairs, who had lived next door to them in Sussex for eight whole years. That, of course, was their old house, the *proper* house, the large Victorian semi with the wooden sash windows and the lovely garden.

She was longing to see Wendy again. Dear Wendy, the only one who'd remembered Ben's anniversary.

Bob Sinclair, a Scot, and his English wife, Wendy, had three children, a little younger than Connie's. They'd been there when Ben was killed and Wendy had been the person who'd got her through those black days. She'd kept an eye on Connie's three while Connie was in emotional turmoil and Roger had immersed himself in work. Every evening Wendy would appear with the Scotch bottle. 'Bob says you're to have a wee dram whenever you feel like it. Never mind the bloody sedatives!' Connie had never been able to drink Scotch since. She wasn't sure if it was the association with Ben's death, or whether she just didn't like the taste.

She'd missed Wendy dreadfully. Wendy had been her rock, her soulmate, and the person who'd taken her by the arm and made her face the outside world again. After Bob and Wendy had relocated three years later, they kept in touch with greetings cards and the occasional phone call.

She'd given them no advance warning of her visit, so Connie decided to find a B&B first and do a spot of sightseeing before getting in contact. She knew they would invite her to stay but she wanted to do some exploring on her own.

There was, of course, proper educational sight-seeing, and then there was Connie-type sightseeing; not the things people *thought* she should see. As a teenager, after a particularly heavy week during a very educational school trip taking in the historic sites of London with accompanying lectures, she'd decided she had to have a free day when she'd escape to explore the zoo and Carnaby Street and all the wonderfully naughty and exotic-sounding haunts in Soho. And, in later years, she'd often exasperated Roger by expressing a preference for people-watching in pavement cafes and exploring interesting alleyways to the interior gloom of museums and churches.

But, as most of the trip so far had been pretty much Connie-type sightseeing, she felt the need for a teeny bit of culture and spent a whole day navigating her way around the city via a Lonely Planet guide and a bus timetable, touring the Royal Mile and the castle. And, all the while, treated to acts by performers of varying degrees of talent, because she'd quite forgotten that this was coming up to the time of the Edinburgh Festival and its Fringe. Interesting though all that was, the next day she headed for Corstorphine and the zoo, mainly to see the pandas, which she loved, and then on to Greyfriars Kirkyard to see the famous statue of Greyfriars Bobby, the Skye terrier who, it is claimed, in the 1800s guarded the grave of his owner, John Gray, for fourteen years, until Bobby himself died and was buried a short distance away from his beloved master. Connie found herself in tears at this sad tale. She loved dogs and wondered if her late lamented Paddy would have been so committed in his grief had he outlived her. Well, probably not – not if he saw another dog, or a cat, or a rabbit. But she knew that Greyfriars Bobby would remain lodged in her memory long after she'd forgotten the relevant facts about poor Mary, Queen of Scots.

It had turned cooler and Connie, dressed only in T-shirt and jeans, decided she needed a long-sleeved sweater. She explored several shops on Princes Street on her way back and finally settled for a buttercup-yellow wool number from a department store, which was reduced to half price and so fitted the bill – and her – perfectly. As she waited for her bus, she watched with incredulity the most amazing troupe of acrobats from Brazil perform some daredevil balancing acts.

She'd memorised the landmarks so she'd know where to leave the bus to return to Craiglarry House B&B, and the very grand Mrs Conon-MacLeod, who wore twinsets and tweed skirts and had Corgis and a hair-do exactly like the Queen's.

'There are fine parts, and not so fine parts in Edinburgh,' she'd proclaimed to Connie in her very precise accent. 'I'm a *Morn-*

ingside person myself.' She pronounced them 'Aidenburgh' and 'Morningsade'. This remark was supposedly sufficient in itself to denote superiority and supremacy. Connie recalled once hearing a comedian on the radio who was poking fun at the various parts of the city. 'In Morningside,' he'd quipped, 'sex is something in which they deliver the coal.'

Plainly he'd met Mrs Conon-MacLeod.

Connie alighted from the bus at the stop alongside the enormous Gerry's Garage with its countless orange flags declaring that you wouldn't find a better used car anywhere else on planet Earth. Be this as it may, it was also an easy-to-recognise bus stop. Even here a lone tenor was belting out 'Panis Angelicus'. Connie was unable to decide if he was part of the Fringe, or had just jumped on the bandwagon. For sure the Bocellis of this world had little to worry about. From here she knew she must turn right down the one-way Billington Street, which led to Garbon Road and Craiglarry House. The only problem was that Billington Street seemed to be filled with a moving sea of yellow-clad ladies waving placards and shouting lustily. Were they also some form of Fringe entertain-ment? This demonstration was blocking the entrance to the street, much to the chagrin of a long queue of furiously hooting, irate drivers. She knew of no other way to go and, as she cautiously approached, she noted that the yellow outfits were sweatshirts printed with the words 'Save Victoria House!' and 'Safeguard our Refuge!' The placards, held high in the air, read 'Men might bash us but they'll never break us!', 'Help us to keep safe' and the like.

Connie had little choice but to push her way through, and she only hoped they wouldn't prove to be too militant. At least she blended in well colour-wise. She'd only gone a few yards before she became wedged between two enormous women, one with a broken nose.

Connie looked nervously at the least intimidating of the two. 'Can you tell me—' she began, only to be interrupted by Broken-Nose saying, 'See, are yew English?' To which the other one added, 'Ach well, she cannae help that. Thae Sassenach women get knocked aboot just as much as us.' She turned to Connie. 'Don't you, hen?'

'Well, yes, I suppose—' Connie was cut short by Broken-Nose again.

'At least ye havena any scars on the ootside.' She indicated her nose. 'Twice that bastard broke it. *And* ma arm!' She rolled up a buttercup sleeve. 'See that? Ah had tae have a *pin* put in there. An' see *that*?' She rolled up the other sleeve to expose a long, jagged scar. '*That* wiz a kitchen knife! An' here wiz me thinkin' it needed sharpening!'

'Goodness!' said Connie faintly.

'If it wiznae for the Refuge we'd likely all be dead,' Broken-Nose added.

'Aye, so we would,' agreed her companion.

Nodding and smiling, Connie managed to squeeze past them, continuing further into this angry tide of womanhood.

A tall, black, very attractive girl, brandishing a placard, had suddenly appeared at her side. 'It's going well, isn't it?' she said to Connie. 'Are you from the Refuge too? Don't remember seeing you before. I'm Julie.'

'No, no, I'm not from the Refuge,' Connie replied. 'I'm Connie, just sort of passing really…' She looked up at the placard. 'Bullied and Battered! But we won't be Beaten!' it asserted as they were carried along slowly by the huge procession of women.

'Well, it's good that you came to support us. We should be on the telly tonight,' Julie continued. She didn't have much of an accent, unlike the others.

'Should we?'

'We need all the publicity we can get, don't we?'

'Well, actually, I—' Connie began, but was interrupted by a woman on her other side who leaned across and asked, 'How's yer bairn, Julie?'

'He's coming along OK now,' Julie replied. 'There won't be any lasting damage, thank God.'

Connie gulped. 'Your child?'

'Yeah, my little Bobby. Six months old he is.'

'I hope you don't think I'm being nosy, but what happened to him?'

Even with a slight lull in the shouting Connie had to cup her ear to decipher Julie's reply. 'My bloke tried to kill Bobby. Did you not see it in the papers?'

'Well, no, I don't actually live round here. But that's *awful!*'

'He wouldn't stop crying, you see. I should've known Kevin would do something because he has such a hellish temper and he'd already broken my arm.'

'*What?*' Connie was appalled.

'He knocked my baby black and blue, trying to kill him. And he even broke Bobby's little leg.'

'Julie!' Connie's eyes filled with tears. 'That's *horrendous*! Oh, the poor little mite – what did you do?'

'I did what I should have done months before. I bashed him over the head with the first thing that came to hand, which happened to be the frying pan I'd left to drain on the sink. It was good and heavy and stunned him enough to let me grab Bobby and get out the door.'

'Where's this wretched man now?'

'In jail, thank God. But he'll be out in a few months, and I don't want to stay at Victoria House forever, so I'm going to get myself sorted. And Bobby's on the mend.'

'I don't know what to say; that's just awful.'

'What about you, Connie?'

'Me? I'm a fraud, only here by accident. But have *all* these women been abused?'

'Yeah, one way or another.'

'Then I'm glad to be with you. What can I do to help? Here, let me take that placard for a bit. Give your arms a rest.'

'Thanks, I'd be grateful if you would as I'm dying for a pee and I've just seen a loo over there.'

Connie grabbed the placard, hoisted it as high in the air as she could, and started chanting along with all the other women. What the hell had *she* got to complain about when some of these poor women were in fear of their very lives? And their children's lives! She had never, mercifully, known that kind of fear, or that kind of treatment. She'd read about it in the papers, of course, and heard some graphic details via the media. *It doesn't happen round here.* Well, perhaps it did.

Connie was now aware of flashing blue lights and scuffles taking place as police tried to clear the street and the traffic chaos. And here she was, yellow-clad and waving a banner with the best of them. And I'm glad, she thought. I'm on their side.

Propelled forwards, Connie spied the line of police who, using loud-hailers, were ordering the women to go home, and being none too diplomatic in their choice of words either.

'Go *home*!' exclaimed the busty blonde who was now yelling next to her. 'Is he *kidding*? That's why we need the bloody *refuge*!'

Connie wondered how many thousands of women nationwide needed protection from abusive partners and offered up a silent prayer of thanks; Roger might have his faults but he'd never, ever raise his hand to her.

She'd now managed to inch forward sufficiently to be within spitting distance of the line of police. She knew this because one woman at the front was doing just that. Connie only needed to squeeze through and then she'd be on her way. And she knew that somehow or other she must try to do something to help these women. As soon as she got back to Craiglarry House she'd get on the Internet to find out what she could do in the way of writing to her MP or signing a petition, perhaps. Could she afford to make a donation? But first she needed to squeeze through the last row of bodies and then she could be on her way.

She'd just made it to the front when she got shoved from behind and stumbled forwards, the placard landing with considerable force on the head of a bulky, red-faced policeman who was trying to restrain a particularly vociferous female. In fury he released her and grabbed Connie.

'I'm so sorry, I tripped—' Connie began.

'And I'm George Clooney!' he snapped, holding her firmly by the arm and manhandling her in the direction of a large police van. 'Get in there and don't say another word! Anything you do or say will be taken down and may be used in evidence against you.' Another equally bulky constable took hold of her other arm and together they frogmarched her into the van, which already contained six women, all yelling abuse at their captors. She hadn't realised that she was still holding onto the offending placard until they prised it off her. That was the moment she saw the cameras. There was a battery of press and TV reporters with a grandstand view.

In the police station the group was informed that they were to be charged with disturbing the peace, disorderly behaviour, assaulting police officers and resisting arrest. While the sergeant was reading out the list, Connie sat down on a bench alongside the other women.

'Ach, dinna look so worried!' The woman next to her placed a comforting arm round her shoulders. 'They'll no likely keep us for long – they just have to put on a bit of a show and look like they're doin' something useful. They're on our side really. What's yer name? Ah'm June.'

'I'm Connie, and I wasn't really in the demonstration!' Connie sniffed frantically to deal with an excess of emotion, trying to avoid wiping her nose on her new yellow sleeve.

'Here!' said her new friend, handing her a tissue. 'Are ye English?'

'Yes,' Connie replied, wiping her eyes. 'And I was only trying to walk through Billington Street to get back to my B&B.'

June threw back her head and snorted. 'Just try an' explain it all at the desk – with a bit of luck they'll let ye go.'

'Or else we'll all be having a night in the cells!' one of the others added cheerfully.

'It was the placard that did it,' Connie explained, 'but I'm not sorry. I'm glad I was with you and I'd do it all again! Not that it was the policeman's fault, of course!'

'Ach well, ye've been arrested in a right good cause,' said June. 'Have ye never been bashed aboot yersel'?'

'No,' said Connie. 'Never, ever.'

'Well, lucky auld you!' June sighed. 'Mind you, it's always the drink. Kevin liked to get in a bit of boxing practice when he got home frae the pub and Ah was the handiest punchbag. It wiz gettin' worse and worse and Ah was feart fer the bairns – Ah hae two wee girls, ye see. Then Ah heard about the Refuge and one night, when he'd fallen asleep after beatin' me black and blue, Ah just picked up the bairns and walked out. The Refuge never turns anyone away, see. Now it's likely to be closed down due to lack of funding or whatever and Ah don't know where in hell we're all goin' tae go. If this bloody government doesn't step in and do something to help us, we're all in the shit.'

The other women all said 'Aye' and nodded in agreement.

'That's awful,' said Connie. 'I just wish that I could help in some way.'

'Well, ye got us some publicity,' said June, 'and it all helps. I expect it'll be on the telly.'

'It'll only be shown in Scotland though, won't it?'

June shrugged. 'Who knows? There's nationwide demos going on today – probably in yer neck of the woods as well. There's hundreds of refuges.'

A tiny Asian lady in an emerald green sari smiled across at Connie. 'Maybe you can put a word in for us somewhere. Your local council? Write to your MP, perhaps?'

'Oh, I'll do anything I can,' said Connie. She couldn't understand how anyone could abuse this delicate little woman.

'Shadnam here had her wrist broken,' explained June.

'I didn't understand what the effect of drink could be,' said Shadnam. 'No one in my family drank.' She snorted. 'I had no idea what he was like until it was too late.'

'Aye,' June added. 'Ye come to dread the sound of his key in the lock. Ye think, how many has he had tonight? How soon will it be until I start annoying him? I know he's lookin' for trouble and it disnae matter what the hell I do, it's going to be wrong. And, if I got as far as the bedroom without bein' bashed aboot, then he liked his sex with a bit of violence too. Of course he's so pissed he can't perform and, hey, that's ma fault as well! And while he's shoutin' abuse and knockin' me aboot, I can hear my wains cryin' through the wall.'

Connie was speechless.

'There's a lot of it goes on, Connie. And it's the women who're that ashamed and try to cover it all up. Thae men just don't give a damn and carry on as usual; go to work if they've got a job, go to the pub whether they've got a job or not, and spend money they havenae got. Get us all into debt.'

The sergeant at the desk shouted out, 'Silence, please!' He beckoned to Connie. 'You, first, come here!'

'I *know* you won't believe me,' said Connie as she leaned wearily against the desk. 'But I honestly was only trying to get through to Gambon Road. The fact I'm wearing yellow is just a coincidence – I only just bought it…' She dug in her bag and produced the receipt.

'And pure coincidence that you bashed one of my officers on the head?' the sergeant interrupted.

'Yes,' Connie replied. 'I tripped. I'm sorry I hit the officer, I really am. But I'm not at all sorry I joined the protest. These women should be heard! And surely the police should be doing more to protect them!'

'OK, OK, enough of the lecture.' The sergeant sighed as he opened a large book on his desk. 'Name and address, please.'

Connie told him.

'And what exactly are you doing way up here in Edinburgh?'

'Well, visiting friends mainly, but today I was doing some sightseeing.'

'And can these friends vouch for you?'

'Well, I haven't got there yet. I'll be visiting them tomorrow but I'm staying in Edinburgh tonight. You can check with my B&B landlady, Mrs Conon-MacLeod. I got off the bus at the big garage and that was the only way I knew to get back. I'm really sorry; I didn't mean to drop the placard on the policeman's head. I was pushed and lost my balance.'

Ten minutes later, after a phone call to her scandalised landlady, Connie was allowed to go free.

'I'm letting you go,' said the sergeant, looking at her over the top of his glasses. 'And, if you ever do decide to demonstrate in future, lady, I suggest you do it in your own neighbourhood.'

Connie turned to wave goodbye to her newfound partners-in-crime. 'I feel so guilty to be leaving you. I'm going to email everyone I can think of. I'm so worried you'll all have to spend the night in prison.'

'Not us,' hollered June. 'The cells are all full, aren't they, Sarge?'

The sergeant looked the other way. 'Be off with you,' he said to Connie, 'or I might just change my mind and keep you in.'

'Bye, ladies, and good luck!' Connie called back as she went out of the door.

'Did you *know* you were on the six o'clock news?' A stony-faced Mrs Conon-MacLeod was hovering in the hallway when Connie returned. 'Eh had *no idea* that you'd come all the way up here just to cause trouble, Mrs McColl. Eh do *not* approve of that sort of behaviour, and eh certainly do *not* want your sort of person in *may* guesthouse. Eh would be most obliged if you could vacate your room tomorrow morning. *Good* nate.'

As Connie headed towards her bedroom she felt that she could hardly blame Mrs Conon-MacLeod for branding her a trouble-maker. Some people did, after all, travel around the country purely to stir up trouble. Nevertheless, Connie was not at all sorry for her unplanned part in the demonstration. And it was extremely unlikely that Mrs Conon-MacLeod had ever been 'bashed aboot', as June had so vividly put it.

CHAPTER EIGHTEEN

SHOCK! HORROR!

A newly shaved and showered Roger McColl studied his tanned torso in the bedroom mirror, turning this way and that, and then leaned forward to study his face at close quarters. The whites of his eyes were bright and his skin smooth and evenly tanned. He'd never realised how natural a good-quality fake tan could look. Then he spotted a couple of eyebrow hairs growing where they shouldn't, so he helped himself to Connie's tweezers and removed the strays. Now, what to wear? It was important to look good when eating at the club later, particularly as Andrea was on duty tonight.

He'd bought himself a new black cotton shirt and it had taken him forever to release the thing from its cardboard insert and the million pins that anchored it. But it looked so good with his crisp white trousers; a nice combination, he thought. A smooth look, quite continental really. No socks of course, just the soft leather Italian deck shoes he'd treated himself to in Eastbourne.

Roger turned back the cuffs of his shirtsleeves twice, just to expose his wrists and his watch. He took a final look in the mirror. Andrea should be impressed. 'Cool', the youngsters would say.

In the kitchen, Roger poured himself a double Gordon's, added a slice of lime (the proper accompaniment to a gin and tonic), three large lumps of ice and half a can of tonic. It all tinkled and fizzed satisfactorily in his glass. He must try not to spill anything on his pristine white trousers, particularly if he hit the red wine later on. Care would have to be taken. Connie was good at removing red wine stains, but he wasn't. Not yet. Where the hell *was* she, anyway? Her absence was costing him a fortune in taxis.

Roger carried his drink carefully through to the sitting room and sat down on the sofa, to enjoy the breeze drifting through the open French doors. He looked around. It was a charming room, and he'd finally remembered to water the house plants this week after Lou had come round and read the riot act while she prodded dusty dry compost and disposed of dropped off leaves. They had survived his earlier neglect and were now looking remarkably perky, rather like he was.

He glanced at his watch. Nearly six o'clock and almost time for the news. As he picked up the remote control he wondered idly what disasters might have befallen the unsuspecting world today.

He sipped his gin and yawned through ten minutes of political arguing and bantering (all as bad as each other; he wouldn't vote for any of them next time) and then refilled his glass during the seedier details of a murder trial. He was comfortably seated again when a report came on about some nationwide protest concerning the impending closure of a chain of refuges for battered women. Battered women, indeed! He'd never known of any women being battered but the ones who were probably asking for it, marrying violent drunks and druggies, getting stoned themselves.

'Even as far north as Edinburgh,' the announcer prattled on, 'women were making themselves heard and, in some cases, resorting to violence.'

And there, in full view of the nation, was his wife, Constance Mary McColl, dressed in lurid yellow and being arrested while clutching a placard on the end of a pole which proclaimed, 'Bullied and Battered! But we won't be Beaten!'

Roger choked, coughing gin all over his white trousers.

※

At seven o'clock Nick McColl wearily entered the kitchen after a long, hard day at work, exhausted by a client who kept changing his mind about designs and building materials. He found his wife in a state of high excitement; in fact she was practically incoherent.

'It's your *mother*!' Tess exclaimed. 'On the six o'clock news!'

'On the six o'clock news? Are you *mad*?'

'No, no, honestly, it was *her*! She was in a demo for battered women in Edinburgh and she got arrested! It might be on one of the other channels if you scroll around.'

'My *mother*!' Nick glared at his wife in disbelief. 'Arrested?' He rubbed his eyes and shook his head. 'Come on, Tess, it'll just be someone who looks like her.'

'No, I swear it was your mother. And she's probably languishing in a Scottish jail as we speak!'

'Scotland! Bloody hell! Has Dad been on the phone yet? Has he seen it?'

'No, but Lou has, and she's absolutely beside herself. She can't believe your dad would have knocked Connie around.'

'Knocked Mum around? Don't be *ridiculous* – of course he hasn't!'

'Well, why would she be protesting then? Tell me that!'

Nick calmed down sufficiently to withdraw an uncorked bottle of Chablis from the fridge and filled the glass to a millimetre short of the rim before collapsing (carefully) onto the sofa with the remote control.

'That must be why she left home,' Tess went on blithely. She was obviously enjoying all this, Nick realised with irritation.

'My dad might have faults,' he snapped, 'but bashing women certainly isn't one of them. There has to be some mistake.'

'Well, see for yourself.' Tess busied herself at the range cooker, turning switches on and off while Nick started a news hunt. He finally found the right channel and sat impatiently watching the day's disasters until, almost at the end, came the report he was waiting for.

'Bloody hell!' he said. 'It *is* Mum!'

Just at that moment Lou rang. 'What are we going to *do*?' she wailed.

'Looks like I'll have to fly up to Edinburgh and sort this out,' Nick said with a sigh.

'There has to be a mistake. And at least now we know where she is. What is she playing at? This beggars belief!'

'Surely Dad would never hit Mum, would he?' Lou sounded close to tears. 'But then *why* would she be demonstrating? She was dressed the same as the others in yellow, so it must have been planned.'

'What does Andy think?'

'Andy thinks it's the most hilarious thing he's ever heard. He's nearly wet himself. I don't know who's infuriating me most, him or Mum.'

＊

Diana McColl rarely cooked although every conceivable gadget was built into her state-of-the-art kitchen, mostly unused. And she didn't often watch the six o'clock news either, preferring to catch the headlines on her tablet or on the TV later in the evening when she got home from the wine bar, or the sushi bar or the tapas bar.

Tonight was an exception because Mark was coming to dinner. And Mark was special. She'd met him on a flight returning from Dubai, where he'd been reporting for Channel 4. A nomad, like herself.

Di looked round in despair at the chaos in her normally pristine kitchen as she tried to make head or tail of the recipe.

He'd invited himself, really, after a particularly torrid lovemaking session on the ultra-smart white sofa she'd recently bought from Harrods. 'I'm sure you're just as capable in the kitchen.' She'd been so busy checking the white covers for any tell-tale stains that she hadn't taken him seriously. However, he kept on and on about it, making her wonder if this was to be some sort of domesticity test.

'I'll bring the plonk,' he added.

If she hadn't been so keen on the wretched man she'd never have agreed to it. In fact, she couldn't quite get her head round the fact that a forty-year-old like herself could become so besotted after so many years of warding off unfancied and unwelcome suitors.

She continued to slice garlic while glancing up from time to time at the TV, which was at eye level on the opposite wall. She rather fancied George Alagiah, who was reading the news. And it was purely by chance that she looked up at the exact moment that her mother was being bundled into a police van, in Edinburgh of all places, having been protesting about violent men. Her *mother*! *Bullied and Battered!*

Di was so gobsmacked she didn't even notice that a thin slice of her finger had dropped into the Le Creuset along with the garlic.

❊

Sue Maloney didn't watch the six o'clock news but her daughter, Laura, did.

'Hey, Mum, get it on iPlayer or something. You really have to see this; it was your friend, Connie McColl, and she was protesting about abusive husbands!'

'You *must* be kidding!'

'No, I'm not, and you didn't ever tell me that her husband knocked her about. What was his name, Robert, Reg…?'

'Roger. His name's Roger.'

'Well, Roger then. And doesn't it just prove that you never really know what goes on in a marriage, do you?'

Sue felt quite faint as she sat down. Her best friend, Connie, had been knocked about! Now that *was* unbelievable. It was bad enough that Connie had taken off without bothering to tell her, but to have been abused by Roger and never to have mentioned it! There had to be some mistake. Sue feverishly scrolled round the TV channels and news programmes and it took a good hour before she found the relevant item, which she then watched dumb-founded. There was Connie, sufficiently incensed to be carrying a placard and even bashing a policeman over the head with it!

Why had Connie never confided in her? Why on earth did she have to go all the way to Edinburgh to make a protest? Was she too afraid of Roger to do something about it locally? None of it made any sense.

When Dave came in looking for his supper, she realised she'd completely forgotten to turn on the oven or set the table. She was too busy emailing Connie.

CHAPTER NINETEEN

HOME TRUTHS

Connie hadn't slept well because her overactive mind kept returning to those poor, abused women. The Refuge was only five minutes away from the stony-faced Mrs Conon-MacLeod's B&B and, as she'd paid her bill the previous evening, she decided to skip breakfast and go straight there.

She introduced herself to the startled and suspicious woman who unlocked the door.

'Ye're no from the police, are ye? Are ye from the Social? Have ye an ID?'

Connie did her best to explain. 'Is June around? Or Julie?' Or, heaven forbid, were they in the cells?

June eventually surfaced, wrapped in a shabby blue dressing gown with two tiny saucer-eyed girls tagging on behind.

'Connie! No, we all got away shortly after you left. Lots of lectures and all that, but the police are on our side really.'

'Well, so am I,' said Connie, 'and I wondered if I could make a donation or something?'

'Aw, Connie, ye're an angel – isn't she, girls?' Two little heads nodded mutely.

So she'd made a donation and signed their petition as well, wishing she could do more to help. She must start buying lottery tickets again; how wonderful it would be to hand over a few million to such a great cause! She'd never understood those wretched people who *did* win the lottery and then refused to let it change their lives. Why on earth not use it to change someone else's life then?

'And is Julie OK?' Connie asked anxiously.

'Aye, she'll be at the hospital. Her wee baby's due to come home later today.' June gave her a hug. 'I'll tell her ye came.'

Connie spent the rest of the morning parked up in a leafy layby while she sorted through the outburst of emails and texts from her scandalised family, her emotions careering from horror to anger, and to barely controllable hysteria. How *could* they think that she represented one of the abused women? How *could* they? Then again she hadn't actually seen the news item herself. She sent placatory email after email, feeling increasingly fed up about their reactions, before finally calling the Sinclairs.

Wendy answered the phone. 'Connie! I don't believe it! Why didn't you let us know you were coming? Roger's not with you? Oh, do come to see us and let us know what you've been up to!' Connie breathed a sigh of relief that they obviously hadn't seen her television appearance.

There followed detailed information as to their whereabouts, which Connie dutifully wrote down word for word, knowing she might well get lost anyway. Which, of course, she did, but she found the general area, and a friendly road-sweeper directed her, with great precision, for the final few miles.

When she arrived, she saw that Wendy and Bob had found themselves another Victorian semi, in a tree-lined road of solid, grey, stone houses.

'Oh, Connie, it's so good to see you!' Wendy hugged her tightly. 'Come in, come in! Bob's bowling but he'll be back shortly. And I hope you're going to stay the night now we have some spare bedrooms?'

She led Connie into a large open-plan living area, littered with books, newspapers and countless colourful wonky pots. 'I've taken up pottery,' she explained. 'Keeps me out of mischief while Bob's at the bowling green.' She removed a huge ginger cat from the settee. 'Sit down, Connie. Tea? Coffee?'

'Coffee, please, Wendy.'

Wendy looked older, of course, but she was lively as ever and she'd even acquired a trace of a Scottish accent.

Connie got scolded, as she knew she would, for not letting them know she was coming and for wasting money on B&Bs. They then exchanged all the family news while they drank their coffee. Wendy, forever the diplomat, asked nothing about Roger.

Connie grinned. 'You're *dying* to ask why Roger isn't with me, aren't you now?'

'No doubt you'll tell me in your own good time.'

At this point Bob appeared; much greyer, bespectacled, but otherwise little changed.

'Connie McColl!' he bellowed, enveloping her in a bear hug. 'How great to see you, and you haven't changed a bit! What on earth brings you up here? Is Roger with you?'

'No, he's not,' Wendy cut in. 'And we were just *coming* to that.'

Bill pulled a face. 'Oops! Have I come in at a bad time?'

'Of course not!' Connie laughed. 'I can tell you both my woes, such as they are.'

Bob consulted his watch. 'Is it time, do you think, for a wee drop of the hard stuff?'

Wendy rolled her eyes. 'It's only half past five!'

'Well, it's half past six in Europe and we're all very European these days. Don't like to think of them opening their bottles over there while we just sit here looking at the clock.'

'No, I'm fine with coffee,' Connie said. 'But perhaps later, since your wife insists I stay the night.'

'Of course you're staying the night! Stay as many nights as you like!'

There followed a refill of coffee, a passing round of shortbread and some general chat before Connie said, 'Well, I just decided to up and leave, you see. Looking back now it might seem to have been a silly thing to do, without warning them. But I needed to get away for a bit and, if I'd given them advance notice, I know they'd have talked me out of it. Roger would have made his annual suggestion of a holiday in Spain, where he could play golf in the sun all day.'

Then Connie told them about Roger becoming increasingly distant, about the endless babysitting, and about the hated bungalow. She told them no one talked about Ben any more, no one remembered the anniversary of his death ('except you, bless you, Wendy'). Or, if they did, they chose not to acknowledge it. Perhaps they thought it might upset her and probably she was being oversensitive. And she knew, only too well now, how fortunate she was to have a secure home and a family close by. They must think she was very, very silly.

'No,' said Wendy. 'I don't think you're silly at all.'

'It strikes me Roger's the silly one here,' Bob said. 'Let's face it, kids generally take their parents for granted. If ours lived nearer I know we'd be roped in for constant babysitting duties too. But I like to think that Wendy and I would sometimes do it *together*. But you have to draw the line; you have your own life to lead, Connie.'

'That's just the thing,' Connie said, 'I haven't. Not until now. Since we've both retired Roger's been at the golf club nearly all day and every day, and I've either been babysitting or staring at the four walls, every one of which I painted myself. I do a bit of floristry occasionally, but that's it. I'm becoming a dull old crone.'

Wendy patted her arm. 'You? Never! Please forgive me for saying this but, when it comes to being dull, Roger takes some beating.'

'*Wendy!*' Bob exclaimed.

'You know it's true!' Wendy snapped. 'He and Connie have always been as different as chalk and cheese. There's nothing wrong with Roger as such, but you know that people are either classed as drains or radiators? Well, Roger's drained you, Connie, and you've let him.'

'For God's sake, Wendy!' Bob was looking embarrassed.

'No, Bob, Connie needs to hear this. And it all stems from Ben's death.'

'*Ben?*'

'Yes, Ben. Before Ben died you were assertive and self-assured.' Wendy leaned forwards and took Connie's hand. 'I'm not suggesting for one moment that a tragedy like that doesn't knock the stuffing out of you. I don't think I could have coped at *all*. But it's a long time ago now, Connie, and you've been a general dogsbody ever since. And it's high time you stopped. Is it because you still feel some sort of guilt about Ben's accident?'

There was a silence before Bob said, 'Bugger it all. Time we had a wee Scotch and something. Drambuie, perhaps?' He got up to go in search of the bottles.

Wendy was still gripping Connie's hand. 'Because,' she said, ignoring her husband, 'you *did* feel guilty; I remember that. And it wasn't your fault; there was absolutely nothing you could have done.'

She passed a box of tissues to Connie but made no other acknowledgement of the tears that had begun to trickle down Connie's cheeks and drip from her chin. 'That man was drunk, Connie, he should *not* have been driving.'

Connie blew her nose. 'I know, I know. But I shouldn't have sent Ben out to get me that loaf. A *loaf*, for God's sake! I could have done without the bloody loaf!'

'He'd probably have gone out on his bike anyway, like he did every day. And why did he take off his helmet the moment he was out of sight? He *knew* he was supposed to wear it. But it wasn't the cool thing to do, was it? None of his mates wore helmets. That's how kids are.'

Connie swallowed. 'But—'

'But nothing, Connie! You've been beating yourself up about it ever since, you *know* you have.'

Bob returned with the drinks. 'You came on a bit heavy there, love,' he said, giving Wendy a reproving frown before he turned to Connie. 'This is a Rusty Nail.' He placed the glass directly in her hand. 'It'll make you feel better in minutes.'

Connie took a sip, feeling the warmth spread through her veins. This was an OK way to drink Scotch. A Rusty Nail… Had she herself become like some sort of nail? She had certainly been holding everyone and everything together since the family tragedy, while her own self was being eaten away. Had her willingness to be at everyone's beck and call *really* been a way of trying to pay for Ben's death? Had she been punishing herself? And for what? Of course it hadn't been her fault but, year after year, she had had that vague feeling that she'd failed to protect Ben. She thought again of Kath in Manchester and her boy killing himself 'on that bleedin' bike'. Kath didn't feel guilty, why would she? Why would Connie? Why would anyone? Roger certainly wouldn't.

'Maybe there's some truth in what you say,' Connie conceded, taking another sip. 'This is very nice.'

'Can't beat Scotch and Drambuie – Scottish nectar,' Bob pronounced.

Wendy took a sip and made a face. 'It's a bit early for this, Bob. But, Connie, it did need saying. You're a lovely person and you've still lots of living to do. Just make sure you do it.'

Several hours later, after a takeaway curry and some beer, Connie entertained her hosts by recounting her escapades since leaving Sussex.

'You see, you really started having fun when you got away from home,' Wendy said. 'You're going to be able to write a book at this rate. What else do you plan to do?'

'Well, as the saying goes, you might as well be hung for a sheep as a lamb. So I'm planning on continuing to head north and having a look at the Highlands before I go home.'

'That's if you decide you *want* to go home,' Bob said, chuckling.

'Oh, I expect I will.' Connie was aware she didn't sound very certain. 'I'm missing the kids and the little ones a lot, you know.'

'And what about Roger?'

'Well, I think we really need to talk, Roger and I. Really talk. We need to thrash out what's gone wrong with our marriage, and it's probably as much my fault as Roger's.'

'Why?' Wendy asked. 'Here you go blaming yourself again. Why shouldn't it be Roger's fault?'

Connie shrugged. 'I should have insisted that we sit down and talk everything through long before now. But perhaps I haven't cared enough.'

'And perhaps that answers your question,' Bob said.

Connie woke early, feeling calm and more convinced than ever that she'd done the right thing in getting away. Wendy knew she was guilt-ridden and Connie remembered that, when leaving Sussex, she'd vowed to renounce all feelings of guilt. Perhaps she hadn't even realised that, for twenty-three years, she'd been harbouring a different sort of guilt. She didn't know. But yesterday's conversation had been cathartic, if a little brutal. And she knew now that she'd only go back home when she was good and ready, and that finally she'd be prepared to confront Roger about their relationship.

But she still hadn't reached her turning point yet, so today she'd head for the Highlands.

※

'I tried to get her to stay another night,' Wendy said as they watched the little green car turn the corner and out of sight.

Bob put his arm round her. 'I think she's finding some comfort in keeping on the move.'

'Was I wrong to say those things to her, Bob?'

'No, of course not. They needed saying. I never cared much for Roger. And he left her pretty well alone at the time of Ben's death, just buried himself in work, as I remember.'

'That was his way of dealing with it. Roger's not a chatty, touchy-feely sort of person, but he's good and dependable.'

'Well, I always thought he was a little odd.'

'Oh, you're always saying people are odd.'

'Only if they are, my love.'

'Well, there's nothing odd about Connie. I think she should have set off on this sabbatical of hers years ago. And do you know what? She insisted on buying one of my pots, the one with the wee birds on it. She loved it, and insisted on giving me a fiver for it.'

'And you say there's nothing odd about her? Perhaps she's dafter than I thought,' laughed Bob.

CHAPTER TWENTY

ONWARDS AND UPWARDS

Connie drove across the Forth Road Bridge, thrilled with the views of the Firth and the imposing red-painted railway bridge alongside. It was so vast and she couldn't imagine how they'd ever found enough paint to cover it the first time round. She headed up the A9, bypassing Perth, and stopped for lunch in Pitlochry, resisting the kilts, the shortbread, the diamond-patterned cashmere and the unbelievable array of Scotch whiskies on display everywhere. She was becoming seriously concerned about money and the continual depletion of her bank account. She'd need to spend many more nights under the stars to continue her travels, if she could only find somewhere suitable.

The further north she ventured the cooler it was becoming, the summer heat having waned somewhat, but it was still fine and clear and Connie drank in the superb views of the mountains, the heathery hillsides and the fast-flowing peat-brown rivers, which she imagined were literally teeming with trout and salmon. None of your farmed stuff round here. But, even in the midst of such beauty, she found herself, as usual, sandwiched between towed caravans, motorhomes, family-filled cars, cyclists and the inevitable quota of juggernauts. She had plenty of time to take in her surroundings and she found herself looking for castles, particularly searching for that red-coloured castle she felt sure she'd seen on the holiday with her parents so long ago. And the more she thought about it the more convinced she was that it was on top of a hill. There were a few greyish ones, and a white one at Blair Atholl, but nothing red. Well, she'd probably imagined it anyway. How could she possibly remember something clearly from more than sixty years ago!

She had just been cut up by one obviously-bent-on-suicide white van driver, causing her to brake sharply, when she saw a young couple walking ahead on the grass verge. She motored on until she found somewhere to pull in, and then she waited. There was something oddly familiar about the boy.

She got out of the car.

'Harry!'

'Connie – jeez, I don't *believe* it!' Harry dropped his rucksack and ran forward to hug the astounded Connie. 'You *still* stretching those wings of yours, then?'

'You bet I am!' laughed Connie, 'and you're still walking!'

Harry's companion, all huge blue eyes and curly dark hair, was standing to one side, staring in curiosity.

Harry finally released Connie and re-joined his companion. 'Hey, Connie, this is Nyree! Nyree, this is Connie; you remember I *told* you?'

Nyree smiled broadly. Connie had never seen so many pretty, evenly shaped, pearly white teeth.

'Great to meet you, Connie! Any chance of a lift?'

'Jump in!' said Connie.

Harry's friend hadn't shown up in Stratford-upon-Avon so he'd headed on to Coventry where Nyree, who was from New Zealand, was visiting some relatives, and where Harry overnighted in a nearby youth hostel. They'd fancied each other on sight at the local Pizza Express (who said romance was dead?), got chatting and decided to get together.

'We've been to some great spots,' said Harry. 'Derbyshire Peaks, Liverpool, even Gretna Green…'

Connie gave a brief account of her own adventures before asking, 'And where are you heading now?'

'We're looking for somewhere to camp out tonight,' said Harry. 'We've invested in a little tent.'

'And a Primus!' Nyree giggled.

'Well,' said Connie, 'I was thinking along much the same lines myself. If I promise not to come too near your tent, do you think we could share a field or something?'

They stocked up with beer, wine and groceries at a tiny roadside petrol station.

As they stowed their purchases in the boot, Harry patted the car and said, 'This old thing's still going strong then?'

'Fingers crossed,' said Connie.

They finally decided to drive down a rough track, sheep scattering in all directions, towards a small copse, where Kermit could be hidden from the road. It was quiet and peaceful, but Connie thought fondly of her little green oasis by the river.

'I daresay we're trespassing,' she remarked. 'These sheep must belong to somebody.'

'What the hell,' said Harry.

'Exactly,' said Connie, as she unloaded the boot.

'So, time for a cuppa?' Nyree suggested.

'Queen of the Primus!' Harry held up a mug. 'Fancy tea, Connie?'

They drank their tea before the two youngsters began to erect their little tent, and Connie found a sheltered spot to lay out her sleeping bag, which had been lurking in the depths of Kermit's boot ever since her departure from the riverside idyll. Later they dined on cooked chicken quarters and mixed salad off paper plates, washed down by a bottle of Merlot.

'Nicest meal I've had in ages.' Connie licked her fingers.

'You sure you're going to be OK all night out in the open?' Harry asked as he gathered up the debris into a plastic bag.

'You bet,' said Connie.

There were no visitors or intrusions of any kind. The sheep kept a respectful distance although some bleating during the night woke Connie from a dream in which she was aware of a *presence*, undefined except for blue, blue eyes, protecting her. She lay, gazing up at the stars, for a very long time, unable to get back to sleep, trying to recall how they looked. And *felt*.

Although Connie sometimes struggled to remember her parents clearly, she had a sensation of once being held by her mother, a soft blur of smiling blue eyes and lily-of-the-valley perfume. Scent – it was always called *scent* back then. And her father, more remote, in his scratchy policeman's uniform with the silver whistle that blew such a shrill note, so different from the deep tone of his dark brown voice with its Geordie accent. Here again she felt their presence very strongly, just as she had done in her riverside idyll.

She could remember seeing her mother, in that long red dress, saying something like 'we won't be very late' to the babysitter as Connie hovered at the top of the stairs in her nightie, clutching Pod, her teddy. She'd no idea how he came to be called Pod.

Her parents' car, returning from the police ball that night, had been sliced in two when a truck, with its half-asleep, beer-sodden driver, had veered across the road and hit them full on. No one thought of drink-and-drive regulations back then. More likely he was persuaded to have 'one for the road' when he tried to leave the pub.

Twice Connie's life had been shattered by irresponsible drivers.

It had taken little Connie some time to digest the fact that 'Mummy isn't coming back'. But of course, there was instantly the question: what to do with a sad little five-year-old orphan? Enter Uncle Bill, with those blue eyes so like her mother's. 'She can come to live with our brood,' he'd said kindly, before disappearing back to Nigeria and the oil for months on end. Aunt Lorna did her best, and Connie eventually adapted to being the 'extra' family member.

'My special girl,' Uncle Bill would say on his visits home. But she wasn't Aunt Lorna's special girl; she was well-dressed and well-fed, if only somewhat rationed in love. When she eventually had children of her own, Connie could better understand the bond. Uncle Bill had died soon after retirement, and Aunt Lorna, or at least the *shell* of Aunt Lorna, gazed at Connie without any sign of recognition when she made her monthly visits to the nursing home. Awaiting death or dinner, whichever came along first.

Even though it was barely light, Connie slid out of her Miracle sleeping bag, which was covered in a dewy sheen. She was too cold to get back to sleep so she opened Kermit's passenger door and draped the sleeping bag over it. There was the promise of another warm day, and it would soon dry once the sun had risen a little higher. The others probably wouldn't wake up for some time yet so she got out the folding chair again and sat, studying the map and trying to decide where she might be going. She was on the A9 so it was probably sensible to continue on to Inverness, which was somewhere she'd always fancied visiting. She'd never been able to persuade Roger to venture any further north than Edinburgh, which was where, he seemed to think, civilisation came to an end.

'With a name like McColl you must have some Scottish ancestry,' she'd said.

'Generations ago,' Roger had replied. 'And they were sensible enough to head south.'

The youngsters woke a little later and they all breakfasted on sausage rolls and instant coffee before setting off for Inverness. Harry and Nyree were aiming to get to John o'Groats eventually, after exploring the Highlands. Connie was none too sure where she was going after Inverness. But they had all day to travel less than forty miles so they decided to explore some of the interesting-sounding isolated villages signposted off the A9.

'I like the sound of Lochmahadoc,' mused Nyree, craning her neck to look back at the sign.

'Let's go there then,' suggested Connie.

Lochmahadoc was a small, grey Highland village spectacularly positioned against a backdrop of heather-clad hills and distant blue mountains. No sign of a loch, though.

Harry spotted a modest hotel. 'Pub lunch later, perhaps?' he suggested hopefully.

But, as they rounded the corner to the signposted parking, nothing prepared them for the sea of trucks, juggernauts and as-sorted vehicles and equipment that appeared to stretch to the ho-rizon. And people rushing everywhere.

'What the—?' spluttered Harry.

Connie parked the car in one of the few remaining spaces. 'So much for our tranquil Highland village – do we *really* want to stay here?'

As they got out of the car they were accosted by a human whirl-wind in the shape of a skinny girl with a wild mop of frizzy red hair, a FCUK T-shirt, tight jeans and cowboy boots, clutching a clipboard.

'Are you the guys from the Extraordinaries agency?' she de-manded. 'Aren't there *four* of you?'

The three regarded each other in bewilderment before Harry found his voice. 'Last time I looked there were just three of us.'

The girl sighed loudly. 'You're not the *extras* then?'

'We certainly aren't,' Harry replied.

'We're short of four fucking extras!' the girl ranted, running her fingers through her already chaotic tangle of hair. 'Casper's going to shit himself if they don't show up soon.'

Before anyone could progress the conversation further, a large middle-aged man with bleached blond hair, dressed in denim, and with a multitude of gadgets on chains dangling round his neck, appeared on the scene.

'Are these the extras, Sam?'

Sam rolled her eyes yet again and shook her head. 'They're just bloody *tourists*, Casper.'

Casper smacked his forehead dramatically and groaned. 'They'll *have* to do. We just can't wait any longer. This scene's got to be shot in sunshine and there's a bloody big black cloud heading this way. And Harvey's going *mad*.'

'Harvey's the director,' explained Sam to the astounded trio.

'Right,' continued the indomitable Casper. 'We need one person serving coffee; the old girl will do. And the young couple need to be sitting at a table drinking the stuff. Like, *pronto*! But we still need to find someone else – oh shit, shit *shit*!'

Connie was flabbergasted and furious. *Old girl*, indeed!

'Just one moment!' She marched forwards to face Casper. 'It's hardly *our* fault your damned extras haven't shown up, so please don't take it out on us. And don't be so bloody *rude*! We know nothing about what you're doing here, and we don't *want* to know because now we're heading for Inverness – *pronto* – thank you very much!'

With that she turned on her heel and headed back towards Kermit, signalling to the others to follow.

'Hang on! Keep your hair on, lady!' Casper wasn't giving up. 'It'll only take a day or two. Give them the lowdown, Sam, and *don't* let them go. And see if you can find a fourth.' He headed back towards the action while Sam rolled her eyes heavenward yet again.

'*Please* – can you help us out?' She'd suddenly adopted a humbler approach. 'You only have to stand around, sit around – background stuff for *The Hamiltons*.' She studied them for signs of recognition. 'The *soap* on Scottish television, you know?'

'No,' the three replied in unison.

'Well,' Sam sighed, 'it's *very* popular north of the border. And two of our main characters – a young couple – have eloped and are supposed to be staying here. We've had to build a coffee shop because they don't do coffee shops in this godforsaken place.' More sighing. 'And we need a minimum of four extras.'

'No,' Connie repeated.

'The money's good.'

'*Money?*' The three stopped in their tracks.

'How much money?' asked Harry.

Sam smiled. 'Seventy pounds a day, plus breakfast, lunch and dinner.'

'We'll stay!'

CHAPTER TWENTY-ONE

SCOTTISH SOAP

Polly, the make-up artist, applied powder to Connie's nose with an enormous fluffy puff. 'Can't have shine,' she said. 'And now we really need to emphasise your eyes.'

'I'll look like a clown,' Connie muttered. 'I'm only supposed to be standing behind a counter, aren't I?'

'Yeah, but we can't have your face in a blur.'

Polly had already worked her magic on the other two, much to Harry's disgust ('Jeez, she's just put *powder* on my face!') and Nyree's amusement. As she selected an appropriate mascara for Connie she glanced out of the window. 'I guess they've finally found a fourth. Sam looks like she's frogmarching some poor guy in this direction.'

Another idiot, thought Connie, who'll do anything for money.

'Now,' said Polly as she put the cap on the mascara brush, 'Sam will take you across to Wardrobe.'

The door flew open. 'Finally found a fourth!' Sam announced triumphantly as she led a tall man through the door. 'This is Dan.'

'*Don*,' the man corrected.

'Yeah, whatever. He'll need the usual, Pol. Come on, you three, we're off to Wardrobe. And I'll be back for you shortly, Dan.'

'Don,' he repeated, smiling at Connie.

For a moment she'd assumed he was one of the actors, as she took in his black hair greying neatly and evenly round each nicely shaped ear. His dark brown eyes reminded her of long-ago summers: the Adonis who greatly enlivened her stay in Greece, or the Italian lothario who'd embellished her holiday in Sicily. Mediterranean Man. Not to be trusted for one minute, so just as well sensible grey-eyed English Roger had come along when he had.

'Now,' said Sam, turning towards Harry and Nyree, 'you two are going to be sitting at a table, in the background, drinking cappuccinos and rabbiting quietly away about anything that comes into your heads. Just try and look animated. Our two characters, who are called Calum and Marie, will be doing their scene right in front of you, but you don't look at them. You two –' she waved a hand at Connie and the newly powdered Don, who had just joined them – 'are in the coffee shop. You, Connie, are behind the counter dispensing coffee from the machine. It's a real one, but you just need to pull a few handles – Casper'll show you. And you, Dan, are the customer, waiting for your coffee and passing the time of day with Connie here. That should be done by lunchtime if nobody snuffs their lines.' She sniffed and sighed again.

Connie emerged onto the set draped in a white overall.

'What's this?' yelled Casper.

'The old girl doesn't look *Italian* enough!' screamed Harvey, the director, whose long grey hair was anchored in a ponytail.

'Best we could get,' snapped Casper.

Best we could get. Old girl. I'm going to give somebody a ticking off in a minute, thought Connie. She had to concentrate very hard on the seventy pounds.

'It's got "Giovanni's" painted above the door, for Chrissakes!' Harvey glared at them all.

'Well, we could stick a dark wig on her then,' Casper shouted, signalling to Sam, who was still rushing around in a demented fashion waving her clipboard.

'We haven't got all day,' yelled Harvey. 'What about the bloke? He looks like he could be Italian. Can't he serve the bloody coffee, and she can be the customer. Get him a white coat, Sam!'

'Can't they just be *Scottish*?' sighed Casper.

'No they bloody well *can't*. Any half decent cafe up here is run by Italians. Now, get in position before this cloud comes over.' With that he signalled to the technicians, causing cigarettes to be hastily extinguished and the murmur of conversation to abate.

Sam led Connie into the improvised coffee shop and removed her white coat. 'Stay here,' she commanded, 'while I get Dan positioned behind the counter and au fait with the machine.'

'*Don*,' he murmured, as he followed her.

'OK,' said Sam, 'now you just need to pull a few handles, like this. See, shot of coffee, frothy milk, hey presto – cappuccino! It's real stuff. Now, you two are to chat to each other in a *whisper*, yeah? Just say any old crap, like you're passing the time of day, yeah? The sound mustn't interfere with the conversation our two lovers out there are having. And you, Dan, are passing the cup across to Connie, got it? Yeah?'

'Got it, yeah,' he said, grinning at Connie. 'I'm *Don*.'

'I'd never have guessed,' said Connie.

'And I'm supposed to be Italian, so watch out! *Buongiorno!* Now, what shall we whisper about, Connie?'

There followed hushing sounds all around and the click of the clapboard, which signalled the commencement of the dialogue between the two eloping characters, Calum and Marie.

'How do you like your coffee, Connie?' Don asked in a stage whisper as he struggled with the rudiments of the machine.

'Preferably in the cup.' Connie tried to keep a straight face as coffee spurted in all directions.

'Well, I've never used one of these damn things before in my life,' he whispered as he set down the cup and saucer, awash with coffee, on the counter. Nobody seemed to have noticed and the argument between the two lovers appeared to be reaching its crescendo, which hopefully meant the end of the scene.

'No proper Italian would slosh coffee around like that,' Connie whispered, noting the penetrating dark eyes, his beautifully shaped hands and the way he… No, no, she thought, I'm sounding like a Mills & Boon heroine. He was just a good-looking bloke, and she thought he was probably well aware of it.

'Well, what you're looking at is half-Scottish and half-English, so you'll have to make allowances.'

'So I will.' She noted his nice teeth too. 'What shall we discuss now?'

Don smiled at her. Really nice teeth, they were. 'You could tell me how you ended up here and why.'

'We were planning to go to Inverness. We just stopped to have a look at the scenery.'

'I just stopped for a wee and a tea,' he said, 'and look at us all now. Are you travelling with the two youngsters? Your son? Your daughter?'

What a flatterer, she thought, or do I really look young enough to be their mother? I suppose I could have given birth in my forties.

'I'm just giving them a lift,' Connie whispered. 'He's Australian and she's from New Zealand.'

'CUT!' yelled the director. The two stars had messed up their lines. More shouting. 'We'll have to do that again.' More coffee. Everyone looked up at the sky, where the black cloud was about to blot out the sun.

'We've *got* to get this in the can!' Harvey was tugging at his ponytail in frustration.

Sam had edged in from nowhere, minus the clipboard this time, and removed the messy cup and saucer from the counter. 'Just as well no one can see this,' she murmured. 'You'll have to do more of this, Dan, when we start again. Yeah?'

'Anything you say, *Pam*,' said Don with a sigh.

'*Sam!*' she corrected him.

'Think of the seventy pounds,' Connie whispered.

Calum and Marie's conversation had turned into a satisfactory full-scale row, with no one forgetting their lines this time, which fortunately meant that the necessary footage was finally in the can seconds before the first spots of rain began to fall.

'Lunch!' yelled Casper.

'Not *you*,' said Sam, reappearing from nowhere. '*You* eat last.'

The four extras were directed to a large caravan nearby, which had two functioning toilets and some comfortable seating. 'You wait in here,' continued Sam, 'until I come to give you the OK. Yeah?'

'Yeah!' they chorused.

While they waited they chatted generally and Connie discovered that Don was an ex-airline pilot who had retired the previous year. 'They chuck you out at fifty-five,' he added, 'but I'd had enough anyway.'

So, he was fifty-six. And he was twice divorced (she'd suspected correctly he was something of a ladies' man), had two grown-up daughters, and lived in Cornwall.

'I've only been there once,' Connie said. 'Where in Cornwall do you live?'

'On the north coast. It's really beautiful there and very wild, particularly in the winter. I bought a place down there years ago for family holidays, and now I live there all the time.'

He'd come up to Scotland to visit his late mother's only remaining sister, who lived in Perth.

'My mother was the Scottish half,' he explained. 'Her sister's eighty-six and quite a character.' He'd then continued northwards because he wanted to visit Inverness again. 'I was born up here when my father was stationed at RAF Kinloss and, when I was a child, we often used to come through Inverness, so I just thought I'd like to visit the place again.'

The food was unexpectedly delicious, and there was plenty of it, even though they were the last to eat. As lowly extras they ate after the stars, the director and most of the crew. And even after the production assistant (Casper) and the runner (Sam). The pecking order, it seemed, was sacred.

'Best lunch we've had in days!' Harry exclaimed, wiping his mouth with a paper napkin.

'*Only* lunch we've had in days,' corrected Nyree.

'Don't know where we'll find room for dinner as well,' Connie said. 'Not to mention afternoon tea.'

'We've got to store it all up for the frugal times ahead,' said Harry. 'Like camels in the desert.'

Don had asked her several questions regarding her reasons for travelling so far north, and Connie had given him little in the way of a satisfactory reply. She'd either fended off the questions or abruptly changed the subject and, as a result, he'd become particularly well informed on Harry's life in Australia and Nyree's enormous family in New Zealand. She had of course told him that she was married and lived in Sussex. At one point Harry had chipped in with, 'But you're getting ready to fly, aren't you, Connie?' Don had given her a questioning look but mercifully, at that point, Sam had ordered them back on set.

Connie wondered why she was so reluctant to discuss her personal life with this man. After all, she'd opened up to Harry and to Kath and to Jeannie. But there was something about Don that she found disconcerting. Those dark eyes of his seemed to bore into her very soul. He was dangerously attractive and the least he knew of her and the sooner she was on her way – solo – the better it would be.

At the end of the day's filming Sam informed them that, for reasons of health and safety, they were forbidden from sleeping in any of the film caravan units.

'You have to find your own accommodation and the hotel's full up with all us lot!' She waved her arms around cheerfully.

'You could try squeezing into our tent,' said Harry, oblivious to Nyree's hostile stare.

'I've rung up and booked the last remaining room in Lochmahadoc's only B&B,' Don said. 'But, look, I've got a big car and I could easily sleep in that. Why don't you have the room, Connie?'

'Oh, no, I couldn't!' He was being gentlemanly to a fault but Connie didn't want to be beholden to anyone, and particularly not to this good-looking stranger. 'My own car's fine. Really. I've got a sleeping bag and everything.'

'She has, you know,' said Harry.

'Really, I've done it before,' she added.

'Well,' said Don, 'let's meet up in the Poachers' Bar of the hotel for a few nightcaps, and we can discuss it then.'

The Poachers' Bar had spent a considerable fortune on taxidermy – from the glass-encased salmon, set against painted views of swirling rivers, to the countless stags' heads gazing vacantly from above, plus two pheasants displayed against a rocky outcrop and one surprised-looking otter.

The owner ('Willie MacKinnon at yer service') was a happy man, pouring all manner of alcoholic drinks to a very thirsty TV crew.

'Shouldn't think he's ever had a crowd like this,' remarked Don, depositing a gin and tonic in front of Connie, as Willie looked flummoxed when one cameraman asked for a Screwdriver. ('Did ye say a *screwdriver*? Have ye no got yer tools with ye?')

'I should think he usually gets a few fishermen and hunters, according to the season,' Don went on, 'and I don't suppose they, or the locals, go in much for cocktails. Just wee drams, and pints with whisky chasers.'

'It reminds me of New Zealand,' Nyree observed. 'Very macho.'

'Well, probably not so very long ago, in this very hotel, the ladies would have sat separately, sipping sherries or lemonade or something, while the menfolk got hammered in the bar,' Don said.

There was standing room only and Connie found herself firmly wedged between Don, Nyree and the otter.

'Perhaps we should go outside?' Don suggested. It was still unbelievably mild for the time of year, even this far north.

'What about midges?' asked Connie, who'd read about those tiny cannibals.

'They really like nice, freckly, Sassenach skin,' said Don, running his fingers up Connie's arm. She laughed, hoping that, in the diminishing light, he would not see her blushes. Why, she wondered, am I acting like a silly teenager?

'But,' continued the subject of her angst, 'I was a good Boy Scout and so, here –' he produced an insect-repellent stick from the pocket of his jeans – 'rub this on your face and arms.'

There was something about the way he looked at her. Or was she imagining it? Well, she might as well enjoy it as it was only for this one evening and tomorrow she'd be on her way.

It was late and they were all tired. Two gin and tonics later, Connie was ready to sleep right there on the floor. When Harry and Nyree started making noises about escaping to their tent, it seemed a good time to take her leave. The bar and garden area were still crowded and noisy and she wondered if she'd hear them from where Kermit was parked, only about a hundred yards away.

'I'll walk you back,' said Don, draining his beer.

'It's no distance,' said Connie, but he paid no attention.

'Are you sure you can sleep in that?' he asked anxiously as he set eyes on Kermit. 'You really are welcome to my room, or to my car. It's twice the size of yours.' He indicated a large, silver Mercedes parked a few yards away.

Connie shook her head vehemently. 'I shall be just fine,' she said, 'but thanks for the offer.'

'Well, goodnight then, Connie.'

'Goodnight, Don.'

Connie then discovered that this insistence of hers on being independent came at a price: hardly any sleep, and aches and pains in every joint. She forgot sometimes that she was sixty-six. She'd never felt worse as she staggered out of Kermit at 6 a.m., having given up on the idea of even fitful dozing. Fortunately the portable loos, which had hand basins, were unlocked and so she was able to have a perfunctory stand-up wash.

Consequently, on the second day's filming, she struggled to keep awake. They all had to be customers in Lochmahadoc's only mini-market while the two lovers were being filmed on the pavement outside. They were instructed to roam the aisles, scan the shelves and drop the selected items into their wire baskets but, as Connie filled hers for the umpteenth time with tins of cat food and packets of cereal, she could think only of Wendy's comments about her 'guilt', and her family's reactions to her unsolicited television appearance. How could *any* of them truly believe that she had personal reasons for demonstrating? No wonder Roger sounded so furious. Then again, he could have given her the benefit of the doubt, surely, or even sent some love. He was plainly very cross.

'That's the second time you've collided with me,' Don murmured, as he reached up for a packet of chocolate digestives. 'You're in a world of your own today, Connie. Did you notice if this place is licenced? I think I might try bagging a bottle of gin and trying for a discount.'

In spite of herself Connie smiled. 'Sorry, I was miles away. Do you think they're nearly finished out there? Because this basket's getting mighty heavy.'

As if on cue, Harvey was heard to bellow his famous 'CUT!' and everyone adjourned for lunch.

'That's it!' he yelled. 'I think we've got all we need. Extras – please hang on until I see the rushes – just in case we need you again later.'

At three o'clock, after another hefty lunch, Sam presented each of them with a sealed brown envelope and dismissed them. They had all been paid for two complete days, and even Harvey spoke to them personally. 'Sorry we had to waylay you like that.'

'You should be flattered,' Sam said as a parting shot. 'He doesn't normally *talk* to extras.'

'We are *not* extras,' Connie reminded her.

'Well, you have been for the past two days, like it or not, yeah?' retorted Sam. 'Anyway, you've been great, and don't forget to look out for this on the telly, probably around January sometime,' she said, walking away as she spoke.

As they headed towards their respective cars Don said, 'Perhaps we can meet up in Inverness?'

'I'm not sure I'll be staying there after I've dropped off these two,' Connie said, nodding towards Harry and Nyree, who were packing their belongings back into Kermit's boot. It was time to move on now. And alone.

'I'd really like to see you again.' Don sounded genuine. Connie didn't respond. 'Well, anyway,' he continued, 'I'm going to do a little shopping in our mini-market over there, and then I'll be on my way too. It's been fun knowing you all.'

There was hand-shaking all round, and he pecked Connie on the cheek.

'Bye, Connie,' he said, 'and I hope you find whatever it is you're looking for.'

CHAPTER TWENTY-TWO

THE TURNING POINT

'That was fun,' remarked Nyree as they headed north over Slochd Summit, purple moorland stretching away in every direction. 'And, do you know, that Sam was actually quite a nice girl once you got talking to her?'

'Yes, I'm sure she was,' said Connie, still mentally editing her email replies and hoping that they'd gone down well in Sussex. She supposed she really should go home now.

'And I think that Don fancied you,' Nyree added.

'Don't be ridiculous,' said Connie. She was far too old to blush, so this rush of blood to the face was obviously some type of geriatric hot flush.

'*Don Juan!*' said Harry, and the two of them dissolved into noisy giggles.

'Just look at this amazing scenery,' said Connie, keen to change the subject. 'And however do you pronounce some of these names?'

As they neared Inverness, Connie looked out for a garage where she could fill up her petrol tank before they hit the city centre. For the last five miles she'd been aware of a faint knocking sound. At first she hoped it was just her imagination but, as she drove on, it became more and more obvious that it was very real indeed, although neither of the other two had made any comment. *Please* Kermit, she prayed, don't go letting me down now.

'Hey, Connie,' Harry said suddenly. 'What's that knocking sound?'

She could see an Esso sign up ahead and hoped fervently that it was a proper garage and not just a filling station but, in any case, it would be somewhere to stop and call out the AA if necessary. Thank goodness she'd continued with her membership. Little chance of help from someone like Foxy around here.

And, there was no doubt about it, the knocking was becoming louder and louder. There goes my lovely 'extra' money, Connie thought, and *then* some probably. Could this be anything to do with Rav running into the bumper? Had he known more than she realised when he gave her his card? No, she thought – he was just fishing for custom.

She was relieved to discover that it was indeed a proper garage – Archie's – and Archie himself, an elderly chubby mechanic in dirty navy overalls, was still working at nearly six o'clock. He emerged from underneath a yellow Fiat, spanner in hand, rubbing his palms on an oily rag.

'Ah cannae do anything tonight,' he told her cheerfully after listening to the description of Kermit's symptoms. 'Ah'm going home for ma tea. But Ah'll have a wee look at it first thing in the morning.'

'Oh, *please!*' Connie was close to tears. 'Couldn't you just tell me if it's safe to drive? I'm sure it's nothing much. *Please!*'

Archie produced a paper cover, deposited that and his sizeable bottom into the driving seat, and revved the engine several times.

He pulled a face. 'Ah wouldnae drive it another inch if Ah wiz you. Ah'll need to hae a good look at that engine, but do ye want to know the honest truth? This car is clapped out.' He got out and walked round it, tapping here and there. 'It's nearly *twenty* years old! I'm telling you now it's probably going to cost a lot more to repair than the car is worth. Ah'm awful sorry,' he added.

Harry put his arm round Connie's shoulders. 'Don't worry,' he said. 'We're nearly in civilisation again and we can work something out.'

'But how are we going to *get* there?' Connie became suddenly aware of the magnitude of her predicament, with all her personal belongings stowed in Kermit's boot, not to mention the youngsters' tent and rucksacks, along with the groceries, the wine bottles, odd coats, boots, the sleeping bag, the folding chair, plus a myriad of miscellaneous objects and general rubbish.

'Aye,' Archie continued, consulting his watch. 'Now ye could've got a bus just an hour or so back, but there'll no be another one today. But ye cannae drive the car like that or ye'll break doon for sure before ye're a hundred yards doon the road.'

For the first time since she'd left home Connie felt utter despair. Of course Kermit was an old car and she had been aware that he might have need of surgery at some point, but she hadn't considered that he might actually *die*; this trusty friend who had transported her along these six hundred or so miles, along with her occasional passengers.

Suddenly there was a yell from Harry – 'Jeez, I can't believe it!' – as a large silver Mercedes saloon pulled in directly behind them.

'It's *Don Juan*!' squealed Nyree.

Oh God, thought Connie, not *him* again. She dug frantically in her shoulder bag for a tissue, and dabbed her eyes.

Don Robertson eased himself out of his car and strolled towards them.

'I thought I spied an elderly green Escort in the forecourt,' he said, 'and I didn't think there could be two like that.'

'We've broken down,' Harry informed him.

'Well, well.' Don turned to Connie. 'And what's the prognosis?'

She sighed. 'According to this gentleman,' she said, indicating Archie, who was making a show of putting his tools away and digging out his keys, 'it appears to be clapped out.'

'Aye,' Archie called as he pulled down and locked the up-and-over door, 'and if you want my honest opinion that's exactly what it is, but Ah'll have a good look at it in the morning. Just lock it up and leave it where it is. Leave me the keys.'

'Just as well I spotted you then,' said Don. 'Let me give you all a lift. Have you got much luggage?'

As she opened up Kermit's tightly packed interior, Connie waved her hand mutely.

'Lucky for you I have a decent-sized boot then,' said Don, apparently unfazed at the chaos. And within minutes he and Harry had transferred the contents of Connie's car into the Mercedes.

'Wasn't that the luckiest thing *ever*!' Nyree clutched Connie's arm. 'Good old Don Juan,' she added in a whisper.

'Tomorrow,' said Don to Connie, 'I'll bring you back here when Archie's had a chance to look at it, and you can decide then what to do. Right now I'm going to take you all into town to find somewhere to spend the night and have a drink.'

There were murmurs of assent from Harry and Nyree, and Connie knew she had little choice. Her mind was in turmoil as she was guided into the front passenger seat of Don's luxurious car, the other two having made a dive for the back with much giggling.

'Now,' said Don, as he got into the driver's seat beside her, 'have you got any accommodation booked in Inverness?'

Connie shook her head mutely.

'But *we* really just want a campsite,' added Harry.

'Well, let's see what we can find.'

What they found, a few miles further on, was an enormous camping and caravan park.

'Ideal!' exclaimed Harry. 'And we can actually afford a pitch tonight because we're so damn *rich*!'

'And we could have hot showers and proper loos,' sighed Nyree.

'Perhaps I could stay here too,' Connie said desperately.

'Are you *kidding*?' Don parked the car at the entrance. 'You haven't even got a tent! And, sure as eggs is eggs, these two aren't going to want you squeezing into theirs! I'm heading into town for a proper meal and a proper bed, and so are you.'

Connie got out of the car while the two youngsters unloaded their belongings. 'I shall miss you.' She gave Harry a farewell hug. 'And I somehow think the chances of my picking you up again are extremely remote.'

'We'll miss you too, Con,' said Harry. 'You've been more than kind. I hope you get the car fixed so you can carry on with this grand tour of yours! Promise you'll stay in touch and let us know how you get on?'

They exchanged mobile numbers and hugged each other tightly one final time.

'You'll be OK with him,' Harry added as he shouldered his rucksack, nodding towards Don, who was rearranging the contents of his boot yet again. 'He's a really nice guy.'

'Well, I haven't much choice,' said Connie, wiping her eyes. Somehow she felt that saying goodbye to these two youngsters was her final link with her spontaneous journey. For sure, she was no longer in the driving seat.

An hour later, after Don had phoned around twenty hotels and B&Bs from his mobile, it was plain that there were hardly any rooms to be had anywhere. They ended up in a motor inn on the outskirts of the city.

'We've only got one twin-bed room left,' said the desk clerk, shoving a half-eaten sandwich into the bowels of his desk. 'You'll be lucky to find anything in Inverness tonight because the place is still crawling with tourists and there's a big political conference on this weekend as well. Scots Nats,' he added with a knowing nod of the head.

'We'll take it,' said Don.

Oh no, thought Connie, this is *all* I need. But the thought of a bed, any bed, was pure heaven after her sleepless night on Kermit's back seat.

After they'd checked in and Don had picked up their bags and headed towards the lift he said, 'I promise to be the perfect gentleman. This was *not* in the plan, as I'm sure you'll appreciate, and I have no ulterior motives. And, besides, you're plainly knackered.'

The room was clean, impersonal and functional and, mercifully, the beds were well separated by a wide unit. She flopped down on her chosen divan closest to the window. 'I must have a shower before I do anything else,' she said, thinking of her brief strip-wash in the public loo early in the morning.

'Fine by me. Help yourself.' He busied himself hanging up a couple of items and making a big point of not looking at her.

Now, thought Connie, I have to take absolutely *everything* into the bathroom with me, because there'll be none of this usual wandering around the room in the raw, or in bra and pants. Clutching a change of clothing and her toilet bag, she headed towards the shower wondering if she should lock the door and, if so, could she do it quietly because she didn't really want him to think that she didn't trust him. But *did* she trust him? *Could* she trust him? Well, what would he do anyway? She certainly wasn't young enough or attractive enough to present much of a temptation, but then Nyree had referred to him as Don Juan, so she'd probably already sussed out that he was a bit of a womaniser. Oh, what sort of mess had she got herself into now? And how was she supposed to wash out her underwear? She couldn't very well leave these greying items dripping over the bath...

But all these worries were washed away by the shower, which was wonderful, and the temptation to put on a nightie and collapse into bed was almost overwhelming. And what would be Don's reaction to that! So instead she put on clean clothes, brushed her hair, and even sprayed a little Chanel behind her ears. She'd left her make-up in the bedroom, and hoped she'd be able to do something about that while he showered.

Connie nearly put her eye out with the mascara brush when, shortly afterwards, Don emerged from the shower with only a towel wrapped round his waist.

'I'm so sorry,' he said, as he delved into his bag, 'I completely forgot to get out some underpants.'

She blinked frantically while cleaning off the smudged mascara, and tried not to stare at his tanned, toned body and the black hair curling fetchingly across his chest. Did he know he was bloody gorgeous? she wondered. Yes, of course he did. And how long was it since she'd openly admired a man's body? Too long; much too long.

Don disappeared back into the bathroom and Connie made some further attempts with the mascara.

They had a rib-eye each, washed down with a bottle of Merlot, at a nearby steak house. It was informal, with most people in jeans. Connie was relieved because she hadn't the first clue where she'd packed her 'going-to-the-theatre dress' or where it might be located in Don's boot.

'In the morning,' said Don, refilling her glass, 'we'll go back to see Archie, after he's had time to give your car the once over.'

'Poor Kermit,' sighed Connie as she took a generous slurp.

'You need to prepare yourself for the worst, Connie. That's an old car.'

She nodded. 'I know.'

'You can get a train from Inverness, you know, which would get you down to London.'

'I know that too.'

Don stared at her for a minute. 'Don't you *want* to go home?'

'Of course I do!' Connie retorted. Then she added, quietly, 'I think I might have reached my turning point. Or, more accurately, I think the turning point has been *made* for me.'

He continued to regard her quizzically. 'Turning point?'

She sighed. 'I wondered when it was coming, when it would be time to go back.'

He didn't speak for a moment. 'You don't have to go back yet if you don't want to. At least, not straight away. I plan to head south at a leisurely pace and you're very welcome to join me. I'd really like your company. No funny stuff – separate rooms and all that.'

'I'll be able to think more clearly when I've had a sleep,' she said eventually. 'But I really should be getting home, I suppose.' She clutched her head. 'But what about all my *stuff*? In your car?'

'Well,' Don said, 'I could always drop that off for you when I get back.'

Connie stared at him, trying to imagine Roger's face if a good-looking man in a silver Mercedes should drive up with her belongings in his boot. 'But Sussex is a long way from Cornwall,' she said after a minute.

'Just as well I like driving then,' he said.

CHAPTER TWENTY-THREE

COFFEE BREAK

Roger had just finished his M&S lasagne when there was a knock on the door. Who the hell is this? he wondered, as he dabbed his mouth with a piece of kitchen towel. And there, standing on the doorstep, was Mrs Henderson in a state of high agitation.

'Oh, Mr McColl, I'm really sorry to bother you but all my electricity's gone off! I think something must have blown it. Could you possibly spare a minute to have a look?'

Roger groaned inwardly but supposed he couldn't very well refuse.

'Just a minute,' he said. 'I may need a torch.' What had the silly woman done? At least he knew where the fuses would be: in the garage, like everyone else's in the modern cul-de-sac.

Roger followed her into the gloomy interior of the garage and shone his torch on the fuses, located the one that had blown and switched it on again.

'There we are,' he said. 'That's all you have to do if it happens again.'

'Oh, Mr McColl, thank you so much! Since my Ed died I dread anything like this happening. He saw to everything, you see.'

Roger wasn't sure when her Ed had died, but it was before he and Connie had moved next door. 'No problem,' he said.

'I've just made a pot of coffee,' she said. 'Won't you come in and have a cup? Please?'

Roger hesitated. He'd been about to make himself some coffee when she came to the door. He supposed it would be rather churlish to refuse.

'Well, just for a minute then, Mrs Henderson,' he said, reluctantly following her into the house. Her lounge was a replica of his own, but with lots of dark furniture and countless ornaments. He sat down on a chintz-covered sofa and looked out at her garden while she went to fetch the coffee. There were military rows of begonias, bordered by equally spaced clumps of alyssum and lobelia against a background of dahlias. The same as last year. Connie hated it, of course. Connie, the great flower expert, liked shrubby, messy, haphazard gardens, but he himself could see nothing much wrong with some precision in the garden, as in life.

'Here we are!' Mrs Henderson had appeared with a tray bearing two flowery mugs, a cafetière of coffee, a jug of milk and a bowl of sugar. 'I do like decent coffee, don't you?'

'Yes I do,' Roger said, surprised at how good the coffee smelled. 'Just a little milk and one sugar please, Mrs Henderson.'

She handed him his mug and duly stirred hers. 'Oh, do please call me Doris. We've been living next door to each other for a couple of years now but have never really got to know each other, have we?'

'No,' he agreed. 'We haven't. I'm Roger, and my wife is Connie.'

'She's still away, then?'

Was it his imagination or was she looking decidedly smug?

'Yes.' He took a sip. 'This is very nice coffee, Mrs... er, Doris.'

'Thank you, Roger. Now, just one minute...' And, with that, she got up and headed back to the kitchen.

Doris reappeared with a cake. 'This is my coffee and walnut cake, Roger. Would you like to try a slice?'

Roger *loved* coffee and walnut cake! Connie didn't bake much, and she didn't like walnuts, so there was little chance of such delicacies at home.

'Thank you, Doris,' he said, sinking his teeth into a hefty slice. 'This is delicious.'

'Oh, good. It's so nice to have someone to share a cake with since my Ed passed away. I usually just make them for the church bring-and-buy sales, you know.'

Well, this woman could certainly bake! Roger drained his coffee and licked his fingers to transport any remaining crumbs to his mouth.

'Another slice, Roger?'

'No, no, I mustn't. But that was delicious.' And I must get to the golf club before a certain person goes off duty.

'More coffee?'

'No thanks, I'm a one-cup man.'

'Aw,' she said, 'just like my Ed. He was a one-cup man too. Pity you never knew him; I think you'd have got on well.'

Roger stood up. 'I must go now, Doris. Thanks so much for the coffee and cake.'

'Oh, any time, Roger.'

CHAPTER TWENTY-FOUR

JUST GOOD FRIENDS

Connie awoke to the hum of an electric razor coming from the bathroom. It took several minutes to get her bearings and check the time. It was only 7.30, but she couldn't believe she'd been asleep for nearly nine hours. Then she remembered Kermit's impending demise and her spirits plummeted. Perhaps the poor car could be repaired for a reasonable amount? But, even if that were possible, how confident would she now feel about driving all the way back in it? And was this indeed the sign she'd been waiting for to indicate that it was now time to turn around and go home?

Don emerged, shaved and fully dressed, beaming. What the hell did she *look* like? She fought the temptation to pull the duvet over her head knowing that, newly awake and minus make-up, she must look ancient.

'Good morning!' he said. 'You certainly needed that sleep, didn't you?'

Yawning, she nodded. 'Did I snore?'

'Not that I heard. Did I?'

Connie rubbed her eyes. 'No idea. I'd have slept through an earthquake.'

'Right,' Don said. 'I'm going to leave you in peace to get up while I suss out where we can get some breakfast and where the nearest laundrette is. If you're anything like me you've probably got a bag of dirty washing stashed away somewhere.'

The man's a mind-reader, she thought.

'So, if you don't mind sharing a machine with me, we could get all that out of the way this morning. Make a fresh start before we visit your friend Archie.'

'I need to dump half the junk in the boot,' said Connie, thinking of all the rubbish; empty bags, soiled sandwich wrappers, old gardening shoes (why on earth had she brought *those*?), and, not least, the deckchair. He must think I'm a bag lady.

'We can do that too,' he said cheerfully.

Two hours later, having got rid of Connie's rubbish (she'd felt particularly sad as the old flowery garden chair was chucked into a container), breakfasted and laundered, they arrived back at Archie's Garage. To give Archie his due, he'd got the car up on the ramp and was poking around in the innards, tut-tutting.

Archie climbed out of the inspection pit, shook his head and pulled a face.

'It's needin' a new engine, truth be told. Ah can get the parts and patch it up, but it's going to cost an arm and a leg. And, let me tell you, there's a lot more that's going to need doing very soon – the clutch, for one thing. It'd be pouring good money onto bad.

Ah widnae drive tae Inverness in it, far less doon tae England. Ye could buy a newer car than this for a lot less than the cost of thae repairs. I've a nice wee Fiat round the back that would do ye fine.'

Connie took a deep breath and shrugged.

'What happens,' Don asked Archie, 'if she doesn't go ahead with the repairs and she doesn't want your wee Fiat?'

'It'll have to go to the knacker's yard,' said Archie, with narrowed eyes. 'And Ah wouldnae charge ye for taking it there if Ah could use some of thae bits and pieces for spare parts.'

There was silence.

Connie said, 'I need to think about this and come back to you.'

'So, let's go and find some coffee somewhere,' Don said, opening the door of his car.

They found a tiny roadside cafe about half a mile away.

Connie stirred her cappuccino thoughtfully. 'Is he on the level, do you think? Should I get a second opinion?'

'I expect he'll make a few quid out of it one way or the other,' Don replied. 'But you could only use it now as a trade-in, unless you're prepared for a big bill. Or are you ready to buy another car?'

She was aware that he was studying her intently; she almost felt those dark eyes boring into her very soul.

'You might want to have a word with your husband?'

Connie shook her head at this suggestion.

'But you can't drive all the way back south in that car the way it is. So, you either take the train, look at the Fiat, or you come with me.'

Connie had picked up her teaspoon and was playing with the froth on the top of her coffee. 'Can I have a little longer to decide? But I don't want to interfere with your plans, Don.'

He shrugged and grinned. 'I'm at your disposal. Take as long as you need, but we'll have to do something about the car before too long because I don't suppose Archie will want to have it sitting indefinitely on his forecourt.'

After a second cup of coffee they returned to Archie's Garage, where poor Kermit had been repositioned out of sight down a side lane. Archie had plainly been breakfasting as he emerged from the gloomy depths of his garage, grunting audibly and wiping crumbs from his mouth with oily fingers.

'Ye're back then.'

Don was about to step forward. 'Let me tackle Archie,' he said quietly.

'No, Don, I have to do this,' Connie murmured. Then, more loudly, 'It's *my* car.' I've let Roger make almost all of my decisions lately, and it's high time I did my own thing, she thought.

Connie turned towards Archie. 'What will you give me for the car?'

Archie regarded her with ill-concealed astonishment. 'Where's yer man, if we're talking business?'

'My man, as you call him, is *not* my man – he's only giving me a lift. Now, can we talk about *my* car please, Archie?'

Archie scratched his chin. 'It's only fit for the scrap heap, so it is.'

'No, it isn't. It's worth a lot if it's done up, it's got an MOT, and two new tyres, one of which I only bought a short time ago. It's got—'

'I'll give ye a couple of hundred quid,' Archie interrupted. 'Because Ah'm in generous mood.'

'I want five hundred pounds,' Connie said, remembering her conversation with Nick the day he checked her tyres.

'It's twenty years old, missus, and it's falling to bits. It's only fit for the scrap heap.'

'Five hundred pounds.'

'If there's one thing Ah cannae be doin' with,' said Archie, 'it's an argumentative woman.' He rubbed his nose. 'Ye'll put me out of business, that's what ye'll do. Three hundred, and that's *it*!'

'Five hundred! You *know* you can do this car up and sell it on. It's got low mileage too – *look*! And it's a *classic*!'

'Ah'll give ye *four* hundred right now, or else ye can take that car away and dispose of it yersel'. And, let me tell you, that's a whole lot more than the car's worth but Ah'm a generous man. Ah'll be on the dole next week at this rate,' said Archie. 'Ah don't suppose ye have the documents?'

'They're in the glove compartment and I said you could have it for *five* hundred,' said Connie, half wishing she'd never thought to bring the paperwork with her, so she'd have an excuse to delay the parting.

Archie paid cash; a roll of dirty twenty-pound notes, but five hundred pounds nonetheless. Connie almost wept as she closed Kermit's door for the last time. It was the end of an era. There was no question about it; she'd involuntarily reached her turning point.

'You probably would've got more on a trade-in,' Don said, as they drove back towards the city, 'but it would have meant buying another car. I think you did very well there to haggle with a Scottish car dealer!'

'Thanks.' Connie sniffed. 'Well, at least I've got enough cash for the train fare to London.'

'And that's what you *really* want to do?' Don turned to look at her briefly.

'Right at this moment I don't know what I want to do. What's the alternative anyway?'

'The alternative is that I show you round some of Inverness and then we head down Loch Ness-side, through the Great Glen, to Fort William, through some of the finest scenery on the planet.'

That sounded much more tempting than a twelve-hour train journey and a furious Roger at the other end. A few more days probably wouldn't hurt. And she was in no particular hurry to face her husband.

'Bring it on!' Connie grinned.

Don took her first to Culloden battlefield and told her about the final confrontation of the 1745 Jacobite rising. As Connie walked over the springy turf she wondered how many bodies might lie beneath her feet. War: the inevitable loss of life, the sons who never returned home, the grieving mothers and widows. Connie shuddered.

Then, Inverness. Connie liked Inverness. She liked the river and the walks on either side of it, and the Notre Dame-style cathedral. But what really knocked her out was the castle – that huge sandstone edifice overlooking the town. The red-coloured castle! She had found it! The castle she'd seen on that camping trip with her parents all those years ago. It was real; her memory had not played tricks! Surely it was fate that had brought her here again! She took several photos hoping that, when she studied them, she might remember other events or places from the distant past. And there, in the castle grounds, was the statue of Flora MacDonald, gazing longingly across the miles from her lofty position towards

Skye and her lover, Bonnie Prince Charlie. Connie gazed at her, and the castle in the background, for a long time.

Don was more concerned about the changes to the city centre. 'They've built a huge shopping precinct!' he said as they drove round. 'Marks and Sparks, and all the rest of them! Whatever happened to all the little local shops? And the whole place is twice the size it used to be! Is nothing sacred? My mother would *hate* it! But Flora there has reminded me of Skye, and the islands. You really should see the west coast.'

They had a snack at Drumnadrochit where, amidst the ruins of Urquhart Castle on the shore of Loch Ness, they stood spellbound by the lake's sheer size and magnificence.

'Of course there's a monster!' Don teased. 'You can see it any night of the week after a skinful of whisky!'

Monster or not, Connie had the sensation that there was a certain magic about this place. She wondered if she'd still feel like that if she were alone, or had her companion got something to do with it? Of course not, she thought; Connie McColl, you're going soft in the head!

Then they went on to Fort Augustus with its Benedictine abbey and even more stunning views back along the loch, where the road crossed the canal via a swing bridge. Connie had a glimpse of the staircase of locks for which this part of the canal was famous, then the three smaller lochs that formed the southern part of Thomas Telford's Caledonian Canal. It was a novelty to be driven, to relax and to be able to enjoy her surroundings as they headed towards Fort William.

'I once came up here with wife number two,' Don remarked. 'And we had a Godawful row right about here somewhere.'

'How could you possibly argue in such a beautiful place?' Connie asked, gazing at the serene surface of Loch Lochy.

'She could do battle absolutely anywhere,' Don replied. 'Particularly after six consecutive days of rain!'

'So you could say that all this sunshine is unusual?'

'You certainly could say that. They must have known you were coming, Connie.'

Next Don took her to see the splendid and very emotive Commando Memorial at Spean Bridge. 'Dedicated to the guys of the original British Commando Forces in World War Two,' he informed her. So many battles, so much sadness, Connie thought.

They managed to find a small loch-side hotel, set in stunning scenery, just a few miles from Spean Bridge, where, much to Connie's relief, they were able to have two single rooms. What would Roger say if he could see me now, she wondered, accompanied by a good-looking younger man in a luxury car? He'd never believe they were booking separate rooms.

'We don't get asked for the singles so much,' said the pretty young receptionist, studying them with open curiosity. 'We serve dinner from seven to nine,' she added, openly flirting with Don. 'And through yonder, we have a lovely wee bar.'

'I think we'll definitely be heading for the lovely wee bar,' said Don as he picked up the keys.

Tartan carpets and shortbread on the tea tray! Highland Moor soap and Scottish Heather bath oil! A mini-bar with countless miniatures of Scotch and Drambuie! Connie reckoned she could spend a very satisfactory evening in here on her own. She'd developed quite a taste for Rusty Nails, thanks to Bob.

Later she joined Don in the furthest corner of the lovely wee bar, in the bay window overlooking the loch and the mountains, out of earshot of the other customers and as far distant as they could get from the very bored-looking youth, wiping glasses desultorily, who was plainly only there to earn money during his summer university break.

In spite of the endless array of Scotches available, Connie was a gin and tonic girl. She gulped down her first, aware of how apt was the cliché about it not touching the sides, and tried to slow down on the second one as she didn't want Don to think he had landed himself an alcoholic passenger. She remembered only too well the last couple of times she'd overdone it recently.

'You're enjoying that, aren't you?'

'I don't normally glug it down this quickly,' she replied, as she drained the glass.

'Are you still upset about the car, Connie?'

'Yes, I am, but it wasn't just a car, you see. It was my freedom my ability to get up and go, if I ever felt the urge, which I did...' Connie sighed. 'And perhaps I owe you some sort of explanation...'

Don regarded her with amusement. 'You owe me nothing at all, Connie.'

But now that the turning point had been reached, Connie felt she badly needed to talk. She told him about leaving a perfectly satisfactory husband, and a perfectly satisfactory bungalow. And she told him about Di, and Nick, and Lou. She even told him a little about Ben and the gap that his death had left in her life. She felt a couple of tears sliding down her cheek, and Don positioned yet another gin and tonic in front of her, along with a tissue.

'I'm just not ready to be living in a retirement bungalow with a man who wants separate beds and who plays golf all day long. I'm just a bloody housekeeper! I'm sorry, it must be the gin,' she said, wiping her eyes, not caring if her mascara had smudged.

'No wife should feel like the housekeeper, especially not one as nice as you!' said Don. 'But gin on an empty stomach has a tendency to make a person maudlin. It's high time we had some food.'

Connie continued to pour her heart out all through dinner. When she'd first met Don she'd been wary about telling him anything. Now she couldn't stop. She told him then about Martin and MMM, finding Harry on the road to Stratford, about Freddy and Baz, about Kath, about the puncture and the three lads, about Jeannie and her memories and then the protest march in Edinburgh.

'You can't have got up to all that mischief in the space of just a couple of weeks,' Don said, laughing.

'Oh, I did,' said Connie.

They ate an excellent dinner in the busy dining room, enjoying the view.

Don leaned towards her. 'How old are you, Connie, if it's not a rude question?'

She thought quickly. 'Sixty,' she lied. She wondered why it was so important that he didn't think of her as old.

company who were looking for tour guides. "Some knowledge of a foreign language an advantage", it said. Anyway, my French was passable, so I applied.'

'So, you've always had a taste for a getaway?'

'I suppose I have.'

'And where did you get away to?'

'Greece. That's the sort of daft company it was. I spoke French so I got sent to Athens. I was supposed to go out there with a girl whose parents were Greek and who *did* speak the lingo but, at the last minute, she didn't show and Freddy was sent in her place. Well, neither of us spoke a word of Greek but we got by somehow and had the most hard-working but hilarious summer imaginable. We've been pals ever since. And I can tell you a thing or two about Greek ruins as well!' Then Connie told him about how much she'd enjoyed her evening with Freddy and Baz.

'I'd really like to see them again on the way back,' she added wistfully.

'And why not?' he said.

'I think they'd expect me to have found an answer to my restlessness, and I *think* I know what I'm going to do, but I'm not a hundred per cent sure yet.'

They sat quietly for a moment or two and then he said, 'You've had more than your share of life's knocks, Connie, haven't you?'

Connie shrugged. 'Compared to some people, perhaps. But I've been lucky in lots of ways. Gosh, when I think of what some of those women in Edinburgh have been through!'

She stared out across the loch. 'What's really upset me is being *ignored*. I used to feel ignored by my Aunt Lorna. She had a brood

'I'm fifty-six,' he said. She'd guessed right. 'And I've been through two divorces, so you're doing very well.'

'I'm doing very well,' she repeated as she demolished the last few crumbs of her liqueur-laden Highland Cream dessert. Was it possible to get sloshed just on the menu? Highly probable after the gins, although she'd refused wine with dinner. 'So, do you think it's OK for me to have a little fun now?'

'I definitely *do* think so. And I'm sure your husband's a very nice man, but I fear he's not *cherishing* you like he should, Connie.'

Cherishing! Now, *there* was a word. I haven't been *cherished*, she thought, and I need cherishing.

'And tomorrow,' Don said, 'we'll sit by the side of the loch there and, because it's so beautiful, your problems will just fade away.'

of her own and didn't particularly want me thrust upon her. I tried to imagine over the years, when my four were young, how I'd have felt if I'd been saddled with someone else's child.' She sighed. 'And then lately I've felt ignored by my own husband although he, of course, would argue with that. He's rarely at home and he doesn't really listen to me when he is. Maybe lots of marriages are like that? I don't know.' She turned towards Don. 'I hope I don't sound sorry for myself, because I'm really not.'

Don shook his head. 'No, I know you're not. And now you've taken matters into your own hands, haven't you, coming away like this?'

'I suppose so. But I'll probably have to go back to Roger eventually.'

'Will you? Why?'

She was aware that he was studying her intently, and she felt herself redden; she hadn't blushed so much since she was at school.

'Truthfully, I don't know,' she said.

It was then that he put his arm around her, and she automatically leaned against him.

'He's a fool to take you for granted,' Don said. 'I took my first wife for granted while I zoomed around the world and she brought up the girls virtually on her own. I flirted with other women. I had an affair. She found out, of course – end of marriage number one. And I can't say I blame her.'

'What about marriage number two?'

'Ah, well, she led *me* a merry dance. She started off by falling in love with local politics, and then with a local would-be politician. He never did get elected but he was loaded, and he didn't leave her on her own for weeks on end either.'

'But she must have known the nature of your job when she married you, surely?'

Don shrugged. 'It probably seemed like a good idea at the time. Anyway, I decided after that that I definitely wasn't good husband material and I'd be better off single.'

'Do you have a lady friend now?' asked Connie, and then immediately regretted it; such a damn silly question and a damn silly expression! *Lady friend* indeed!

'No,' he said. 'Not just at the moment.'

She laughed, not daring to meet his eye. *Not just at the moment!* He couldn't possibly be considering *her*, could he? Ten years his senior! Of course, she'd told him she was sixty but, in any case, she was far too old for such goings-on. And she was a married woman to boot. She'd never, ever considered having an affair, even if someone had fancied her, which they hadn't. But would it be so wrong? Everyone seemed to be at it these days, according to the media. Nobody batted an eyelid any more. No, no, no, Connie McColl, she told herself, that's not what this pilgrimage is all about. You're trying to find yourself, not someone else. And then, all at once, against her reasoned thoughts, she was very aware of stirrings in places that hadn't been stirred in years.

Connie turned involuntarily to face Don, knowing by instinct that his eyes and his lips would find hers, which they did, and she surprised herself as she clung to him.

'I would very much like to make love to you, Connie,' Don whispered. He was disarmingly polite as well!

'Oh yes,' Connie heard herself say. 'I think I'd like that very much.'

'Well, we might get arrested here, so why don't we head for Fort William, and the Road to the Isles?'

Connie McColl, she thought, what have you done *now*? Ask him to take you to the nearest station and get straight onto a train back south. Or maybe just *one* night? No. She'd insist he take her to the station. *Insist* upon it.

As they headed towards Fort William, all she could think was: can I still remember how to *do* it? Have I dried up completely? Will I be able to climax? (She could count her climaxes on one hand – and they were ancient history anyway.) Will he think me old and wrinkly? What the hell, Connie thought, I want this man, so I'll take a chance! Just this once I'm going to follow my heart…

CHAPTER TWENTY-SIX

SUCH INCONVENIENCE

Nobody had ever told Roger that toilet rolls didn't reproduce themselves, that towels didn't wash themselves or that sheets had to be changed regularly. He sighed; things certainly couldn't go on like this. He could just about cope with basic groceries – or the lack of them – because Lou and Tess occasionally remembered that it was advisable for him not to starve to death. And there was the golf club, but eating there so often was mighty expensive. Not only that; people were beginning to talk. 'Haven't you got a home to go to?' they'd quipped at first, but not now, not after seeing the thunderous expression on Roger's face. They obviously knew things were amiss. They may even have noticed his budding friendship with Andrea. At least no one appeared to have seen Connie on the television, so that was something.

'Isn't your lovely wife back from her hols yet?' the obnoxious Nigel Babbington-Smith asked, treating them both to large gin and tonics after he'd thrashed Roger that afternoon on the golf course.

Roger wanted to kill him. He ignored Nigel. 'Lime!' he snapped at Phil, the barman on duty. 'You *know* I always have lime – not bloody lemon.' He fished the offending slice out of his glass and dropped it into a discarded crisp packet lying on the bar. Andrea would have known about the lime.

'Does it make much difference?' Nigel asked, taking a large gulp of his own, a smug, self-satisfied smirk all over his face.

'Yes, it bloody well does!' Roger snapped.

He picked up fish and chips on his way home and wondered when exactly his lovely wife *did* intend to return from her so-called 'hols'. Nearly three weeks had passed and he was none the wiser. Mrs Henderson next door had waylaid him yet again yesterday while he was mowing his section – and hers – of the communal grass at the front.

'Mrs McColl still away?' she'd asked pointedly.

'Yes,' he'd murmured, through gritted teeth. With a bit of luck she hadn't seen Connie's appearance on the news either.

'Well, never mind,' she said. 'I've just made another little coffee and walnut cake, which I know you like. So you just wait there a minute…' And she dashed into the house and out again with a polythene box. 'Here we are!'

Inside the box was half a cake and Roger would stick pins in his eyes before he'd ever admit it, but he'd eaten the whole lot at a single sitting in front of *The One Show*.

Now he set his fish and chips down carefully on the kitchen table. His diet was becoming increasingly unhealthy and he'd gained three pounds during the past week. At least Connie always had a balanced meal on the table and made sure he got his five-a-day.

But he didn't have time for all that palaver, and he was none too sure if mushy peas counted as a vegetable or not, although he was pretty sure that chips didn't. And what about the pickled onion?

This was doing his self-improvement scheme no good whatsoever. But, when a man's been deserted and left to fend for himself, what else would you expect? What about cruelty to husbands, eh? Well, as of tomorrow he would get back on some sort of diet again. Perhaps the Atkins this time. In the meantime, he'd work this lot off on his rowing machine. But was she *ever* coming back? Connie could walk through the door at any minute. The uncertainty was driving him mad.

⚛

Diana McColl was in a quandary. Mark had asked her to move in with him, which she really wanted to do, and she also desperately wanted a chat with her mum. Connie had always been a good listener and was very open-minded. Since she'd taken herself off on this sabbatical or whatever it was, Di had realised just how much she missed her mother and their weekly chats on the phone. She'd thought a couple of times of calling her on her mobile but then decided against it. Some sixth sense warned her that this was not a good idea, that her mother needed a break from all the family pressures. Dad wouldn't understand that, of course. He was a good man but incurably conventional. She supposed that's what came of having been an accountant; even in retirement everything had to add up and be correct. But Mum had a quirky side to her and a good sense of humour.

Di was *sure* she would move in with Mark, into the Dockside apartment with its river view (if you hung over the balcony and looked sharp left). After all, they were two of a kind in the same crazy sort of business, reporting for the media and living out of suitcases for half of the year. They both loved their jobs; they didn't want conventional ties, kids or animals. They just wanted to be in the same bed, in the same flat, whenever they both landed back in the UK. Dodging around from her flat to his was driving her nuts; whatever she wanted to wear always seemed to be in the wrong place, and the flats were miles apart, involving six stops on two different Underground lines.

But Di was realistic. She was well aware that the most supposedly idyllic relationships could go awry and it would be reassuring to keep a bolt-hole. The obvious thing to do would be to rent her flat out, but that might stop her from heading back if – heaven forbid – she should ever need to. Decisions, decisions. *Where are you, Mum?*

❀

'I've taken on two days' work,' said Tess McColl.

Nick lowered his *Daily Telegraph*. 'Doing what? Nursing?'

'What else would I be doing? Nursing, of course, home nursing.' Tess slammed the door of the fridge. 'But now it's a problem because your mother normally looks after the boys on Wednesdays and Thursdays. And I thought she wouldn't mind Fridays as well.'

'Did you ever tell Mum that you were planning to go back to work part-time? And that she'd be looking after the boys *three* days a week?'

'How was I supposed to know she'd do a runner? And what am I supposed to do now? I had no reason to expect her to change her routine. After all, she's only got to take one to school and one to nursery and collect them again afterwards.'

'Perhaps,' Nick sighed, 'she'd prefer to be doing other things three days a week. Perhaps, having brought up four kids of her own, she doesn't necessarily want to start all over again.'

'Well,' said Tess. 'That's typical of you. *Mummy* can do no wrong.'

'I rather hope she can, Tess. I'd like to think of her living a little before she gets too old.'

'And what's wrong with her life as it is?'

'Why don't you ask Tracey Bragg in the village to look after the boys? They say she's great with kids.'

'In case you hadn't noticed,' Tess said drily, 'nurses do not get paid an exorbitant hourly rate and, by the time I paid Tracey or anyone else, I'd probably be working for a couple of quid an hour.'

'Well, that's a couple of quid more than you're earning now. And it's not as if I don't earn enough. Honestly, Tess, there's no need for you to work at all.'

'You don't understand – I need to feel *fulfilled.*'

'So, what's wrong with feeling fulfilled on two quid an hour? And isn't looking after two great little boys, going to the stained-glass workshop, Pilates and art appreciation classes fulfilling enough? Christ, Tess!'

'You men never understand! I suppose I should talk to Connie myself, woman to woman. You know how much she loves the boys.'

'Get on with it, then. No point in sounding off at me!'

✻

It was 10 p.m. and Lou had finally managed to get the baby to sleep.

'Too late for a drink?' Andy asked, turning on the BBC News.

'No, it isn't,' Lou snapped. 'I'll have a white wine, and fill it up.'

'Been another tough day?' Andy sighed as he removed the Sauvignon Blanc from the fridge and poured them each a glass.

'It damn well was! She hasn't slept at all – not closed her eyes for one minute all day. Everyone else's babies sleep for an hour or two in the afternoons – it's what keeps mothers sane. And I don't recall Tess ever having a problem with her two.'

'Ah well, that's Tess for you.'

'What do you mean by *that*?'

Andy turned down the remote control; there was little chance of concentrating on the news. 'Isn't she your typical earth mother, or whatever they're called these days?'

'*Earth mother!* Lou spluttered as she set down her glass. 'She's never in the house! Anyway, what's that got to do with it? Are you insinuating that I'm *not* a natural mother?'

Andy sighed. 'Of course not, Lou. You're a lovely mother.'

'Stop patronising me! And anyway, Mum spends half her life looking after Tom and Josh – which is far more than she ever does here – while Tess goes to her endless bloody classes.'

'Not at the moment, she's not!' snorted Andy as he turned up the volume.

'I suppose you find that amusing!'

'Just that your ma's gone walkabout, and that's an indisputable fact, my darling.'

'And leaving her family without a backward glance! Poor old Dad!'

'"Poor old Dad" my foot! He's never at home anyway – practically *lives* at the golf club.'

'Yes – and now, in case you haven't noticed, he expects me to go over there and clean and tidy up for him! On top of everything else!'

'Well, tell him to get a cleaner or something.'

'That's typical of you! You've never liked my father, have you?'

Andy gave up on the news. 'Are we having that old argument again?'

'You've *never* liked him, Andy. You think he's dull and boring – just because you work in advertising with a bunch of nutters. You sneer at anyone in an ordinary job but, let me tell you, my dad earned a good living and looked after us well.'

'I'm sure he did. Just a pity he seems to have had a humour bypass.' He took another swig of his drink. 'I don't know why you don't get in touch with your mother instead of ranting at me.'

'I'm going to do that, but right now I'm heading up to bed,' said Lou, picking up her glass.

As she slammed the door the baby let out a lusty yell.

'Now see what you've done!' she hollered back at Andy.

CHAPTER TWENTY-SEVEN

DON JUAN

On the short drive to Fort William all Connie could think about was that kiss, which had unlocked stirrings deep inside her. Stirrings that she barely remembered existing. She felt excited and naughty and what the hell! She couldn't believe she could *want* this man, so *much*! This man she hardly *knew*! What's happening to me? she wondered. She glanced sideways at him. He seemed unperturbed. Well, he probably did this sort of thing all the time.

'We'll be able to see Ben Nevis properly,' Don said as they drove along. 'Believe me, it's not that often you can actually see the summit. We've got to make the most of this fine weather.'

They had an excellent view of its imposing height as they stopped for coffee in Fort William. But, as she sipped her drink, Connie could only think that she should get a train home, or south, or anywhere for that matter, without delay. She wondered how frequently trains ran from Fort William to London. She'd ask him to take her to the station just as soon as they finished their coffee.

'I was thinking,' he said. 'We might make a little diversion and head for the Road to the Isles.'

Connie nodded. 'That sounds great.'

'It's the most beautiful drive from here to Mallaig,' he said. 'The most scenic in the UK. And I can show you beaches that can rival the Caribbean any day!'

What about my train? Connie thought. But perhaps we can go there and come back in a couple of hours. And perhaps we can't. Or won't. And do I really want to get on the train? Will I be able to resist him? Why should I resist him?

'Sounds lovely,' she said into her coffee cup.

Don leaned across the table and gently lifted her chin up so she was looking directly at him. 'Let's go then,' he said.

'Yes,' she agreed.

'It's magnificent, isn't it?' Don asked, as they drove along. 'We're extremely lucky because ninety per cent of the time you can't see a damn thing due to the awful weather.'

They got to Glenfinnan. 'This,' he told her, 'is where Bonnie Prince Charlie rallied his clansmen for battle. And that,' he added, pointing out of the window, 'is their monument.'

And there, at the foot of the towering mountains, at the head of Loch Shiel, stood the tall, imposing monument, the tribute to the many men who'd fought and died, he told her, for the cause of Charles Edward Stuart.

Connie was mesmerised by the surrounding mountains, the rough heather-clad terrain, the intense green near the loch, the blue of the water. And so much history!

And all the time she was aware of his proximity and his hand brushing against her leg when he changed gear. She should really get on that train – but tomorrow, or the next day.

Just over an hour later they were in Mallaig.

'This is the end of the Road to the Isles,' he said, taking her hand as they parked above the town. 'From here you can get the boat to all the islands. And that, over there, is Skye, where your friend Flora MacDonald was looking towards.'

Connie felt she was running out of adjectives as she studied the glorious panorama.

'I know I promised you Caribbean-type beaches and, charming as this port is, there's no sand, so let me take you to Arisaig.' He opened the car door for her. 'I want to show you my favourite place. It's not far.'

Arisaig did indeed have beaches to outdo the Caribbean, Connie thought, although she'd never been to the Caribbean, of course. But surely even the Caribbean couldn't rival these spectacular views out across the sea to the little islands.

'This is stunning!' Connie exclaimed. This place is seducing me, and he's about to do the same. Bugger the train!

'Arisaig,' he said, 'is not only beautiful, but has its own special place in history too. During the Second World War, at Arisaig House, Churchill created a secret guerrilla army of saboteurs and assassins who were trained to smuggle themselves into Nazi-occupied Germany. This whole area was sealed off – no-go. It's a hotel now, but there's an exhibition at the visitor centre.'

'Oh, I'd love to see that,' Connie said. 'I'd no idea.'

'No one had any idea,' Don said. 'That was the whole point.'

They parked alongside the beach.

'Do you know what?' Connie said. 'I feel I want to run barefoot along that sand!'

He laughed. 'Then we shall!'

Within minutes they'd kicked their shoes off and were running, giggling, along the fine powdery sand, watched with interest by some strolling couples and several encampments of kids building sand castles.

'They filmed *Local Hero* round here,' Don said, as they slowed a little. 'Remember the film, with Burt Lancaster?'

'Mmm,' she said, out of breath. In fact she could only think of Burt Lancaster in some old film, rolling about on the beach with Deborah Kerr. She'd better not mention that.

'Can we slow down now?' she gasped. 'Don't forget I'm older than you, and I'm way out of condition.'

'You're in very good condition,' he laughed, as they tumbled down on the sand, and he put his arms round her. 'How long is it, Connie, since you've run along a beach barefoot?'

She thought for a moment. 'Not since Greece – a long time ago, before I was married.'

'That,' he said, 'is tragic. Everyone should run barefoot on the sand. Regularly.'

'Yes,' Connie agreed. 'They should.'

She couldn't imagine Roger running along the beach, giggling. And collapsing in the sand! Roger had been paranoid about getting sand in his clothes, between his toes or, horror of horrors, in the picnic, as he set up deck chairs and wind breaks, then gathered the herd together, plastering them in factor ninety-nine or something, before making his way cautiously to the water's edge.

There must be daft couples who do things like this, Connie thought: enjoying each other's company, laughing at silly things, running barefoot on the beach. But not Roger and I, she thought. Not in a million years.

'And,' Don stroked her cheek, 'after they've run barefoot on the sand, they should go to bed and make wild, passionate love.'

She turned her face to his, and he kissed her.

'I noticed a "Vacancies" sign half a mile or so back,' Connie said. 'Why don't we see if it's still there?'

They walked, her hand in his, back to the car, brushing themselves free of sand as they went.

La Vista had one double room available for two nights only. It was separate from the house, across the yard in what used to be a milking parlour, they were told by the plump young landlady. Would that be all right? Yes, yes, it would be just fine. They liked the idea of the privacy of the milking parlour. 'Och, as long as it disnae rain,' said Morag. 'Ye can get awful wet just coming across for yer breakfast.'

It was ideal, Don said, and it wasn't going to rain.

Ripping off their clothes, sand flying everywhere, they crashed onto the bed. Afterwards Connie couldn't remember ever having had sex like it. Certainly not with Roger, who didn't do much in the way of animal passion. Don was different. She refused to think about how long and how often it must have taken him to perfect his techniques, and she could scarcely credit her own fevered reactions either. Don Juan, Nyree had named him, and she wasn't far wrong. She relished every inch of that tanned, beautiful body, those deep dark eyes. That slightly lopsided grin, the square jaw, his wicked sense of humour – the whole bit – a walking, talking cliché, that's what he was. The way he listened when she spoke; *really* listened, or seemed to anyway, as though what she was saying was of major importance. She realised he was a ladies' man, of course; Don Juan, Casanova – what the hell. Just for a day, or perhaps a few, he was going to be *this* lady's man. Connie felt infused with new life.

What had she *done*? It was as if someone had opened up the floodgates to let everything flow out, carrying away all her inhibitions and insecurities and hang-ups. And he didn't *have* to be with her; he could have packed her onto that train in Inverness. Indeed he should have done, because what was she now – a fallen woman? Did they call them fallen women these days, or *wanton* ones? Whatever they were called, she was one of them now. After forty-one faithful years!

She should really stop this right now. There had to be a way to get home as soon as possible. In fact the train would be just fine. *Tomorrow*, though. She'd go home on the train tomorrow. They'd have tonight together. Just *one* night.

'Now,' he said, propping himself up on one elbow, 'we'll go to see the sunset.'

This, Connie thought, is complete Mills & Boon.

'Oh, yes,' she said.

They showered together and he didn't appear to notice the flab, the stretch marks, the wrinkles. She was pleased to note that he had his own quirks as well – the beginnings of a beer belly, and he was ever so slightly bandy.

'Why ever did we waste two whole nights in separate beds?' he asked, as they got dressed. 'You're a cracker!'

A cracker! Connie McColl was a *cracker*? Well, that was a new one. She was rather pleased at being a cracker.

'We'd better think about getting something to eat now,' he said, as he put on his shoes.

'Fish, perhaps?' suggested Connie.

'With chips?' he teased.

'Why not?'

'With a pickled onion,' he said, laughing.

'And a pickled egg,' she added.

Sunset comes late in Scotland in summer, and so, after the fish and chips, they bought a bottle of wine, took two plastic glasses from their bathroom, and headed towards the sea, where they found a vacant bench just a few yards above the beach. Connie snuggled up to Don as he deftly opened the bottle with a smart little corkscrew he withdrew from his pocket.

'Do you know,' she mused, 'that a million years ago I spent ages trying to find a wine I liked with a screw-top because I hadn't thought to pack a corkscrew?'

'Very remiss of you,' he agreed.

'And a million years ago,' Connie continued, 'I could never even have *imagined* sitting in a beautiful spot like this, with a man who wasn't my husband, and with whom I'd just made the most fantastic love.'

'A lot happens in a million years,' he said, handing her a glass of wine and kissing her gently on the mouth. He put his arm round her and she leaned back against him, sipping her wine.

The sun was slowly slipping down towards the horizon as they gazed out at the panorama of sea and islands. It was one of the most beautiful views that Connie had ever seen as the sun finally disappeared behind the Small Isles in a riot of red and pink and purple, with the mountains of Rum and Skye ablaze with colour. And then, as darkness fell, they wandered back to La Vista, hand in hand.

When Connie woke just after six the next morning it was already bright and sunny outside, and slivers of sunlight were peeking in through the chink in the curtains. She surveyed her still sleeping lover and thought she'd like to make love again, and again. This whole thing was surreal, ridiculous, totally crazy. Whatever had happened to sensible old Connie McColl? Furthermore, she didn't care, and that train from Fort William could wait until tomorrow.

She eased herself from his arms and tiptoed across to the window. What a beautiful spot it was and what perfect weather!

Don opened one eye. 'Come back to bed, please,' he said. And she did.

It was another beautiful day, and surely *one* more day couldn't hurt. Of course she couldn't live in this dream world forever and besides, she missed her kids and their little ones. But she couldn't even begin to *think* of Roger. Because what would he think of her brazen adultery? Would he want a divorce if he had any inkling of what sort of woman his wife had become? Did *she* want a divorce?

She wouldn't even have admitted such a thing to herself just a week or two back.

They stopped at the visitor centre on the way to the beach to see the exhibition. Connie could scarcely believe that such clandestine and controversial goings-on had ever taken place in an area of such scenic beauty. But, of course, over the centuries, this entire area had been a battleground of one sort or another. What must it have been like, Connie wondered, to have been born into such a turbulent period of history? One clan fighting another and perhaps your entire family slaughtered in front of your eyes? There but for an accident of birth and all that, she thought. And, of course, it still went on daily in other parts of the world. You should thank your lucky stars, she thought, for your safe, secure, civilised life in Sussex. But you still have to do battle with yourself, she considered, with your feelings and your failings   although she guessed that those fighters from the past never had the time or the inclination for all this self-analysis.

Don unearthed two large beach towels from the depths of the boot of his car, and spread them out on the grassy verge at the edge of the sand. Connie stripped off her top and shorts, and laid down beside him in her swimsuit. It was a one-piece, black, Marks and Spencer; a sensible choice for the older woman, of course, but Connie was beginning to wish it was pink, or turquoise, or emerald green because Don was wearing a very tiny, racy pair of royal blue trunks.

He leaned across and kissed her gently.

'Tell me,' he said, 'how you're feeling. Happy?'

'At this moment, very happy,' Connie replied.

'But at other moments?'

'Not sure,' she murmured. 'Very confused.'

He began to stroke her breasts. 'Am I adding to the confusion?'

'Yes,' she moaned, 'you are most definitely adding to the confusion.'

'Ah,' he said, continuing to stroke.

Connie removed his hand. 'You,' she said, 'are turning me into a sex maniac.'

He laughed. 'Have you never been a sex maniac before?'

'Never.'

'Never?' Don turned to face her. 'Not even on your honeymoon?'

'Not even on my honeymoon.'

'Bloody hell! And you've had four kids!'

Connie sighed. 'Lie back and think of England – isn't that how the saying goes?'

'You are *kidding* me, Connie!'

'No, I'm not!'

'Why the hell did you ever marry him?'

When she didn't respond he said, 'What am I going to do with you, Connie McColl?'

'I have a suggestion, but probably not here on the beach!'

Don was noticeably in the same state of arousal as she was. 'I think we should cool our ardour with a quick dip, don't you?'

Connie gazed out to sea. 'I know it *looks* like the Caribbean, but that water will be freezing!'

'The way I feel right now, the colder the better! Come on!'

⚛

It would be their last night. They found a little bistro in which to sample the local seafood, and drank some excellent Chablis.

'I could stay here forever, just like this,' Don commented, holding her hand across the table. 'Just a pity that Morag has the room booked from tomorrow.'

Connie sighed. 'It's time I moved on. This has been a lovely two days, and I shall never forget it.'

Don studied her for a moment. 'Where shall we go next, Connie?'

'*We* are going nowhere, Don. I should get back to Sussex just as soon as I can find a train heading in the right direction.'

'You don't need a train, Connie. I'm heading south. I plan to visit my elder daughter, the one I told you about who lives near Cheltenham? I'm sure she wouldn't mind my having company.'

He'd told her about Katy in some detail. 'They live in a virtual sea of yuppification,' he'd said. 'The latest is they've just installed a hot tub in the back garden in which to poach their visitors. In addition to the swimming pool, of course. And they've got the obligatory farmhouse in the Dordogne, naturally. Real wankers' – sorry, bankers' –lifestyle.'

Connie smiled to herself as she visualised arriving there with Don. (*'Hello, Katy, this is my latest and most ancient paramour!' 'Oh, Daddy, how lovely! Do come in!'*)

Now she removed her hand from his clasp. 'No, Don. It's a sweet thought, but I should be on my own now.'

He looked bewildered. 'Have I upset you?'

Connie laughed. 'On the contrary! I'm having one of the best times of my life – truly!'

'Then why?'

'Because I have to make some decisions and you provide far too many distractions! You've woken up bits of me that have lain dormant for years, but at least I know they're still *there*!'

'Can we wake those bits up again, do you think, when we finish our coffee?'

'I'll give the idea due consideration,' Connie said, draining her cup.

CHAPTER TWENTY-EIGHT

HOMEWARD BOUND

Connie agreed that Don could take her to Glasgow to catch the train. There would be more trains going to more destinations from there and Connie had also long nursed a desire to visit the Glasgow School of Art and see first-hand the works of Charles Rennie Mackintosh. But she felt sad at leaving Arisaig. It might only have been a couple of days but she felt a different person from the dithering Connie who'd first arrived here. And, she hated to admit it, but she felt sad too at parting from Don.

As he took their bags out to the car and Connie was checking that they'd left nothing behind in their love nest, her mobile whined. Connie preferred it when phones rang properly. Anyway, she wasn't going to answer it; they, whoever they were, could leave a message and she'd get back to them. But she couldn't resist checking.

'Hey, Connie!' said the voicemail. 'Harry and Nyree here! We just wondered how you were and *where* you were. It would be great to speak to you.'

Harry and Nyree! Connie suddenly yearned to hear those young sing-song voices again. Why hadn't she thought to call them before now? They must indeed have wondered what she'd got up to. Oh boy, wouldn't they just *love* this!

'Hello? Harry, hi! I'm so glad you called – it's really good to hear from you.'

'Great to talk to you too, Connie. We wondered how you're getting along?'

'Oh, I'm fine. What about you two – where are you now?'

'We're hunky-dory. Been all the way up to John o'Groats. It was awesome, really beautiful. We've got bikes now and we're heading south again – somewhere near Perth at the moment.'

In the background Connie could hear Nyree's urgent whisper. '*Ask* her! Where is she?'

She knew what was coming.

'What about *you*, Connie? You home yet? How did you get on with, you know, what's-his-name?' They remembered his name perfectly well. Giggles and more whispering. ('*Don Juan!* from Nyree in the background.) 'Yeah, Don, the one who gave you the lift?'

'Well, strangely enough, I'm still with him. In Arisaig, on the west coast of Scotland, just at the moment.'

There was a moment's silence. 'Oh, wow! I mean that's *great*, isn't it? You still being together, I mean. *Jeez!* An audible 'Wow!' from Nyree in the background.

'Well, yes. But we don't plan to be together much longer, Harry. Anyway, you and Nyree, what are your plans?'

'We're planning on heading south. Getting some work in the south or south-east, hopefully, before we head for France in the middle of October.'

'Well, we must organise to meet. I'd love to see you again.'

'We'll be in touch, I promise you. And, you know what? We're even thinking of tying the knot when we get back home. How about *that*!'

'That's wonderful! Congratulations, you two!' Connie said, laughing.

'Perhaps you could make your next walkabout Down Under, and come to our wedding! We've got a lot of catching up to do. Sounds like you certainly got those wings of yours stretched!'

'Ready for take-off,' said Connie.

As they drove back towards Fort William the sky darkened, the heavens opened, and everything became clouded in grey mist. Connie could barely decipher Loch Shiel and the monument. Nevertheless, one way or the other this was a monumental trip, and this very special part of the Highlands would forever occupy a piece of Connie's heart.

'I like it like this,' she said. 'It's atmospheric. I can imagine all those clans killing each other off in the doom and gloom.'

And the top of Ben Nevis was well and truly hidden, as Don forecast, when they headed towards Glencoe.

'This,' Don informed her, 'is where the Campbells butchered the MacDonalds, who'd given them hospitality. To this day there's bad feeling between these two clans.'

The rain was torrential now, the mist rolling down the hillsides, and Connie could well imagine scenes of carnage in this gloomy glorious glen. Then it eased off a little as they got to the Trossachs and skirted the side of Loch Lomond, so Connie could see the beauty of the bonny banks.

As they approached Glasgow's grey urban sprawl, Connie didn't find the grey skies quite so appealing. Back to buses and trucks and traffic lights; streets of terraces and semis, blocks of high-rise flats.

Everything was grey. Even the cars seemed to be silver or dark-coloured until there, in a street of rather dreary semis, a little patch of bright red caught Connie's eye.

'Stop!' she ordered Don. 'Can you pull in somewhere, please?'

'What the—?'

'*Please*, Don!'

He grunted as he pulled off into a side street. 'What could you possibly want to look at round here?'

As they got out of the car Connie took him by the hand and led him back round the corner.

'Look!' she said.

'What?'

'That little red Ford!'

Don sighed with exasperation. 'It's just a Ka for sale. What's so special about it?'

'The notice on the window says "For sale – £500". I want to look at it, Don.'

'You're not thinking of buying another old banger, are you? Who the hell would rescue you next time you break down? It's even older than Kermit!'

'It looks immaculate.'

Connie walked round it several times, peering into the windows, while Don squinted in, hoping to read the mileage. It was bright crimson, pristine, no bumps or dents. 'I expect it's had a re-spray,' Don said dismissively.

'I'm going to the door,' she said.

'You're nuts!'

She ignored him and walked up the path of the neat little garden and rang the doorbell. As she waited she looked at the well-weeded rose beds.

The door opened a couple of inches and an old man looked out, keeping the chain on.

'Excuse me,' Connie asked, 'is that your Ford Ka out there for sale?'

'Oh, aye, indeed it is.' The old man removed the chain and opened the door fully.

'Would it be possible to have a good look at it, please?'

'Aye, I'll just go get the key.' He shuffled back inside and reappeared a couple of minutes later waving the key. Connie noted his neat collar and tie, V-neck jumper, cords and carpet slippers. He must, she reckoned, be nearly ninety.

'How many owners has it had?' Don asked, taking the key from Connie and opening the door.

The old man looked confused. 'Owners?'

'Yes,' Don said patiently. 'How many people owned this car before you?'

'Oh, I see. Well, nobody did. I've had it from new.'

Don was studying the dial. 'This mileage seems very low.'

'Well, we didn't use it that much,' said the old man. 'When Maggie was alive we'd maybe take it out for a run at weekends. We went to Dundee once. And we'd go to Tesco once a week, of course.'

'And why are you selling it now?' Connie asked.

'Well, to be truthful, my eyesight's not what it was and I'm not feeling safe to drive any more. I'm ninety-two, you see. But I'll be that sad to see her go! We called her Rosy because she was the exact colour of the Loving Memory rose in the garden.'

'Rosy!' Connie repeated. 'I *love* that!'

'I only put that sign on the windscreen this afternoon,' the man said. 'I didn't think it would sell so quickly. Would you like to come in? I can show you its service history and everything.'

'Thanks, I'd *love* to come in,' Connie said.

The old man looked from one to the other, sensing discord. 'I'm Jim McWhirter,' he said, holding out his hand to Connie.

'And I'm Connie McColl,' she said, shaking it. 'And this is my friend, Don Robertson, who's giving me a lift to the station – who *was* giving me a lift to the station, I should say.'

'Oh, I see,' said Jim, looking doubtfully at Don who, sighing, followed her indoors.

'I'll just go put the kettle on,' he added, as he showed them into his tidy little lounge. 'And I'll dig out all the car stuff.'

With that he disappeared and they could hear the sound of a kettle being filled and then the opening and closing of drawers.

'Are you seriously planning to buy that?' Don asked.

'Yes, I am,' Connie replied, a little irritated at Don's lack of enthusiasm, but more and more convinced that this was meant to be – this little red car that had caught her eye, that had only been up for sale for one afternoon, and was the colour of a Loving Memory rose. She'd had a Loving Memory rose in her own garden years ago, before the move. And, roses again! She thought fondly of Kath's tattoo and Jeannie's bouquets.

'So, why didn't you buy Archie's yellow Fiat then?'

'I wasn't ready to replace Kermit straight away, and I didn't think I'd find any car for five hundred pounds.'

'Well, you get what you pay for,' Don said.

'This feels right.' Connie looked round and lowered her voice. 'Do you see this room, how clean and tidy it is? Did you not notice those rose beds out in the front garden? Why should his car be any different?'

At this point Mr McWhirter reappeared with a file of papers, which he handed to Connie.

'Have a look through that now, while I make the tea,' he said. He established how they liked their tea and came back again a few minutes later with hot mugs and a plate of ginger biscuits.

Connie had found receipts for everything that had ever been done, and the car hadn't needed much work because Jim had had it fully serviced every year, even when he'd only done three or four thousand miles. It had new tyres and it had a year's MOT.

'And what nice tea!' she exclaimed.

Jim beamed. 'Everyone says that. It's because I make it the old-fashioned way, you see, with tea leaves.'

He even made proper tea!

'You'll want to take it for a wee drive,' Mr McWhirter stated. 'You could take it round the block where there's not much traffic, and then you could put your foot down on that road beside the park.'

'You'll probably still manage to get lost,' Don remarked. 'Shall I come with you?'

'No, I won't get lost. But I could do with your opinion of it when it's running.'

A few minutes later the little car purred into life and Connie found her easy to drive. 'Don't forget, I'm used to Fords,' she reminded Don as they turned the first corner.

Don was still amazed at the low mileage on the dial which, he now conceded, was very likely genuine.

'More tea?' Jim McWhirter asked on their return.

'No thanks, Mr McWhirter. But I would very much like to buy Rosy, so I'll need to arrange the tax and insurance.' She fumbled in her bag, and looked at her watch. 'Can I pay a deposit and come back tomorrow morning?'

'Och, I'm not needing a deposit,' said Jim McWhirter.

'I insist,' Connie said, handing him fifty pounds from the unspent roll of notes Archie had given her.

'Well, that's very kind. I'll just come out now and take that sign off the windscreen.'

There would be one more night together.

'We'll stay at Blythswood Square,' Don insisted. 'My treat.'

And, as they checked into the luxurious room in the iconic hotel, he added, 'You won't find any sand in the sheets round here!'

'Pity,' said Connie. She loved the luxury, but her heart still hankered for their special room in Arisaig.

Later they wandered down Sauchiehall Street and opted to eat in a multinational restaurant which served food from every corner of the globe, and as much of it as you could eat. Don seemed to have an enormous capacity for worldwide cuisine, but Connie was forced to give up after moderate portions of India, Italy and

Mexico. And, afterwards, they drank coffee and liqueurs in the sumptuous hotel bar.

'Here's to you, Connie,' Don said, raising his brandy goblet. 'And to your new car. And, I hate to admit it, but I think you've got a winner there.'

Connie grinned. 'I think so too. And thanks, Don, for everything.'

'Why are you thanking me? I've enjoyed every single minute we've been together. Truly, Connie.'

'Me, too.'

'And now?' He leaned towards her and took her hand. 'Where will you go now?'

Connie had been considering exactly that all evening. 'I'm on my way back home,' she said, 'but I'm not in a hurry.'

'So, you'll go back to Sussex?'

'Eventually.'

'Hmm. Have you come to any kind of decision?'

'Oh, I definitely have,' Connie replied. 'But right now I think it's high time we went to bed.'

After they'd made love in the morning, Connie, with ripples of pleasure coursing through her body, knew she'd never forget these past few days. Then she wondered how long it would have taken her to become exhausted by it all because she was, after all, sixty-six. But would she ever tire of this man? Would she ever develop the proverbial headache? *Not tonight, darling.* She had no idea and she certainly wasn't going to hang around to find out. The whole point of an affair such as this was that it should never become stale.

After an enormous Scottish breakfast Connie found a bank, withdrew some extra cash and organised her road tax and insurance. They even managed to fit in a visit to the Willow Tea Rooms and the Glasgow School of Art to admire Mackintosh's beautiful architecture and Art Deco designs. But, all the time, her thoughts kept returning to the little red car, feeling more and more confident that Rosy would be a worthy successor to Kermit.

She liked Glasgow too, with its impressive buildings, great shops and restaurants, and the friendliness of the people. She didn't even notice the rain, and only wished she could stay longer. When her life was settled she'd come back and explore the city much more thoroughly.

It was nearly two o'clock before they got back to Jim McWhirter and Rosy.

'I hope you'll be as happy with it as we were,' he said, handing her the key and looking suspiciously moist-eyed.

'I'm quite sure I shall be, Mr McWhirter,' said Connie, and kissed him on the cheek. What a lovely old man!

She drove the Ka round the corner into the side street where Don had parked, and there followed some ten minutes of transferring Connie's belongings from the boot of the Mercedes.

Don consulted his watch. 'How far are you planning to go this afternoon, and have you decided on which route you're taking?'

'Well, I'd like to keep off motorways,' Connie said, digging out her map, 'and I'm in no hurry.'

'Will this help?' Don produced a box from the boot of his car. 'I bought this for my younger daughter's birthday, but I've plenty of time to get another one.'

'Oh, Don!' Connie gasped, as she looked at the satnav.

'From what you told me,' Don said, 'I gather you're pretty good at getting lost.'

'I'm improving all the time,' Connie laughed. 'And this will be invaluable, but please let me pay you.'

'Don't be ridiculous. It's a gift from me to you, and perhaps it'll help you find your way back to me. If you ever need to.'

She put her arms round him. 'Thank you, Don. This is one of the best presents I've ever had.' And she realised that, in spite of her initial reservations, this unexpected man had come along at exactly the right time in every sense.

'Let me set it up for you,' he said, 'and show you how to enter the address you want.' After he'd explained the basics he asked, 'Why don't I follow you for a few miles just to make sure you're OK?'

'I'll be fine, Don.'

'I don't doubt that. OK then, why don't we take a stroll in that park we passed when you were doing your trial run? Before you go...?' He looked at her imploringly.

'That would be nice.'

She was in no hurry. She'd make her way south and stop when she was tired. She had a yearning to see Jeannie again, to tell her of her decision. But she'd have that stroll first.

The park had well-tended flowerbeds and a pond. Apart from a couple of kids who whizzed past them on skateboards, there were few people around and they found a bench beside the pond from which to watch the ducks, who waddled towards them hopefully.

'Sorry, we've no bread,' Connie said to them.

'You're not sorry about anything else, are you?' Don asked, putting his arm round Connie's shoulders.

'Not at all,' she replied. 'But I did lie to you about my age, you know. I'm sixty-six.' She didn't dare look at him.

'Do you mean to tell me I've been cradle-snatched?' he asked.

'I'm afraid so,' she said ruefully.

'Don't you know that some men prefer older ladies, and that they often make the best lovers?'

'Or that we're bloody grateful!' she added, and they both burst out laughing.

'And now,' he said sadly, 'we've come to the parting of the ways.'

'We've had a lovely few days, Don. Thank you.'

'Nothing to thank me for,' he said, stroking her knee. 'I've told you before – if I hadn't liked you I'd have put you on the train in Inverness.'

'Well, I'm glad you didn't.'

'So am I. And, Connie, promise me that you'll call me if you ever need me…'

'I will,' she replied. 'But I think you came along at my hour of greatest need.'

'Well, you never know.'

'No, you never know.'

They stood up and he put both arms round her. 'It wasn't just sex, you know, Connie.'

'I know,' she said. 'I've enjoyed our time together more than I can say. And I really hope that eventually you find some lucky lady to settle down with – third time lucky and all that!'

He kissed her gently.

She smiled. 'Goodbye, Don.'

He released her from his grip. 'Goodbye, Connie McColl.'

She turned and walked quickly away from him to where she'd parked her little car, hoping he wouldn't see the tears in her eyes.

CHAPTER TWENTY-NINE

HELPING HAND

Connie was heading south-east, along B roads, in watery late-afternoon sunshine. This was the Scottish Borders region again, and she bypassed signs for Peebles and Galashiels before crossing the River Tweed in the early evening. For the first few miles Connie had replied to the satnav in the same way as she'd initially done with other disembodied voices, until it dawned on her that there really wasn't much point in saying 'thank you', or 'Sorry, I missed that turning.' She could recall, years ago, saying 'thank you' to an ATM as she withdrew her notes, and the sniggering of the youngster behind her. The only problem now was that the satnav lady kept ordering her back to motorways, which Connie was trying to avoid.

There were still swathes of wild montbretia here and there, flowering by the wayside, heralding the beginning of a coppery autumn glow. Summer was ending. Her journey must end soon too. She missed her family, particularly the grandchildren, and hoped they hadn't forgotten her. Thomas wouldn't, but what about Joshua? She tried to remember how a three-year-old's mind functioned. How quickly did they forget? Would he give her the cold shoulder like Hector, their old cat, had? It was a long time ago now, but Hector would give them a chilly stare whenever they returned from holiday, eager to make a fuss of him. 'Did you miss us, Hector?' the kids would ask as they tried to stroke him. Hector would arch his back, lift his tail straight up in the air, and march away icily. His body language was clear. *How could you have gone and left me?* He'd keep his distance for several days, deeply offended, until eventually the creature comforts of being constantly stroked on someone's knee, and sleeping on everyone's beds at night, along with his favourite tuna dinner, won the day. But he'd made his displeasure known. 'Poor old Hector!' they'd say the following summer, as off they went again, leaving him to the mercy of some obliging neighbour. Surely the boys wouldn't be like *that?* Then again, perhaps everyone would be like that.

She'd left Scotland behind, but she would come back again. Now she was in Northumberland she'd been thinking about Jeannie, ever since she'd passed signs for the intriguing-sounding villages of Little Dancer and Great Dancer. Connie wondered if this might be some sort of message. She'd like to see Jeannie again; Jeannie had advised her not to give up on her marriage and Connie wanted her to know that she'd reached a decision.

Connie pulled into a layby and dug out her phone. If she answers, I'll ask if I can pop in to see her. If she's out, that means that it wouldn't have been such a good idea anyway.

Jeannie answered.

'Oh, Connie, I've thought about you such a lot!'

'I've got lots to tell you,' Connie said.

'Good things?'

Connie was aware of a frailty in Jeannie's voice. 'Yes, lots of good things. But I'm heading in your direction right now and wondered if it would be possible to pop in for a little while?'

There was a slight hesitation before Jeannie replied, 'Yes, I'd like that very much.'

'Are you sure?'

'I'm absolutely sure.'

When the door opened, Connie tried not to gasp. Her little friend had shrunk to skeletal proportions in the space of a couple of weeks, and there hadn't been much of her in the first place. But it was the greyness of her complexion that really shook Connie.

'I'm so glad you were able to come,' Jeannie said, as Connie bent to hug her gently, terrified she'd break one of these tiny bird-like bones, and trying not to show how shocked she was.

'I've brought you some Scottish heather honey,' Connie said, 'and a few wee miniatures of whisky.'

'Thank you, Connie.' As she entered the sitting room, Jeannie turned and said, 'You'll probably gather I haven't been too well.'

'I'm so sorry. What's been the problem?'

'Well, I might as well tell you. I've had cancer for some time, since long before I met you, and it's accelerated recently.'

'Oh, Jeannie…'

'And I'm driving my doctor mad. He's wanted me to have treatment for months, but I've refused. Can you imagine – chemo at my age? Do I want to look in the mirror and see a bald old coot? Just for the sake of a few extra, not very pleasant, months?'

'Sit down, Jeannie!' Connie ordered. 'Let me put the kettle on.'

'Oh, would you mind? And after that long drive you've had!' But she seemed grateful to sink into the chair.

Connie was glad of a few moments in the kitchen to compose herself at the sight of her friend virtually disappearing in front of her eyes. Even the walk to the door had clearly exhausted her. She made tea and, remembering Jeannie didn't have mugs, set out the tray with the elegant china cups and saucers.

As she sat down and watched Jeannie take her first shaky sip, Connie said, 'Tell me about all this.'

Jeannie rolled her eyes. 'It's so damn tiresome,' she said. 'It started in the breast and now it's gone all over the place, and I just wish it would get on with it.' She smiled. 'Don't look so shocked, Connie – I'm nearly ninety and I've had a lovely life.'

'But ninety's not that old these days...'

'Of course it's old! It's ancient! Don't go telling me ninety's the new seventy, or some other rubbish! And all my friends have gone now, so it's lonely at times. I don't mind dying one bit, so long as I don't have to go into a hospital or a hospice. I know they're wonderful places, but what I really want is to drift off right here, in my own little flat. Anyway, that's more than enough about me. Now, tell me how you've been getting on.'

Connie told her, with as much detail as she could remember, and was pleased to see Jeannie laugh at some of her escapades, particularly tickled by the bit about being rescued by Don and her sexual awakening during the tour of western Scotland.

'I don't want to shock you,' Connie said, 'but I've never had sex like it!'

Jeannie squealed with laughter. 'Good for you! And not before time! He sounds lovely. What have you done with him?'

'Yes, he was lovely, but a bit of a ladies' man. I left him in Glasgow.'

'Did you fall in love with him, just a teeny bit?'

'Not really. Well, a *very* teeny bit! And I loved feeling alive again, truly alive. I only wanted to feel that I might still be passably attractive to the opposite sex because, before I left home, I was feeling completely invisible. And I'd no idea sex could be like that! Can you *imagine* – after forty-one years of marriage and four kids.'

'I never had the marriage or the kids, Connie, but I had the sex, and the love to go with it. Seems to me you never get it all.'

Connie drained her cup. 'Well, some people seem to.'

Jeannie smiled. 'But not you and I.'

'More tea?'

'Wouldn't you prefer gin? Or one of those whiskies? I've several bottles of gin in the cupboard, which I'm not going to be able to do justice to, so why don't we make a start now?'

'I'm driving – usual story.'

'Where are you going now?'

There was something uncannily familiar about this conversation, Connie thought.

'Well, I'm heading south,' she said vaguely.

'Home, do you mean?'

'Well, I won't make it home by tonight,' Connie replied, knowing that the full length of England lay ahead. She planned to visit Freddy again as well, but that would be tomorrow.

'Then why not stay here?'

'Don't tell me: you have all these meals in your freezer! Haven't we had this conversation before, Jeannie?'

'We have, and we're having it again. But I'm not much company these days. I go to bed early with a thousand and one pills and, anyway, it can't be very comfortable for you on that sofa.'

There was such sadness in her voice that Connie immediately said, 'I can make myself very comfortable in here, and I'd be more than happy to have a quiet night and catch up with my reading, and watching TV.'

'Are you sure?' There was no disguising the delight in Jeannie's voice.

'Of course I'm sure. Now, shall I get us those drinks?'

Later they got through a bottle of red wine. That is, Jeannie took tiny sips from one glass, and Connie demolished the rest. She'd found some pasta meals in the freezer, along with garlic bread, and set the table for supper.

Jeannie could only manage a minuscule portion of the bread, and Connie realised she was no longer able to eat.

'I don't want to be sick all night,' Jeannie explained cheerfully.

Connie, feeling decidedly squiffy after the gin and the wine, wandered out to Rosy and extracted the Miracle and the mat from her boot. On her return, she found that Jeannie had dozed off in the chair.

What do I do now? she wondered. Leave her be, or wake her up and help her to bed? As if on cue, Jeannie suddenly opened her eyes and glared at Connie, shouting, 'And who the hell are *you*?'

Connie was nonplussed for a moment, before picking up both of Jeannie's hands in hers. 'I'm Connie, remember?'

There was a short silence while Jeannie appeared to re-focus. 'Of course you're Connie,' she whispered, 'of course you are.'

'And it's time you went to bed. Let me help you.'

'Thanks, dear, but I can still manage. You don't mind if I do leave you now, though?' The old lady got up shakily and headed towards her bedroom. She turned. 'Goodnight, my dear. And I can't tell you how much your visit means to me.'

When Jeannie was safely in her bedroom with the door closed, Connie put her head in her hands and wept for her poor friend.

Later on, Connie watched snippets of television while attempting a sketch of Don. She'd taken some photos in Arisaig, but they didn't quite catch his expression, his roguish charm. Then, feeling weary, she laid the mat and the Miracle on the floor, instead of risking a crick in her neck on the sofa, and slept well. She woke at about six and lay listening to the sounds of early morning traffic, watching the dust motes dance in the beam of light where the curtains didn't quite meet. The place needed cleaning. She wondered if Jeannie noticed, or cared. Who would do the cleaning? Did Jeannie have any kind of home help? Probably not, and she was rapidly losing the battle to cope on her own.

Jeannie's doctor was right. She should be in some sort of care. And then Connie thought about dying in a geriatric ward somewhere, surrounded by people she didn't know, with not even the visiting hour to look forward to. Because who would visit Jeannie now? She had no family that Connie knew of, and she herself had said that she'd outlived all her friends.

I can't leave her, Connie thought, unless she's desperate to be on her own. She can't have very long and she wants to die in this little flat with the posters on the walls to remind her of happy days, and the roses on the table to remind her of her lover. Surely I could stay a little longer? Perhaps a nurse might call in daily if she becomes completely bedridden? And, let's face it, she's so tiny and frail that I could easily carry her if I have to. And everyone at home has coped perfectly well without me for weeks now, because nobody's indispensable. Not even me. Not in Sussex anyway, but I'm needed here. And I'll start by giving this place a good clean and washing that window.

At eight o'clock the bedroom door opened and Jeannie emerged, heading for the bathroom next door while she steadied herself against the wall with her hand. Connie watched her anxiously, but decided not to interfere. In the kitchen, she looked around Jeannie's meagre supplies: half a small loaf, out of date by three days, two mouldy carrots, a pint of milk and a black banana. Dear lord, she'd need to do some shopping straight away.

'Connie?' Jeannie, still in her nightie, was standing in the lounge, looking considerably perkier than she had last night.

'Good morning, Jeannie. How did you sleep?'

'Not too bad – off and on. But so nice to know that someone was here.'

'I was just about to make some tea,' Connie said.

'I should be—'

'No, you shouldn't! Sit down!'

When Connie appeared with the tea tray a few minutes later she asked Jeannie, 'What exactly have you been eating?'

Jeannie pulled a face. 'Oh, I don't eat much. Just a bit of toast now and again. Oh, and sometimes I have a Cup-a-Soup. They're very nice, you know.'

Connie sighed. 'Your loaf's out of date, and you need some serious nourishment. Who does your shopping for you?'

'Well, Audrey next door's quite good. She knocks on the door once a week or so, and I ask her to get me bread, milk, that sort of thing. I'm fine, really.'

'No, you're not fine. I shall go out later and get some groceries for you. Didn't I pass a supermarket on the way here?'

'That would be Sainsbury's. But I can manage fine, and I don't want to delay you when you have such a long journey ahead of you.'

Connie sipped her tea. 'I'm not planning on going anywhere.'

'Whatever do you mean?' Jeannie's eyes widened.

'I'm staying right here.'

'Don't be ridiculous! Why would you do that?'

'Because nobody on this planet needs me as much as you do right now. And because I *want* to stay.'

'For how long?' Jeannie appeared completely confused.

Difficult one to answer, Connie thought, then said, 'For as long as you'll have me.'

'I can't have you doing this, Connie. Dr Ryan's right; I should go into some sort of care. It's very selfish of me to expect other people—'

'It's not selfish,' Connie interrupted. 'It's *exactly* how I'd feel. You and I are very independent.'

'But what about your family?'

'What about them? I've been away for weeks and they're all getting on perfectly OK, as I knew they would.'

'And what about your husband? What was his name again – Roger?'

'Yes, Roger. Roger's inconvenienced by my absence, of course, but I hardly think he's weeping, wailing or gnashing his teeth for my return. So, I'm staying right here.'

'Oh, Connie!' This time Jeannie wept happy tears.

CHAPTER THIRTY

TEAMWORK

They'd established a routine of sorts in the four days since Connie's arrival. She'd found Sainsbury's; she'd stocked up on things she hoped were nourishing and that might tempt Jeannie's tiny appetite. She dusted, vaccumed, changed and laundered Jeannie's bedlinen. And all the time Jeannie protested. 'Connie, I can't have you doing all this!' 'Connie, there's no need to iron the sheets!' 'Connie, you must be bored witless!'

Connie ignored her. 'Will you please be quiet? You're supposed to be an invalid!' And Jeannie had gratefully acquiesced.

But although Connie made soups and a casserole, Jeannie ate almost nothing and, on the fourth day, she decided to stay in bed. Connie sat with her, read out snippets of interest from the newspaper, and told her more about her family.

'Will you go back?' Jeannie asked.

'Oh yes, I must go back. I need to face the music.'

'Don't settle for a second-rate life, Connie.'

'I won't.'

'Did I tell you it's my birthday next week?'

'No, you didn't.'

'I'll be ninety.'

'I know. We must celebrate,' Connie said.

'If I'm still here I'd like you to get me some champagne. I used to drink champagne all the time.'

'You shall have champagne.'

'Now, in the meantime there's one or two things I need to wind up so I wonder if you could ring Huw Davies – he's my solicitor. You'll find his number in the book over there.'

The following day there were three visitors. The first was Huw Davies, the solicitor, ruddy-faced, Welsh and a large, untidy sort of a man, but absolutely charming. He beamed at Connie as he emerged from the bedroom, his tie askew and his briefcase open.

'Well, we've sorted out a few things about her will and all that. She should have done this years ago. I'll need to call again in a few days, Mrs er…'

'Connie.'

'Oh, right, Connie. And it might be an idea if I had your particulars, please.' He cleared his throat. 'Just in case I need to contact you about anything: the funeral, for instance. You may want to come to the funeral?'

'I most definitely will.'

The next visitor was the doctor. Dr Ryan was young and brisk, and he tut-tutted as he emerged from Jeannie's bedroom. 'She should be in the hospice, you know,' he informed Connie as he packed away his things. 'It's a lovely place and she'd get first-class treatment.'

'I know she would,' Connie said, 'but she wants to pass away here.'

He looked around, but said nothing for a minute. 'I under-stand you'll be looking after her?'

'Correct.'

'Well, that's very noble of you but it's going to become more difficult. She's going downhill fast and she's becoming inconti-nent, as no doubt you're aware. I've arranged for a commode to be delivered this afternoon, so hopefully that may help.'

'I'll do my best, doctor. And she hardly eats, you know, so there can't be much to come out.'

'Well, the nurse will call each morning to give her a jab, and I've already increased the dosage of the other painkillers.'

'She never complains,' Connie said. 'I've heard her moan to herself, but she never complains.'

The third visitor knocked on the door in the middle of the afternoon; a tall, formidable-looking woman, wearing a long floral dress and a wide-brimmed sun hat.

She looked at Connie with some surprise. 'Oh, good!' she ex-claimed. 'She's decided to get a home help at long last! I've been nagging her for months, you know. Do you do her shopping as well? I do hope so! I can now be relieved at last of my neighbourly duties.'

'I'm Jeannie's friend,' Connie replied. 'And I shall be doing everything from now on.'

'Oh, how lovely that she thinks of you as a *friend*! Makes your job so much easier, I'm sure! Anyway, I must be off, but do tell her that Audrey called and send her my best.'

'Oh, I will,' said Connie, noticing with some satisfaction that the woman's dress was caught up in her knickers at the back as she walked away.

❊

By the end of the week Connie knew that Jeannie wouldn't be getting out of bed again. She slept a lot and, on one occasion, she woke up and said, 'Oh, hello, Emma! I thought you were dead!' At other times she was still completely lucid.

'Connie,' she said on one occasion, 'don't forget the champagne for my birthday, will you? And do you know what else I'd like? I'd like a packet of fags. I used to smoke like a chimney – all us girls did.'

'Do you think that's a good idea?' Connie was aware of the wheezing in her lungs. Then, seeing Jeannie becoming agitated, she added, 'Yes, of course, I'll get you some cigarettes.'

The following morning Jeannie had soiled the bed and, as Connie grappled with the laundry, the nurse appeared for her morning visit, complete with syringe and incontinence pads. 'Comes to us all!' she said cheerfully.

Jeannie was now deteriorating very quickly, and most of the time she was in a world of her own. And then there was the awful moaning when her pain became unbearable, and which often went on all night. Connie felt lucky if she got more than a couple of hours' sleep at a time, and often that was all she got. She'd hold Jeannie's hand, wipe her brow with a cool cloth, and wished she knew what else to do. And Connie could feel her own eyes welling up, feeling she should be doing more, but what? She'd given up trying to get Jeannie to eat, but kept her as hydrated as possible with sips of water. She begged the doctor for more painkillers but was told that Jeannie was already on the maximum dosage of morphine. So what, Connie wondered, would happen if she exceeded the dose? Would she die? Would that be so terrible?

But Jeannie wanted to be ninety and, somehow or the other, Connie wanted her to achieve her aim. She'd have surely done this for her own mother, who'd been denied the chance of becoming thirty, never mind ninety. And she began to think of Jeannie as the mother she hardly remembered, as she struggled daily with the commode, the washing, the worrying and the lack of sleep.

The roses, which had been delivered on the first of September, were still looking fresh and Connie transported them through to Jeannie's bedside, at an angle where she'd be able to see them. Roses! Red roses! And then it came to her. *Kath!* Kath would know what she should do. Hadn't Kath worked as a carer? Surely Kath would have some tips on how to care for the dying, and manage the pain.

Please be at home, Kath, she thought as she looked round for her phone. Please don't be on holiday or something. Or visiting that wayward son of yours.

Kath was at home.

'Bleedin' hell, Connie! Where are you now?'

'Listen carefully, Kath, and I'll tell you.' Connie then proceeded to give her a summary of the past few days: Jeannie's pain, the endless laundry, the lack of sleep. 'And I really just need some advice, Kath.'

'Connie, she should be in hospital!'

'I know that, but she wants to die at home. And I'm going to see that she does. But it's hard going, Kath, and I desperately want to do the right thing. Not only that, she's ninety in a few days' time and she's asking for champagne, and a *cigarette*! Would that be so wrong?'

Kath snorted. 'Of course it wouldn't be wrong! Good luck to her! But Connie, I'm worried about you. You *sound* knackered.'

'Oh, I'm fine, really.' Connie tried to keep the wobble out of her voice. 'Sorry, Kath, I'm just a bit over-emotional through lack of sleep. Pay no attention to me!'

Kath was silent for a moment. Then she said, 'Know what, Connie? I'm coming up to help you. *Newcastle*, did you say?'

'But, Kath—'

'No buts! You need help, and I like helping. I'm coming, and that's that. I'll get a bus from here first thing in the morning, but I'll need picking up from the bus depot at your end.'

'Kath, I didn't mean for you to—'

'I know, I know. But I'm coming, OK? I'll phone you in the morning when I know the bus times.'

'I don't know how to thank you.'

'Aw, sod off, Connie! Ain't that what mates are for?'

Connie felt an enormous wave of relief wash over her worried body. What a gem Kath was! After all, she didn't know Connie that well, and she didn't know Jeannie at all. Here, surely, was a true friend.

CHAPTER THIRTY-ONE

DAUGHTERS' DECISIONS

From: Diana McColl

To: Connie McColl

Hi, Mum,

I've lost track of where you might be, but rather hope you're on the way home – if only because I'm busting a gut to know what you've been up to!

I'm moving in with Mark this weekend, so everything is in a state of chaos. And don't forget the bed is still available here for any time you want to use it.

I really love this guy – he's lovely and I think you'll like him. He's certainly fascinated by *you*!

Not much in the way of family news: Tess has finally decided to do two night shifts nursing a week, so that lets you off the hook for babysitting (poor old Nick!) and Lou's little horror has finally stopped squalling all night and they're all a bit better tempered as a result. Dad says the woman next door is trying to woo him with coffee and walnut cake! Did you know he was crazy about coffee and walnut cake – if not the woman next door?

Hope all is well with you, Mum, and I'm longing to see you again. We all are.

Look after yourself, and come home soon.

Much love,

Di xxxx

Di's new paramour sounded nice. Connie hoped that her daughter was doing the right thing, and felt incredibly guilty that she hadn't been around to talk things over. But, hey, Di was forty! She was quite old enough to make up her own mind! But, still… perhaps she should have been around… everyone needs their mum from time to time. Not that *she'd* had that choice. Nevertheless it might be time to give them some idea of when she might be coming home.

From: Connie McColl

To: Roger, Di, Nick, Lou

Hi, Everyone!

You must all be wondering if I'm ever coming home, and I am, but not just yet. In fact I'm not sure when, so bear with me. I am on the way back but have stopped off to help a friend in need, so it could be a few weeks yet.

Thanks for your email, Di – your new man sounds nice and I look forward to meeting him.

It certainly sounds as if you're all getting along just fine and, to a certain extent, sorted yourselves out too.

And, Tess, two night shifts a week seem much more suitable than day shifts. And probably better paid.

I'm so pleased little Charlotte's colic seems be on the wane at long last!

And yes, Roger, I have finally sorted myself out. Every mile of this trip has opened up my eyes and my heart. We all need to do that sometimes.

With much love to you all.

Xxxxxxx

﷽

At last, Lou thought, there was some prospect that her mother might finally be heading back. Hopefully she'd sorted herself out and would be content to be at home and enjoy her family, like most women of her age. But perhaps she, Lou, *had* been a bit hard on her and, much as she hated to admit it, her father wasn't the easiest person to get along with.

From: Louise Morrison
To: Connie McColl
Hi, Mum,

Sorry if I've been sounding off a bit in my last few emails. I was in a bit of a 'low', but shouldn't have taken it out on you. Things have improved greatly since Charlotte's now sleeping soundly through the night (Hallelujah, fingers crossed and all that!!), and we've all caught up on our shut-eye and are a lot less tetchy. And I think she's going to be walking soon!

I suppose there's no point in asking the exact day/week you might be planning to get back now that you're such a free spirit. But it's good to know that you are on your way back.

Apparently Tess has given up on the idea of working during the day and is going to do a couple of nights instead. I wonder why she didn't think of that in the first place? Probably because you were available so much.

I realise I often ask a lot of you, Mum, and I'm sorry. I miss you so much. I love Andy to bits but you know what he's like: everything's a joke and he doesn't listen. I'm told that most men don't, so perhaps he's not so unusual. And I realise Dad wasn't all that easy to live with either. I go over a couple of times a week but he makes no effort to keep the place tidy and wouldn't dream of saying 'thank you', even though I do his laundry and everything. Not that he's ever at home to say anything.

I'm so looking forward to seeing you, and soon, I hope, although I'm still not sure why you took off in the first place. Never mind!

Lots of love,

Lou xxxx

CHAPTER THIRTY-TWO

THE BIRTHDAY PARTY

'Blimey!' Kath said as she laid down her small suitcase and looked round Jeannie's lounge. 'It's like going into a bleedin' theatre!'

'She was a dancer,' Connie explained. 'She danced all over the world. And she was really lovely – just look at some of these pictures.'

'Well, sounds like she's going to be dancing with death shortly. When did you say this birthday of hers is?'

'In three days' time, and I honestly don't know if she'll make it or not as she's so weak. She's asleep now, but I'll take you in there as soon as she wakes up. Now, what can I get you?'

Kath glanced at her watch. 'I suppose it's a bit early for gin, but that was a long bleedin' journey with the bus stopping everywhere.'

Connie laughed. 'You shall have gin! But I don't have orange, I'm afraid, so it'll have to be tonic.'

'Beggars can't be choosers,' Kath said, plonking herself in an armchair. 'How are you coping with the toilet and all that?'

'Well, she's light as a feather, and I've been doing my best to get her to the commode on time. But the nurse has given me some incontinence pads now, so there's not so many accidents. I've actually had to go out and get some extra sheets.'

'Oh, Connie! You're a star! But I'm here now, so no worries, we can do this together!'

Connie had, of course, worried about leaving Jeannie for the half hour it had taken to collect Kath; she'd worried about finding the bus station and she worried about where Kath was going to sleep. But Kath assured her she'd be fine on the sofa. All Connie could feel now was relief. Someone to share the responsibility with, someone to talk to, someone to laugh with. Because here was Kath, with her hennaed hair, her bejewelled kaftan and her purple trousers, happily slurping a gin and tonic.

Just then a little voice called out from the bedroom. 'She's awake,' Connie said.

Kath put down her glass. 'She might have waited till I finished me gin!'

The room was warm and Jeannie lay propped up on pillows, covered only by a sheet, her emaciated body cruelly outlined.

'Blimey!' said Kath matter-of-factly.

'Jeannie, this is —'

'PETRONELLA!' Jeannie's eyes lit up. 'Oh, I'm *so* pleased to see you again. I'd know that hair anywhere!'

Kath was taken aback for a split second. 'That's me!' she said, winking at Connie.

'Were you dancing last night?' Jeannie asked. 'I wasn't allowed to, you see, because Connie here keeps me in bed.'

'Oh, she's *like* that,' Kath said. 'Yeah, I danced all last night. Wondered why you didn't show up.'

'I'll be there tonight,' Jeannie said. 'But right now I need a pee.'

✳

Kath took over. She gave Jeannie a bed bath, she hoisted her on and off the commode, and she chatted away about the dancing she knew nothing of.

When Connie entered the bedroom, Jeannie said, 'I'm so glad you brought Petronella along! Wherever did you find her?'

Just then the doorbell rang. Huw Davies, tousled as usual, was accompanied by two young people.

'I hope this isn't an inconvenient time,' he said breezily, 'but we were on our way to a conference in Gateshead and this was on our route. There's one or two things I need to sort out with Miss Jarman.' Seeing Connie looking at his two companions, he said, 'Ah, yes, Clare here's my secretary, and young Norman is learning the trade, so to speak. I need them as witnesses to her will, you see.'

Connie and Kath waited in the kitchen until they heard the three leave the bedroom.

Huw Davies handed Connie his card. 'Please phone me,' he said, 'if anything happens. I'll be arranging everything.'

'Thanks, I will,' Connie said.

'She's looking quite perky today,' was Huw Davies's parting shot, as she closed the door behind them.

'What was that all about?' Kath asked.

'She's leaving all this lot to some theatrical charity,' said Connie. 'They look after aged actors.'

'So why aren't they looking after *her*?'

✳

Kath settled very happily on the sofa, so much so that she snored loudly and continuously all night. Connie took herself, the mat and the Miracle into the tiny hallway, where she camped outside Jeannie's door.

Jeannie was sleeping most of the time now, but tomorrow was The Birthday, and it looked like she was going to make the big nine-o after all. At times she was still fairly lucid, looking rather quizzically at Kath, and at other times she was in the world of Petronella and Paris and Paul. Paul was waiting for her, she informed Connie. He was right there, with his hand outstretched, but she couldn't quite reach it.

'When's my birthday?' she asked Connie.

'It's tomorrow, Jeannie.'

'Oh, good. Have you got my champagne? And my cigarettes?'

Connie couldn't get her head round the fact that, no matter how confused Jeannie became ('away with the fairies', as Kath described it), she never seemed to forget about the champagne or the damn cigarettes.

So they bought a bottle of Bollinger and a packet of Silk Cut. They decided to buy a top-notch fizzy because, after all, it was a special birthday, and they'd be drinking most of it themselves anyway. And they surely deserved a treat.

'Don't worry,' Kath said. 'I've got a friend who'll see off these fags.'

It was mid-morning before Jeannie awoke.

'Happy birthday!' Connie said, bending down to kiss her wrinkled cheek. 'You're ninety today!'

'And I'm still here.'

'You're still here. And, if you could manage a few spoonfuls of porridge, we'll bring in the champagne later.'

'And my cigarette?'

'And your cigarette.'

Jeannie obediently but reluctantly agreed to a couple of spoonfuls, pulling a face each time. Connie could remember exactly the same process years ago with a tiny Nick. ('Yes,' she'd said. 'Just a few more mouthfuls and we *will* go to the swings.')

There were three birthday cards. One, featuring red roses, from Connie; one funny one with two old dears reliving their youth on the front from Kath; and one proclaiming 'You are 90 today!' from Huw Davies.

In the middle of the struggle with the porridge Jeannie fell asleep again, waking only when the nurse arrived with her syringe. It was a different nurse from usual and Jeannie had sworn loudly at her because she thought she was Paul's (long-suffering) wife.

'She's just told that nurse to go forth and multiply,' Connie sighed as she closed the door. And, exhausted by her outburst, Jeannie was asleep again.

She woke again at four o'clock in the afternoon.

'Are you ready for your champagne, Jeannie?' Connie asked, as Kath heaved her from the commode back onto the bed.

'Yes, I am. And has Petronella here got my fag?'

'You bet,' replied Kath.

Connie had carried a tray with three glasses, the Silk Cut and an ashtray, while Kath followed behind brandishing the bottle of Bolly. Jeannie's eyes lit up at the small explosion as Kath pulled the cork and filled the glasses with the fizzy. They propped the old lady up, draped a towel round her neck, and pressed the glass against her lips. And Jeannie took a sip, and then another, and then another.

'Cheers!' they said. 'Happy birthday!'

Kath then removed a cigarette from the packet and lit up. 'Haven't done this in bleedin' years,' she said, coughing. 'Here you are, Jeannie.'

'Oh, thank you, Petronella!'

Connie prayed she wouldn't try to inhale, which of course she did, followed by a bout of violent coughing. Then she recovered sufficiently to have another sip of champagne.

'We're in Singapore, aren't we?'

'Yeah, of course we are,' Kath replied.

They were suddenly aware of Jeannie struggling to get out of bed.

'Where are you going?' Connie asked anxiously.

'I have to dance tonight,' she said crossly. 'You *know* that!'

Connie would never forget what happened next. Kath put down her glass, bent over, picked up the old lady and, holding her firmly under the arms, waltzed her round the floor. And Jeannie threw back her head and laughed; a proper throaty laugh. Then Kath laid her down on the bed again, wiped her brow, took a swig of her drink and winked at Connie. 'Anything to oblige.'

The invalid lay bright-eyed and smiling as Connie pressed the glass to her lips again. She took a tiny sip but declined another puff of the cigarette.

'I've just seen Paul,' she told them.

'Oh, good.'

'The Taj Mahal is so beautiful,' she said.

'Blimey!' muttered Kath. 'We were in Singapore a minute ago.'

'Stick around,' Connie said, 'and it'll save you a fortune in air fares!'

Jeannie had fallen asleep again.

They transported everything to the lounge and Kath refilled their glasses.

'That was a lovely thing you did back there,' Connie said, 'Dancing, I mean. That made her really happy.'

Kath snorted. 'If only she knew! I've got two left feet – never been able to dance properly in me life!'

They finished the bottle of Bollinger and, as Kath lay back and dozed, Connie decided to check on Jeannie.

The old lady was lying very still, the ghost of a smile on her face. A breeze had got up and Connie crossed the room to close the window. Then something made her glance at Jeannie again.

She knew, even as she sat down to watch the rise and fall of her chest, that there would be none. Because Jeannie had gone to join the dancers, to drink champagne and to be with her lover.

The doctor signed the death certificate, Huw Davies organised the undertaker and, that evening, Jeannie finally left her much-loved flat. It was late before Connie and Kath finally got round to finishing off the last of Jeannie's freezer meals, washed down with a bottle of her very good red wine.

Connie had felt sad for only a short time. After all, Jeannie had got her wish. She'd reached her ninetieth, she'd died in her own

flat and her passing had been relatively peaceful. Who could ask
for more?

'Shall we open another bottle?' Kath asked.

'God, Kath, I've had more than enough! But you go ahead if
you want.'

Kath opened another bottle. 'Yeah, well, I'm planning on getting
hammered. I keep wondering who's going to mourn the old girl.'

'I certainly will,' Connie replied.

'Yeah, me too,' said Kath.

'I think we made her last days as nice as we could,' Connie said.

'Of course we did,' said Kath. ''Cos if she'd been in a nursing
home or somewhere they wouldn't let her have a bit of fun like we
did. She'd be told to stop dreaming and they'd try to make her face
reality – you know, where she is and what's happening. Cruel, I call it.
Hope that, when my turn comes, I'll have someone like us around.'

Kath waved the bottle at Connie, who shook her head, before
filling up her own glass.

'Huw Davies said he'd keep us informed,' Connie said.

'Don't like funerals.'

'No,' Connie agreed. 'But at least Jeannie had a good long life.'

'Not like our boys.'

'I always hoped there was a heaven,' Connie said. 'I wanted to
think of Ben riding his bicycle in some sort of celestial paradise.'

Kath gave one of her snorts. 'He'll have Jeannie dancing around
him now! You don't really believe in all that, do you?'

'No,' Connie replied. 'I don't. But I can quite understand that
people need to believe their loved ones have gone somewhere. I
know I did at the time.'

'You know what I fancy? Re—, er, re-in—' Kath was having trouble with words and wine.

'Reincarnation?'

'Yeah, that's it! Maybe Billy's come back as a motorcycling champion somewhere in the world.'

'Or a fly on the wall,' Connie added.

'Christ, Connie!'

'Well, maybe there's a points system. You earn enough for good behaviour in this life, you get a leg-up in the next.'

'Load of rubbish, all of it!' said Kath. 'Sure you won't have a teeny drop more?'

Connie shook her head. 'It would be nice to think there was a heaven and Jeannie's up there dancing right now with her Paul.'

'Wherever she's gone to, let's raise a glass to her.'

'To Jeannie!'

CHAPTER THIRTY-THREE

BACKTRACKING

They left the flat at noon the following day.

'What'll happen to all this stuff?' Kath asked, as she packed her bag, looking round at the pictures and the ornaments.

'Well, I'm taking this,' Connie said, lifting a framed poster of a young Jeannie in Paris off the wall. 'I must have a memento.'

'I'll just take the gin,' said Kath, rummaging in the cupboard.

'And just look at this!' Connie exclaimed as she tidied up Jeannie's bedroom. The roses, which had still looked fresh the previous day, had withered overnight. There were dead petals everywhere.

'Funny, that,' Kath said.

Huw arrived at midday to lock up and collect the key. 'I'll let you know about the funeral just as soon as I know myself,' he said. 'And thank you for being here, Mrs McColl and, er '

'Call me Connie, *please*. And this is Petronella.'

The little red car was tightly packed with Kath and her suitcase, Connie's remaining belongings and Jeannie's poster wedged in the back seat. The idea had been that they'd leave early; Connie would drop Kath off in Manchester and get to Freddy's before too late. But, apart from the fact that the solicitor hadn't appeared until noon, Connie wouldn't have left any earlier, bearing in mind the amount of wine they'd put away the previous evening.

'So you'll spend the night at my place,' Kath said. And Connie set the satnav for Packingham Street. They stopped for a meal on the way, and arrived at Kath's at seven o'clock.

Kath made a large pot of tea, which they drank thirstily, before bringing out the gin bottle.

'No alcohol for me tonight!' Connie said. She felt exhausted, physically and emotionally. It had been a tough time – two weeks to be exact. But she'd always be heartened that she'd made that phone call and that she'd decided to stay. Most importantly, she'd followed her own instinct. She was doing that more and more now.

'A penny for them?' Kath asked, as she poured orange into her gin.

'Oh, just thinking about life,' Connie replied. 'And how glad I am to have known little Jeannie, and you too, Kath. And how grateful I am that you came to help me – and an old lady you'd never even set eyes on.'

'Blimey!' said Kath. 'It was just nice to be useful.'

'You were indispensable, Kath.'

They sat in silence for a while, each wrapped in their own thoughts, before Kath asked, 'What now, Connie?'

'What do you mean?'

'Tomorrow, when you leave here, where are you going?'

'Oh, I'm going to visit my friend Freddy. He lives down in Gloucestershire and I promised to call on the way back.'

'Are you putting off going home, then?'

'Not at all. I'm just seeing everyone on the way back that I saw on the way up. Backtracking, if you like. Makes it neat and tidy somehow.'

'And then you'll go home?'

'Then I'll go home.'

'And life will go on as usual?'

'Oh, no, Kath! Life couldn't be the same again.'

'I'll be in touch,' Connie said, hugging Kath the next morning. 'And that's a promise. Just as soon as I find out when Jeannie's funeral's going to be.'

'Yeah,' said Kath. 'I'd like that.'

As she drove south she thought not only about Jeannie and Kath, but also about Don and everyone she'd met on her travels, all of whom had given her a better understanding of herself. Unknowingly they'd helped to release this new, more determined Connie, less guilty, less dithery. And she thought about her family too and how she longed to see them all. How lucky she really was to have them!

And how lucky she was to have a satnav which guided her, without a hitch, to Freddy's door.

After he'd hugged her and exclaimed about how well she looked, how tanned she was, and how amazing it was that a car could change from safe-old-green to red-for-danger, he said, 'Darling! We've been *desperate* to know what you've been getting up to! Tell us all!'

Connie, back on the red sofa with red wine, gave them a brief résumé of her adventures, punctuated by hoots of laughter from her hosts.

'This Don sounds divine!' Freddy exclaimed. 'Why on earth did you let him go?'

'Or, better still,' said Baz, 'you could have brought him here with you.'

Connie laughed. 'It was never going to be a long-term relationship,' she said. 'It wouldn't have suited either of us. But we'll probably stay in touch.'

Freddy hooted. 'Wonder what The Roger would have to say about *that*?'

Then she told them about Jeannie.

'What a lucky old girl she was to have you looking after her while she popped her clogs!' Freddy remarked.

Connie smiled. 'Believe it or not, I think I got just as much benefit from it as she did. It reminded me how precious life is.'

'So, you're going home?' Freddy asked, twirling his glass.

'Yes, tomorrow.'

'And how long will you have been away altogether?'

'Must be nearly six weeks.'

'Do they know you're coming back?' Baz asked.

'Well, they know I'll be coming back *sometime*.'

'Don't you think you should phone?'

'No, I don't think so,' Connie replied. 'I have my key, so I can let myself in if Roger's out. And I don't think he'd go so far as to change the locks.'

Freddy raised his eyebrows. 'And you think this little expedition of yours has changed things in some way?'

'It's changed me,' said Connie. And how! she thought. In fact, it's changed my attitude to everything. Life is for living, and that's exactly what I plan to do from now on.

There followed another highly entertaining evening, a wonderful dinner and a few more glasses of wine, before heading for the four-poster again. But sleep eluded her this time, as she tossed and turned, her mind in turmoil. She'd made her decision. She couldn't, wouldn't endure this marriage any longer. But how to tell Roger? How could he possibly understand her need to be free? *I'm sorry, Roger, but I only came back to tell you I'm not coming back* – how ridiculous was that! *Roger, I'm sorry but I think we've reached the end of the road... This may come as a shock to you, Roger* – (would it?) – *but I've decided I need to be on my own...*

He'd probably be pleased to see her back. What if he took her in his arms and told her how much he'd missed her? *Perhaps I haven't been very attentive of late*, he might say. *I'm so sorry, Connie...* What would she say then? *Roger, we need to talk...*? Yes, it might be best to tell him gently. After all, they'd been together a very long time and he was the father of her children. She might not want to live with him any more, but she couldn't bear to think of hurting him.

And how would the family take it? Di would probably understand, Nick would worry and Lou would be furious. *Silly old people!* she'd say. *What does it matter at your age?* But it *did* matter. It mattered very much because the dwindling years that were left were precious, not to be wasted. It would be an enormous wrench, but she had to do it. And somehow or other she had to tell Roger.

Finally Connie drifted off, about three o'clock, into a restless sleep and was quite relieved to get up at eight. She was then persuaded to have one of Freddy's famous bacon butties, and they begged her to stay for lunch. But Connie wanted to be on the road. She'd stop for a meal on the way, because she wasn't at all sure of what sort of reception she might be about to get in Sussex.

※

There was no sign of Doris Henderson as Roger let himself in his front door and dumped his clubs in the hallway. He'd been very tempted to stay on at the golf club to eat but he knew that would mean downing a few beers and then, of course, he wouldn't be able to drive home afterwards. Life was inconvenient enough at the moment without losing his driving licence. Anyway, Andrea wasn't on duty today.

He poured himself a generous measure of gin, topped it up with tonic, and then discovered there were no limes. Damnation! There was a wizened-looking lemon lurking in the back of the fridge, so he supposed a slice of that would be better than nothing. Then he opened the freezer door, stared at the rapidly diminishing collection of frozen meals and decided he didn't fancy any of them. Perhaps he should have picked up some fish and chips again on the way home, but his waistline was continuing to expand as a result of his calorie-filled intake and he was becoming a bit bored with the rowing machine. And golf wasn't the most energetic game when it came to losing a few pounds. No limes, no dinner! He carried his drink through to his armchair in the sitting room. Perhaps he'd boil a couple of eggs later on. Feeling extremely sorry for himself, he reached for the remote control, when the doorbell rang.

Roger groaned. Who now? Probably Lou again, come to lecture him on keeping the place tidy and watering the plants. He looked guiltily at the sad *ficus benjamina exotica* on the windowsill.

Drink in hand, he opened the door. He almost dropped the glass. 'It's *you…*'

CHAPTER THIRTY-FOUR

THE LIBERATION OF CONNIE McCOLL

Connie pulled up outside the hated bungalow. Roger's car was in the drive, so the inevitable moment of confrontation could be postponed no longer. Would she *ever* be able to remember her speech? Although she'd been practising it as she drove along, it was likely that she'd be so nervous it would all come out back to front or she'd forget it altogether. She parked Rosy and walked up the path, noting that the windows needed a clean but at least the grass had been cut.

The door was locked. That was strange, but perhaps he hadn't felt well and had gone for a lie down? She dug out her key and unlocked the door. The hall was tidy; no discarded shoes or bags, only an expensive-looking leather jacket hanging next to her hoodie. When had he bought that? And where was he? Connie could hear voices, so he must have a visitor. Damn, damn, damn, that was *not* in the plan. The confrontation might have to wait. She thumbed quickly through the pile of mail on the hall table. She'd deal with that later. And there was a package, containing what could only be a book, from a certain Martin Kerr with an address in Oxford.

She realised she'd never known his surname. How lovely that he'd remembered! She would definitely be in touch.

Connie opened the lounge door. But there was nobody there. Then she realised the voices were coming from the bedroom and, as she approached the door, she distinctly heard Roger's voice asking, 'Did you hear a noise in the hall just then?'

One of the kids must have come round and perhaps they were decorating the bedroom, which was the only room in which she hadn't yet dabbled with the Dulux. She'd told them she liked pale yellow, so perhaps they'd got to work while she was away? Maybe they wanted to do something nice for her after all. She wondered if they'd got the colour right; not that it mattered now of course. Hoping that there wasn't a paint pot directly behind the door, she opened it carefully.

The scene before her eyes would be imprinted in her mind forever.

Every sordid little detail: her husband, Roger McColl, standing there stark naked and regarding her with horror, an impressive erection rapidly dissipating. And, emerging from *her* bed, which was pushed up right next to his, was this gorgeous, young, bronzed creature, firm of body, long and slim of leg, dark-eyed and Latin-looking. Really bloody beautiful.

Connie couldn't think of a thing to say. She looked from one to the other and back again. Roger, in the meantime, had begun to frantically pull on a pair of tiny magenta-coloured underpants, little more than a *thong*! Whatever had happened to the Y-fronts he always wore? And how had he come by that all-over tan?

'I didn't know you were coming back today,' he said eventually in a cracked voice.

'That much is obvious,' Connie said. She had an urge to laugh; she'd never seen anything quite so ridiculous in her life. This was the type of farce you might still see in the theatre, and even in the theatre it would take some believing.

'This is Andrea,' Roger said, struggling into a T-shirt and indicating the beauty who had crawled back under Connie's duvet with its nice new John Lewis cover.

'Well, this is a surprise, Andrea,' Connie said at last. 'You'll have to forgive me if we don't shake hands.'

Andrea remained silent.

'And where did you two lovebirds meet, may I ask?' she asked icily, amazed at her own composure. Perhaps she was experiencing some sort of numbness, born out of sheer disbelief. This just could *not* be happening. 'No, don't tell me,' she continued, 'it *has* to be golf…'

'Andrea's Italian,' Roger said, as if that explained everything. 'He's been working as a steward at the club for the summer.'

'And he just fancied a lie-down in my bed?'

'I'm sorry, Connie. We'll leave in a minute.'

'No, Roger, no need for you to leave. You stay right here with your boyfriend. Do you honestly think I'd sleep in this room tonight – or *ever* again?'

Connie knew her composure was now crumbling and she had to get out, and away, as quickly as possible. Shaking, she staggered back towards the front door.

'Connie!' Roger followed her, still wearing only the T-shirt and those ridiculous pants. 'We must talk—'

'No, Roger, there's nothing to say. Please get out of my way.'

She headed out of the door with as much dignity as she could muster and, slamming it behind her, stood with her heart pounding, in a state of shock, on the front path.

'Coo-ee!' shouted the old bat next door. 'Have you had a lovely holiday?'

The bile, which had been steadily rising from her stomach, had now reached the point of no return. Connie threw up onto the patch of grass that belonged to Roger, gave an appalled Mrs Henderson a wave, and collapsed into her car.

She had to get away from here. Anywhere would do. Then Connie remembered the large, tree-lined layby on the London Road, just a few minutes' drive away. She'd park there for a bit and try to come to terms with what she'd just seen. And decide what on earth to do next.

There was only one other car in the layby, where a family with two young children were having a picnic. Why, Connie wondered, would you want to have a picnic in a fume-laden layby on a busy dual carriageway when there were acres of beautiful countryside all around?

She switched off the ignition, opened the window and took a long swig from her water bottle. There was only the hum of the traffic through the trees, and one of the children howling. The world hadn't stopped; life went on as usual.

Realisation flooded through her veins like the fast-flowing river. This, she thought, must be it. This is what's been wrong with my marriage, surely. But why had she not known? Once or twice she *had* suspected he might have been having an affair but could never find proof of any dalliance. No lipstick on the collar, no receipts for dinners out or flowers sent. Was Andrea the first? And how could you live with a man for forty-one years and have no idea that he might be gay or bisexual?

So, why had Roger married her? Perhaps he liked both men and women? Or was it because Roger McColl, that pillar of the community, must always be seen to be doing The Right Thing? And how he'd disliked Freddy! Was that because he thought Freddy might see through the veneer? Had he fooled Freddy too, and would Freddy have told her even if he suspected? So many questions… but perhaps in time they could all talk about it.

Connie took another gulp of water. Oh, Roger! All at once she felt deeply sorry for her husband. Nowadays he could surely be himself. He wouldn't have needed to hide behind the convention of marriage, or been straitjacketed by his own obsession with the appearance of respectability. Poor Roger! He'd always closed his mind to *anything* he couldn't deal with. It wasn't only Ben's death.

But what about the children? *What* on earth do you say to the children? Well, she'd say nothing. Or, perhaps something like, *Your father and I have decided to go our separate ways,* or some other soothing cliché. Let Roger do any explaining. Connie felt incredibly sad. There was much wrong with the modern world but at least you could be whoever or whatever you wanted to be.

And it had been the right thing to do, to get away; to allow both Roger and herself the space they needed to face up to the lives they really wanted to live.

And now, perhaps, she could also stop feeling guilty, once and for all. In the meantime, she'd need somewhere to stay. Somewhere to plan the rest of her life, even another adventure perhaps! She got out her phone and found Di's number.

CHAPTER THIRTY-FIVE

UNCAGED AND FLYING

'What I don't understand, Mum,' said Di, as she mixed two large gin and tonics, 'is why you won't tell me exactly what Dad has *done*? I can appreciate that you want to strike out on your own but this wasn't in the plan – coming here, I mean. Don't tell me he's got another woman?'

'No,' said Connie shortly. 'He hasn't.'

That would be so much easier to explain. But Roger was their father after all and it was surely up to him to inform his offspring of his sexual preferences. Connie's instinct had always been to protect her children and there was still a certain loyalty to her husband, even now. The kids would have to find out for themselves. Perhaps. For who knew how Roger would live his life from now on? For herself, she could only feel an overwhelming sense of relief. She was shocked, of course, and she'd have a hard job explaining why she'd left, particularly to Nick and Lou. Because she'd had no idea; never suspected for one moment. But in hindsight she began to wonder if Roger had been living another life alongside the one he had with her.

'OK, Mum, so you've definitely left?'

'Yes, I've definitely left. I'm sorry, darling, but your dad and I were never very compatible and these few weeks on my own have made me realise that I need to move forwards, alone. But I won't stay here any longer than I have to. I just need a couple of days to sort myself out and decide what to do next. Now, tell me about this man of yours – Mark, is it?'

Diana sighed. 'Well, Mum, he's *gorgeous*! I can't wait for you to meet him and I've been so looking forward to talking to you about everything. The thing is, we're moving in together.'

'And are you certain of the way you feel about him?'

'Well, yes… but—'

'No buts. If you love him and want to move in with him, do it. You don't get too many chances of happiness in this world.'

'I hoped you'd say that, but the thing is I'd really like to keep this place as a bolt-hole, just in case… you know?'

'I *do* know,' said Connie.

'So, do you think I should rent it out on short-term lets? I just want to know that I could come back without too much delay if I really had to.'

'Excellent idea, Di. I shall be your first tenant.'

'*You*, Mum?'

'Why not? I'm going to need somewhere for the next few months to sort myself out.'

Di didn't speak for a moment and then she said, 'You might not miss Dad, but what about Nick and Lou, and the babies?'

'Weekends.' Connie had never thought so quickly and so confidently in her life. 'I'll go down and stay with them, turnabout, at weekends. I can look after the little ones so they have some time to themselves to go out for a meal or whatever. It's another very good reason to be up here; babysitting will be on *my* terms from now on. And not *every* weekend, of course.'

Connie smiled to herself. She could almost hear the rushing and gushing of that icy cold river, the sighing of the wind across the loch, the sound of the Atlantic waves breaking on the sands at Arisaig. All would need to be visited again, along with the friends she'd made along the way. And, perhaps, even a wedding Down Under.

'I may well have other things to do,' she said.

CHAPTER THIRTY-SIX

TALE END

'So, you've definitely left him, have you?' Kath asked as they walked, arm in arm, towards the crematorium.

'Yes, Kath, I've finally left him. I'd made up my mind to leave anyway, but let's just say that my unexpected arrival really clinched it. Sometime I'll tell you about it, but not here, not now.'

'Where are you staying?'

'At my daughter's flat in London. She's just moved in with her man, and was about to advertise for a tenant.'

'Blimey, Connie! That was meant to be!'

'Yes, I think it was.'

They hadn't travelled up to Newcastle together because Connie had flown and Kath had arrived by train. They'd agreed to meet at the station and take a taxi from there. Much as Connie loved her little red car, she'd had enough of driving for a while.

Huw Davies was waiting for them, clutching a large bouquet of red roses.

'So glad you made it, ladies,' he said cheerfully, shaking hands. 'Just for a minute there I thought I might be the only mourner.

These arrived this morning; aren't they beautiful? But I suppose I'd better notify the sender that there'll be no need for any more. I thought you might like them.'

Of course! It was the first of October.

'No,' said Connie. 'They're for Jeannie. They should go with her.'

'Seems a waste,' Huw Davies said sadly.

'It's what she'd have wanted.'

'Oh well. The undertaker should be here any minute.' He glanced at his watch. 'But may I take this opportunity to have a quick word in your ear, Mrs McColl?'

'Connie.'

'Yes, OK, Connie.' He took her elbow and guided her a few yards away. 'Now, I was her executor as well as her solicitor, so I just wanted to let you know that you'll be getting a letter in the next week or two with all the details. But I might as well tell you now: Miss Jarman has left half her estate to you.'

'To *me*?'

'Well, it won't be a fortune as she had very few savings, but the flat should be worth quite a bit. Good area, you know. Oh, and she did say something about you perhaps making a small gift to, er, Petronella, is it?'

Connie was convinced there must be some mistake. 'But she told me she was leaving everything to some charity or other.'

'Well, she *was*. But she changed her mind. They're only getting half now. Do you remember I called a couple of times while you were there?'

'Yes, but—'

'It'll all be in the letter. Ah, here's the hearse.'

Kath, who'd been edging ever closer and plainly trying to eavesdrop, looked at Connie enquiringly. Connie, stunned, shook her head and walked back towards the hearse, as the tiny coffin was lifted out and carried into the crematorium, the spray of white roses she and Kath had ordered wobbling on the top. When the coffin was laid down, Connie took the bouquet from Jeannie's long-dead lover and placed them on top too.

'Goodbye, little friend,' Connie said softly as Jeannie took her final curtain call to the strains of the can-can.

Kath could keep silent no longer. 'What was *that* all about?' she whispered as they walked back up the aisle.

'I'll tell you that later too.'

Then she linked arms with Kath and they emerged into the afternoon sunshine.

A Letter from Dee

Thank you so much for choosing to read *The Runaway Wife* and I hope you enjoyed reading it as much as I enjoyed writing it. If you did, and want to keep up with Connie's adventures, just sign up with the following link. Your email address will never be shared and you can unsubscribe at any time.

www.bookouture.com/dee-macdonald

And, if you did enjoy Connie's journey, I'd be grateful if you could write a review as I'd love to hear what you think and your feedback is invaluable. You can get in touch via the links below.

Don't forget, Connie's travels aren't over yet!

Dee

AuthorDeeMacDonald

@DMacDonaldAuth

ACKNOWLEDGEMENTS

With many thanks to my editor, Natasha Harding at Bookouture, and to my agent, Amanda Preston at LBA, for their enthusiasm, patience and invaluable advice. And thanks to all the other lovely people at Bookouture too, Kim in particular.

Thanks to my husband, Stan, who has patiently endured my long writing sessions, and to all my friends for their support and encouragement.

A special thanks to my friend and critic, Rosemary Brown, without whose expertise this book would never have taken shape.

Finally, thanks to my late mother, Anne, who encouraged my seven-year-old self to write 'wee stories' to help pass these long Scottish winters. She really was the instigator of all this!